DS Gallier

The Black Country Policeman

Vengeance...

Or Justice?

Thomas J.R. Dearn

DS Gallier

The Black Country Policeman

Vengeance...

Or Justice?

Paperback Edition First Published in the United Kingdom in 2023 Amazon KDP Publishing

eBook Edition First Published in the United Kingdom in 2023 Amazon KDP Publishing

A big thankyou to my good friend Aid-the aide! His advice, experience and knowledge has been inspirational and this book could not have been written without him...

For Dad and Grandad… Always the first two men to read my novels… Gone but never forgotten… R.I.P.

November 1967

It was sick and it was wrong, but it was vengeance... An eye for an eye and a tooth for a tooth...

He was the kind of copper who liked to smash a villain's face through a door or window before he arrested them, but ultimately, he was one of the good guys...

"Thank you! Your sympathy makes all the difference..."

Chapter 1

Her dress was particularly short in a style that was typical of the 1960s and an abundance of make-up masked an innocence that was barely 18 years of age. Her eyes were blue and afraid and her straw like blonde hair clung to a face that was pretty in an overtly ordinary way. Her virginity was a valuable commodity and her captor, a dark and evil man in his middle-aged years had not yet decided what he was going to do with her. *Should he capitalise upon her value and 'farm' her out to the highest bidder? Or should he enjoy the young, innocent nectar for himself?* He could certainly afford the latter option, but he had very particular interests and fetishes that were overwhelmingly unsavoury. *He liked innocence, he liked youth, the more youthful the better, but often he preferred male youth...* It all depended on whomever took his fancy at the time...

Waterloo Sunset by the Kinks had been a number 2 hit record in the British charts in mid-1967 and the song depicted a romantic scenario of two lovers passing over the river Thames near to Waterloo station in London. As the young girl shivered in her mini dress in the cold, November surroundings of a Tipton public house, she could not help but feel melancholic upon listening to the somewhat romantic sentiment of the lyrics 'Terry meets Julie' as the song played on the pub's jukebox. She was being pimped by a loathsome and disgusting local gangster, her innocence being stolen and wasted for ever... *Would she ever be able to experience real romance? Like in the song?* She had no choice but to do as she was told. Her financial reward would be meagre, but if she did not do as she was told then her father would be beaten and tortured... *She had no choice...*

"Is it ok if I smoke a cigarette?" She looked up at her captor with childlike eyes and the wicked man displayed an instant irritancy to her question.

"No…" He was smoking himself but he did not even look at her as he spoke and she instantly remained silent. Through the nerves of the situation, she was desperate to use the toilet, but she dared not ask permission to go to the ladies.

The pub in question was built in 1923 and was named the Doughty Arms. A public house had stood there on the corner of Hurst Lane and Sedgley Road West in Tipton since the mid- nineteenth century and was originally known as the Five ways Inn until it was demolished in the early 1920s to make way for the new building which would become the Doughty Arms. The pub was named after local Councillor William Woolley Doughty who had been chairman of the Tipton Urban District Council. Much later, in 1987, the pub would be bought by Colm 'Mad' O'Rourke and renamed The World-Famous Pie Factory.

"That poor wench dow stand a chance…" Sat opposite the gangster and his captive was Detective Sargeant Reggie Gallier of the West Midlands Constabulary. Prior to its formation just twelve months previously in 1966, Gallier had been a detective in the Dudley Borough Police force that had existed from 1920 until the 1st of April 1966 when all of the Black Country Police forces had been joined together to form the new West Midlands Constabulary. This in turn would later be replaced by West Midlands Police that would be formed in 1974 to combine the Black Country region with nearby forces in Birmingham and Coventry. He was the kind of copper who liked to smash a villain's face through a door or window before he arrested them, but ultimately, he was one of the good guys. Born in the summer of 1935, Gallier had been brought up on the Moat Farm Estate, Tipton, though to everyone who knew, it was known as the Lost City on account of there only being one road in and one road out. Typical of many of the young scallywags in the vicinity, he had grown up tough and had demonstrated a particular talent for fighting and street violence. He also held a strong passion for football, but he wasn't very good at it so he used his fighting prowess and aggression to more than make up for a lack of technical talent on the field. In the '50s, he had fallen in love with Rock 'n' Roll and became an

Elvis Presley worshipping Teddy Boy before his prompt and decisive dumping into National Service where he served in the Army in the recently conquered Germany as a military Policeman. He had shown no particular interest in becoming an MP, in fact, as a youngster he would have cringed at the thought of joining up with the 'cozzers', but his aggression and talents for fighting made him the perfect match for 'sorting out' the unruly British 'Squaddies' who had descended upon the night clubs of the decadent and vibrant German port of Hamburg in the 1950s. Upon his demob back into civilian life in 1956, Reggie Gallier took the 'easy option' and simply transferred to a safe and familiar job as a bobby on the beat in his hometown of Tipton working for Dudley Borough Police force.

"We're off duty Reg… Just drink your beer and smoke a fake…" The man sat at the small table alongside Reggie Gallier was his friend and colleague, Detective Constable Tony Giles.

"I know mate, it just makes me sick… Mecks mar blood boil…" The more beer he consumed, the more angered Gallier became and he soon found that he was making a point of trying to stare down the notorious and powerful criminal who was sat alongside his pretty and petite captive.

"You do know who that is don't you?" Giles spoke again as he raised a cigarette to his narrow lips. He was a tall and gaunt looking policeman in his early 30s with a pale complexion and eyes that were permanently suspicious.

"Of course I do…" Gallier smiled and then took a long gulp of his beer, never once releasing his intimidating gaze upon the much feared villain who was sat opposite with the girl and several young men who were part of his organisation. They were all well dressed and trying hard to 'play the part' of the dapper English gangster. They had read about Ronnie and Reggie the Kray twins in all of the papers and they were trying to mould themselves upon the Cockney brothers, however, the boss, the man who sat with his timid prey at his side was a hardened criminal who descended from a family of ruling and highly influential

Wolverhampton crime figures who had existed long before the illustrious brothers Kray. His name was Cedric Tanner... "One of these days ar'm gunna nail his bollocks to a shit house door!" Gallier's eyebrows lowered as he drained the dregs of his beer.

"Fuck off Reg, Tanner's got more dirty coppers in his pocket than yow've got wenches mate..." Tony Giles found Gallier's comments amusing and he made a sarcastic reference to his colleague's legendary prowess with the ladies. Reg Gallier was 32 years old and had not yet settled down and married. *But he was Reggie Gallier, he had many wenches at his beck and call...* He pushed the side parting of his dark brown and thinning hair into place and maintained his gaze upon Tanner. Reginald Peter Gallier was about six feet tall with broad shoulders and a wide face that was finished off with a sharp and impressive, chiselled jaw line that alongside his piercing blue eyes, helped him to maintain his impressive record with the ladies. Between his work, the beer, fags and his devotion to the Hawthorns, home of his beloved football team, West Bromwich Albion, Reggie Gallier had more than enough going on in his life to keep him fulfilled. He ignored Giles's comment and after fetching another round of beers from the bar, continued to spread his eyeballing between the shortness of the girl's dress and Cedric Tanner... *That poor young girl was nice, she really did not deserve to be contaminated by the likes of scum like Cedric Tanner.*

"What the fuck am yow lookin' at?" After a short time, Gallier's eyeballing of the feared gangster had become so intense that Tanner could not help but make a comment. Reggie Gallier shrugged.

"Ar don't know... But it's a lookin' back..." Gallier replied smugly and Cedric Tanner immediately rose to his feet and strode across the barroom to the small table at which the two policemen were sat.

"So... You're a couple of tough guys ay?" Tanner pulled up a chair from a nearby table without asking permission. Waterloo Sunset had finished playing on the jukebox and the familiar intro guitar riff to 'I feel fine' by the Beatles began to play... "I love the Beatles..." Tanner changed the subject drastically and Gallier and Giles looked at each other with a slight confusion.

"Ar fuckin' hate the Beatles..." Gallier did not mince his words as he responded gruffly and Tanner laughed.

"Yes, you're either a couple of tough guys or you are very, very stupid... But that gets me a thinkin', I know all of the tough guys around here... They all work for me... So answer me this... What is your business and what are you doing in here eyeballing me in front of my associates?" Tanner's tone was surprisingly friendly and Gallier spotted an opportunity to try and gather some intelligence... *Tanner obviously didn't know that they were police officers!*

"You're the one they call Tanner? Is that right?"

"Yes... Ar'm Cedric Tanner and everyone knows me... By the way yow talk I can tell that you're a local lad, so I'm sure that you already know exactly who I am..."

"Me and mar mate here figured that you might be on the lookout for some new talent for your organisation." Gallier took a drink of his beer and continued to stare into the villain's eyes. "What kind of business are you in Mr Tanner?"

"My business is my business aer kid... But you look like the kind of bloke who can handle himself..." Tanner grinned and shot DS Gallier a somewhat flirtatious wink. The detective shivered inwardly and then repeated his question as his colleague Tony Giles looked on awkwardly.

"But if we were to do a bit of work for your organisation Mr Tanner, we would have to know what kind of business you and your boys are in... Prostitution? Extortion? Drugs?" Gallier already knew that Tanner was heavily involved in all three of those rackets, particularly drugs. The gangster was short and stubby with jet black hair that was neither long or short and he had a pair of unnerving and menacing black eyes that looked like two pieces of charcoal in fresh white snow. In a typically 1960s fashion, all three of the men sat at the table were dressed in sharp black suits with elegant, skinny ties.

"You really are a nosy bastard aren't you... Maybe I should have my boys take you outside to mar Jag and let them beat you to a pulp in front of your lady friend here?" Tanner gestured patronisingly towards DC Giles. "Would you like that boy?"

"And maybe I should put your face through this table and dance the Fandango on your head?" Gallier kept his cool, but how he longed to perform such an action. Tanner began to laugh.

"Yow got balls kid... What's your name fella?" Before Gallier could respond, his colleague, Tony Giles opened his mouth and Gallier groaned inwardly.

"His name is Gallier, Detective Sargent Gallier so you better watch your mouth Tanner!" Giles was defiant, but Gallier was furious... *His cover was blown and he would not be getting anything out of the odious villain.* Tanner nodded knowingly.

"Of course... Ar should have known... A couple of pant sniffin' pigs..." Tanner laughed and then proceeded to make loud pig like grunting noises and in that moment, Reg Gallier didn't know who he wanted to hurt the most, Cedric Tanner or his best mate Tony Giles! Tanner suddenly stopped laughing and a look of pure evil came over him. "You listen to this Detective Sargent Gallier..." Tanner lowered his head to the policeman and spoke in a hushed voice. "You see that little girl over there?" Tanner pointed to the scared young girl in the mini dress who had been sat besides him earlier. "I hadn't quite decided what ar was gunna do with her... But now, thanks to you, I have decided... I want you to know this Detective Sargent, that as a direct consequence of your antics here tonight, I'm gunna take her home, and I'm gunna fuckin' hurt her... I'm gunna fuckin' hurt her real bad and it's all because of you... Ar just wanted you to know that Gallier..."

"Maybe I should take her with me and get her to give evidence against you Mr Tanner?" Gallier knew that it was already a lost cause and Tanner spat mocking laughter again.

"She won't go with you... Besides, if she did, that would be very bad for her family... You see, I'm untouchable Mr Gallier... Nobody will

dare give evidence against me... Not a word... You are welcome to try?"
Tanner held up his hands and looked back towards the girl, but Gallier
knew that he was helpless to intervene... "I have a lot of very powerful
friends Mr Gallier... Friends way over your head... Just remember this...
It is because of your actions here tonight that she is gunna get an
induction into 'womanhood' that believe me, she will never forget..."
Tanner's eyes were fierce and violent and Gallier bit into his own bottom
lip with sheer frustration and anger before Tanner spoke again. "Now, ar
suggest that yow pair of pigs finish your drinks and fuck off!" He
sneered one last time and then stood up and walked back over to his seat
amongst his fellow gangsters. He sat down next to the girl and almost
ceremoniously rubbed his hands up her exposed thigh in such a way that
the poor frightened teenager shivered and felt desperately
uncomfortable. Far worse was to come... Reggie Gallier had seen
enough.

"Come on... Let's get the fuck out of here..." He drained his beer
and stood up. He was still livid with the actions of his colleague, but it
was late on a Thursday night and he did not have the energy for an
argument. *As usual, he would be going to work Friday morning with a
hangover and all he needed to do now was sleep.*

The two policemen left the Doughty arms and headed towards
Gallier's 1963 Ford Zephyr 4 that was parked outside on the car park.

"Look!" Gallier suddenly stopped dead in his tracks and pointed
to an elaborate, brand-new Jaguar mk X. "This must be Tanner's Jag..."
A sinister smile suddenly appeared upon the detective's face and he
pulled out his car keys and approached Tanner's luxury saloon. "Nice
motor this..." Gallier nodded sarcastically before digging his key deep
into the shiny paintwork of the front wing and then dragging it
backwards alongside the entire left-hand side of Cedric Tanner's car. He
dug deep and the sound of the damage made a distinctly high-pitched
scraping sound that caused DC Tony Giles to grimace. Gallier found the
action particularly satisfying and when he was done he turned and

smiled at his colleague before climbing into his Ford Zephyr and making the short journey home...

Chapter 2

Tony Giles did not live in Tipton. He was originally from Rowley Regis and had become firm friends with Reggie Gallier when the pair served together in the Military Police as part of their national service in the 1950s. When they left the military, they had both joined up with their regional police forces, Gallier with Dudley Borough Police and Giles with Staffordshire Constabulary. Although Tipton and Rowley were barely four miles apart, in the '50s, they came under separate police forces and although the two men remained friends and had both found success in their chosen careers, it was not until 1966 and the amalgamation of their forces that the two pals reunited as colleagues.

Not long after returning from National Service, Tony Giles had married his childhood sweetheart and had settled in a small, terraced house in Highfield Road, Blackheath. Consequently, Giles would often drink in many of the pubs around Blackheath, but a regular favourite of his was the Shoulder of Mutton public house in Blackheath town centre. It stood on the corner of Birmingham Road and was a popular drinking establishment with locals.

"Ar cor believe that yow've got me coming over here for a pint mate..." It was Friday night and Reggie Gallier found himself sat in the Shoulder of Mutton drinking beer with his good friend.

"Well after what happened last night over in Tipton, ar thought it was best that we give the place a wide birth tonight..." Tony Giles supped his ale from a 'jug' beer glass and Gallier shook his head, even though he knew that his friend was probably right. *It grieved him to think that he had avoided one of his local Tipton pubs on account of that bastard Cedric Tanner... But it was probably only fair that sometimes he drove over to Giles' local every once in a while!*

"Well just as long as you know that it ay because of that bastard Tanner that I've come over here tonight Tony... Ar told yer last night mate, ar'm gunna nail that bastard one of these days... Yow mark mar words mukka..." Gallier was deadly serious and he cast his eyes around the crowded bar for signs of local talent. "Yow got any nice wenches in here aer kid?"

"Ar'm a married man Reg... Dow ask me..." Giles shook his head and smirked, knowing full well that there was one woman in particular he was hoping to introduce his friend to. She was a pal of his wife and was particularly attractive, he figured that Gallier would probably be impressed and he looked around for signs of the women.

Up until 1841, Blackheath, Bleak Heath, or Blake Heath as it was also known was nothing more than a small group of farmhouses and Inns on the road between Oldbury and Halesowen. It was with the success of major local employers, Thomas William Lench and electrical engineers British Thomson-Houghton that in the early twentieth century, the town began to prosper and grow as it became commonly known as Blackheath.

"That dow stop yer from just appreciating a nice wench though does it mate?" Gallier looked at his watch. The night was young.

"There's somebody that ar want you to meet Reg..." Tony Giles looked away as soon as he spoke. He did not know how his friend would take to the idea of being 'set up' on some kind of blind date!

"What?" Gallier was interested. "Work stuff?" His ears were immediately alerted and his eyes looked around in search of some shady looking character. *Maybe there was a new grass, or police informant as it was officially known that he could carry in his pocket?*

"No..." Giles laughed almost sheepishly. "Nuthin' like that mate... It's a bird... A wench..."

"Am yow havin' a fuckin loff mate?" Gallier almost spat his beer across the room. *He did not need Tony Giles to set him up with women!*

"Yow'm gerrin' on a bit Reg... It's time you settled down with a good woman... I mean, how old am yer now?" Giles had been avoiding the subject but he decided to dive headlong into the matter at hand. Gallier laughed.

"You know me, ar like to play the field dow I Tony… Besides, with work, the beer and the Baggies, I ay got time for settling down or any of that bull shit…"

"Yow can work too much Reg…" Giles emphasised the oo in too much. "Let's face it, every time yow gew out yow gew out lookin' for a fight… Yow cor deny it Reg… Sometimes you have to switch off and think of things other than ramming a villain's face through a wall!" He took out a cigarette and continued to look for signs of his wife Jenny and her friend who were due to be meeting them there in the Shoulder of Mutton. His wife had even arranged for her mother to baby sit their kids.

"That's exactly why I go up the Baggies ay it… It helps me to switch off from work…" Gallier could not believe that 'HE' was being set up with a woman! *He was not desperate!*

"Yes, and then you think about getting' kaylied and smashin' a wolves supporters face through a wall instead of a villain!" Giles laughed as he took his first drag of his cigarette.

"Dow yow mention the bloody Wolves around me Tone, for fucks sake!" Gallier smiled. He was no football hooligan and the reason why he loved football so much was that it *didn't really matter… Nobody was gunna die as a result of some football match and nobody's life was gunna change… It didn't matter at all… But it did!* Football was a chance for him to be away from the pressures of work and to think about something else instead of whatever case he was involved in at that time. Nailing villains was an unhealthy obsession, an addiction, and Reg Gallier was well and truly addicted…

Both Tony Giles and Reggie Gallier were typical Policemen. Even when they were off duty, they noticed and studied every person that came into the pub. Over the previous decade they had sent many villains down and it was certainly not unlikely that one of those criminals could walk into the pub and attempt a form of vengeance at some point. They had to be constantly on their guard and be in a constant state of readiness. As a result, both Giles and Gallier noticed instantly as Tony's

16

wife Jenny entered the pub alongside a female companion whose appearance surprised Reggie Gallier pleasingly...

"Who is that?" Gallier eyed her as she neared their table and Giles was happy that his 'blind date' set up had the potential to be a success.

"Her name is Lucy... I thought yow weren't interested mate?" Tony Giles raised his eyebrows mockingly.

"Ar day say I was!" Gallier shrugged and waited for the female duo to reach the table. She was by no means thin or skinny, but she certainly wasn't fat or overweight either and her face was pretty and her red dress was short and only just covered her pleasing curves.

"Reg, this is my wife's friend Lucy... Lucy this is my good friend and colleague Reggie Gallier..." Tony Giles did the introductions and he winked at his wife as the two women sat down at the table.

"What can I get you two ladies to drink?" Gallier tried to play the gentleman and Tony Giles could tell that his friend was certainly interested.

"A gin and tonic please..." The two ladies replied almost in unison and Gallier stood up to walk over to the bar. Somewhat ironically and cornily, Love is all around, a hit record for the Troggs in November 1967 was playing on the pub jukebox and Tony Giles also stood up and followed his friend.

"Ar'll give you a hand Reg..." The two men walked over to the bar and as Gallier began to order the round, his friend nudged him discretely. "So what do you think mate?"

"A nice arse and a cracking pair of..." Before Gallier could complete the sentence he suddenly stopped speaking as embarrassingly, Lucy appeared beside him at the bar.

"Could I please have a packet of pork scratchun's too please?" She was polite but confident as she spoke and Gallier nodded enthusiastically.

"A wench after my own heart!" He stooped as if to playfully tap her on her shapely behind, but she ducked backwards and gave him a sarcastic and playful look.

17

"Its gunna teck more than a G and T and a packet of scratchun's mate!" Her playful aura of 'hard to get' added to his attraction and in his mind he had already decided… *He would give her a gew!*

The night passed favourably for Reggie Gallier and his new love interest and by ten o'clock the pair found themselves dancing slowly together at the Regis Club in nearby Old Hill. She was of a similar age to Gallier and as he admired her large blue eyes that were partially covered on the one side by her perfectly styled brown hair, he could not help but wonder what her back story was. *Why was she still on the shelf like him?*

"So how come you ay married Lucy?" He was a copper, he did not beat around the bush so he launched straight into the obvious question.

"I could ask you the same question…" She pushed herself closer to him as they danced and he knew that his luck was in.

"I've been very busy with work… I've always put my career first… But I certainly ain't gunna get anymore promotions!" He offered a little of his professional life and she was intrigued. She knew exactly what he did for a living and it excited her and made her feel safe…

"Why not? I heard that you are very good at what you do?"

"I ay the type for senior roles… I'm a Sergeant and I put a lot of bad people behind bars, but I dow speak the Queen's English, I dow play golf with the toffs and more importantly, I dow teck bungs from gangsters…" Gallier had consumed a good few alcoholic beverages and he immediately regretted his last remark. *It was not like him to be so honest in such a situation… He must really like her!*

"So you're saying that everyone in the police who is above the rank of Sergeant is bent?" She did not mince her words and he liked that.

"I didn't say that Lucy…" He immediately backtracked on his initial statement and for once in his life he felt like he was the one being interrogated! "Besides, it was me that asked you the question!"

"I was married…" She shrugged and her facial expression seemed to change slightly. "But he was a bastard who liked to slap me around after a few drinks so I left him…"

"Is he still around? I can sort him out for yer? No problem…" He had only just met her but he already felt a desire to protect her. She was completely unimpressed with his comment.

"You know, every bloke I meet says exactly that… Like I'm some possession that needs protecting…. I'm a big girl, I can look after my fuckin' self, thanks…" She pulled away slightly but the fire in her eyes was alluring. Gallier was used to pretty little women that fell at his feet and did all the chasing. *This woman was different.*

"Glad to hear it…" Gallier was a bad dancer but after a few beers he was happy to move clumsily across the floor in the hope that he might get lucky. "So do you think that maybe I could see you again? If I promise not to batter your ex-husband?" He tried to turn his earlier comment into something of a joke and he was relieved when she laughed, *he had not blown it yet!* "Or maybe I could see you later tonight?" *He was definitely pushing his luck…*

"Er no… I'm definitely not that sort of girl… It's gunna teck more than a few G and Ts and a packet of scratchuns, I already told you that!" She raised her eyebrows. *Maybe he had pushed it too far for now!* She pulled out a pen and a small piece of paper from her shiny leatherette handbag and scribbled a number down before handing it to him. "Call me…" She gave him a warm smile before lowering her lips to his and remaining there for just about long enough for him to decide that he definitely would be calling her in the future. She tossed her eyebrows again and then turned to leave the club… *Maybe it was time he started to take women a little more seriously!*

The next day was Saturday the 25th of November and as usual, Reggie Gallier watched West Bromwich Albion play from the Rainbow Stand that had been built at the Hawthorns seven years earlier in 1960. The Baggies were playing Tottenham Hotspur in the First Division and

Gallier was particularly happy to see his team win by two goals to nil. Whenever they won it affected his mood positively for the rest of the day and as he walked back towards his car that was parked on the Soho Road alongside the ground he was thinking about going home and telephoning Lucy. Throughout the cold walk back to his vehicle he thought of it and then eventually decided against the idea. *It would make him look too eager and besides, he wanted to celebrate with a few beers in the pub!*

As he neared his Ford Zephyr, something suspicious caught his eye. A young girl of around 16 years of age was slumped over the bonnet and he prepared to give her a 'mouthful' and a lecture for daring to touch his motor!

"Oi!" He drew alongside the car and grabbed her. "What are you doing?" He pulled her upwards from off the bonnet but the expression upon her face and the pale, deathly white shade of her skin gave him reason for concern. "Hey Sweetheart, what's wrong? Yow ok bab?" Her eyes rolled in her head and she tried to speak before suddenly vomiting violently all over his brown leather shoes. Straight away he could tell that she had taken some kind of substance. *This sort of thing was becoming more and more commonplace, local kids were being flooded with drugs and more and more of them were ending up in hospital or worse.* "What have you taken?" He demanded an answer and she somehow managed to mumble the words 'fuck off'... He resisted the urge to try and shake some sense into her and instead flagged down a nearby member of the St John's Ambulance who had been providing medical support at the match. "Where did you get it?" As the medic approached, Gallier tried to question the girl but he she was in no condition to answer questions. "I think she has taken something... She will probably need her stomach pumped..." As the medic reached them, Gallier offered his thoughts. He had no medical training himself, but he had seen plenty of teenagers who had fallen into such a state through the misuse of drugs.

"Ok mate... We will get her into hospital... Thanks for alerting us..." The medic appeared competent and Gallier felt a sense of relief. *It was his day off, he didn't want to waste valuable drinking time driving some druggie kid into hospital!* But of course, if it was necessary, that is exactly what he would have done...

As he drove the short distance back towards his hometown of Tipton, Gallier continued to shiver in the November cold and hoped that the car's heater would hurry up and start to work. For short journeys, this would never happen... He thought about the girl he had just seen and the increasing problems with illegal substances. It made his blood boil. Ordinary villains, men who robbed banks and ran protection rackets were bad enough, but the men who supplied drugs to youngsters, knowing that their poison would either turn them into addicts or even worse were a significantly lower form of scum. *How he would love to round up the drug dealing gangsters, like he had rounded up unruly squaddies in Germany, and then personally beat the shit out of each and every one of them...* His thoughts turned to Cedric Tanner... Everyone knew that Tanner was the drug dealing, gangster number one in the Black Country and Reggie Gallier was going to make it his personal duty to *bring the bastard down...*

Chapter 3

The autumnal rain beat against the windscreen of Gallier's Ford Zephyr and the brisk wind took hold of the fallen yellow leaves and thrust them against the side of the car. It was dark outside and Reggie Gallier composed himself as he sat and glared at Cedric Tanner's Jaguar that was also parked on the car park of the Doughty Arms in Tipton. He thought extensively of the young girl he had found slumped against the bonnet of his Ford less than an hour earlier. *Drugs were getting a tighter grip upon the youth of the day and it simply was not fair that many parents were having to bury their offspring whilst drug dealing gangsters like Tanner were getting richer and more powerful by the day...* For a mad moment, a wild fantasy entered Gallier's mind. *If he was not a police officer, if he was just an ordinary member of the public, he could embark upon a violent spree as an unhinged vigilante, tracking down scum like Tanner and murdering them in horrific and extreme ways...* He smiled at the thought and then returned to reality, slightly disturbed at the pleasure and sense of satisfaction thoughts of such violence gave him... He had to retain his composure. *He did a good job... He wasn't bent or crooked like many of his colleagues and he could sleep easy at night knowing that he was a force for good. He did catch 'bad guys' and he did achieve some form of justice for many...* However, he did not sleep well... Insomnia was a constant battle and copious quantities of alcohol were his only ally against a condition that blighted his entire existence. Work had consumed him and as much as he liked to pretend that he didn't really like his job and that he could 'take it or leave it', the reality was that every night he would be haunted by the faces and predicaments of the people that he had not been able to help. Desperate people, the poor souls that had fallen victim to the *scum that walked the streets* and had never gained any sense of closure or justice. People like the young girl Cedric Tanner had paraded in the Doughty Arms just days previously. *What had even happened to her? Would she ever find happiness? Would she ever find normality?*

As he closed his eyes and listened to the rain fall, literally dozens of corpses flooded through Reggie Gallier's mind. Victims... Innocents... People that had been beaten and robbed... Women that had been raped and murdered... Children that had been neglected or worse... He knew many coppers that were immune to it... *But then again, they all pretended to be...* Cold, matter of fact men who dealt with things as part of their job in much the same way that a greengrocer would deal with fruit and vegetables. As far as tough exterior, physical fighting prowess and ultra-assertive police brutality was concerned, Reggie Gallier was the hardest of the hard, but inside he was quite the opposite. It was this sensitivity and fragile nature that made him so aggressive and passionate. He was emotionally weak and it was these characteristics that not only made him a highly volatile and violent policeman, but also affected his relationships with women... He was very much the womaniser, but this method of 'having fun' with the girls and not allowing them to get too close was all part of his own self-preservation. When he was in the army and stationed in Germany, he had been madly in love with a Tipton girl whose parents ran pubs and when the relationship had ended prematurely, it had certainly affected him and hardened his exterior in ways that he would never let another living soul know... *But he was Reggie Gallier and anyone who messed with him would get smashed!* He opened his eyes and glared forcefully at Tanner's Jag again... *Cedric Tanner had started something... Cedric Tanner had used a young innocent girl as a pawn against him and Cedric Tanner continued to flood the streets with drugs that were making an absolute mockery of THE LAW!*

He looked at his watch and realised that the night was still young. How he longed to wait for Tanner to emerge from the pub so that he could jump on him and beat him to a pulp on the pub car park... *But what would that achieve?* If it was ever discovered that he (Gallier) had been the perpetrator, then he would lose his job and his mother and father would be in grave danger from the risk of revenge attacks from Tanner's organisation. *Tanner was scum... His (Tanner's) father had been scum and their entire organisation were all scummy parasites who fed off the good and innocent folks of Wolverhampton and the Black Country. Besides, Cedric Tanner could probably take a beating as well as the next villain, it meant nothing to them...* For years, so called tough cops like Reggie Gallier had tried to control villains by beating them at their own game. Pulling them into police cells and then kicking them senseless, but villains were getting cleverer and with the rise in drugs they were getting richer... They could telephone their solicitors and it was no longer a simple, old-fashioned game of 'cops and robbers' where Gallier had to chase the 'bad guys' in their mk11 Jaguars before beating them down like the 'good sheriff'. It wasn't like that anymore and as villains were becoming more complex and sophisticated, the blunt weapons of the law, men like Reggie Gallier were quickly becoming relics of the past...

Eventually, Gallier pulled himself out of the car and walked towards the rear entrance of the pub. He had no exact plan of what to do, but it was getting cold outside in the Zephyr and besides, he needed a beer! Once inside, he turned into the main barroom and was somewhat relieved to see that a vast open fire roared in the middle of the far wall. Adjacent to it was an old-fashioned wooden bar where a middle-aged barman served numerous customers. It was Saturday night and as per usual the pub was heaving with revellers who were looking to spend their hard-earned wages. Gallier didn't mind the crowd. He knew that Tanner and his boys were sat in the corner in their usual spot and he knew that the abundance of people in the room would help him to blend anonymously and not be recognised by the gangster. Reggie Gallier was certainly not afraid of the man, but at present he had no plan so it would be a case of simply sitting back in the shadows and observing the villains until he could think of an idea that would prove more effective than simply beating Tanner to a pulp... He pulled up the collars of his black overcoat discretely and waited patiently at the bar to be served.

"Hello Reg... I ay seen you in here for a few nights..." The barman eventually greeted him and Gallier hoped that the man was not on Tanner's pay roll. The last thing he needed was for the bar staff to alert the villains to his presence.

"Ar bin busy ay I mate... Pint of Hanson's mild and have yow got any pork cobs?"

"Sorry Reg, no pork, but there will be some tomorrow after mar Mrs has cooked Sunday dinner... Ar've got cheese and onion or ham and pickle?" The barman pointed to a selection of bread cobs but Gallier shook his head disappointedly.

"Nah leave it... I might have a bag of scratchuns' later..."

"Ok Reg..." The barman pulled the dark frothy beer and placed it upon the counter.

"Oh, and give us a large scotch chaser..." Gallier nodded upwards towards the optics that hung behind the bar and the barman pulled a double measure of Bells blended whisky into a glass.

"Celebrating the win am yer?" The barman nodded to Gallier's blue and white football scarf and the detective managed a brief smile. He had all but forgotten about the match and the afternoon's victory against Tottenham Hotspur at the Hawthorns. He downed the whisky in one and then moved into a discreet area of the barroom where he could keep an eye on Tanner's party without being noticed. He sat down and made himself comfortable before pulling out a cigarette. The atmosphere was thick with tobacco smoke and he had not enjoyed a smoke for all of thirty minutes! He lit up his cigarette and enjoyed the feeling of the thick smoke filling up his lungs as he eyed two young ladies that entered the room. The first one was petite with long brown hair, a moderately pretty face that was covered in freckles and a skirt that was so short that it stood out despite the popularity of the mini skirt in the 1960s. The second girl wore an equally as revealing outfit, however, she was thicker set and her face was almost pig like with bright blonde hair that had been curled tastefully. She wore an abundance of makeup in an attempt to try and make herself prettier and Gallier estimated that both girls were probably in their middle twenties.

"Is anyone sitting here bab?" The first and prettier girl suddenly spoke to Gallier and the policeman smiled and decided that he would probably try and cheer himself up by sleeping with her.

"No love… Teck a seat…" Gallier pulled the chair back for the brunette and was disappointed when her significantly less attractive accomplice sat down as well. "Can I get you ladies a drink?"

"Babycham please…" The chubby girl with the blonde hair responded first and much to Gallier's disappointment the prettier girl suddenly turned around as she recognised a male friend in another part of the pub.

"Er, not for me thanks… I've gotta go and see a friend over there." The brunette gave her fat friend a wink and then rushed off to greet her male acquaintance. Gallier groaned inwardly and felt as though he had been 'set up'. *How he would much rather be having a drink with Lucy from the previous night!*

"Am yow gunna get me that Babycham then? My name is Kate…" the chunky girl was polite and came across as being particularly friendly and Gallier noticed that she at least had a nice smile.

"Maybe in a minute love… Let me finish my pint first…" Gallier looked away and diverted his attention between the short-skirted brunette who was now on the other side of the room and Cedric Tanner and his band of merry men. Tanner was by far the eldest man at his table. His accomplices were young 'pretty boys' who were immaculately dressed in sharp suits and were all competing and baying for their master's attention. "So then Kate… What is your friend's name?"

"Her name is Gemma… But we ay here to talk about her bab… Lets talk about me…" Kate's eyes were blue and as she fixed Gallier with her best attempts at a seductive gaze, he noticed that her breasts were particularly large. He grunted laughter and then tossed his eyebrows before diverting his gaze back to Cedric Tanner's table. Kate noticed his lack of interest and then discretely placed her stubby hand onto his knee that was concealed under the stable. "So what is your obsession with Mr Tanner? Am yow one of them as well?"

"What do you mean? One of them?" Gallier was surprised by the comment and became suddenly alert to his female companion. *Just what did she know about Cedric Tanner?*

"You know what I mean... A poofter, a shirtlifter... Mr Tanner likes girls and boys dow he..." Kate grinned sheepishly. Up until that year (1967), homosexuality had been against the law in Britain and a stigma, an aura of 'wrongness' and an embarrassment still surrounded the realms of gayness.

"I didn't know that Kate..." Gallier lied. "Let me get yow that Babycham and then you can tell me all the gossip about Mr Tanner!" The lawman suddenly summonsed up a degree of interest in his unattractive companion and he stroked her exposed and chubby thighs in a way that instantly excited her. *She would have her uses after all!*

"So am yow one of them?" Gallier returned from the bar with another pint of beer for himself and a Babycham for Kate and the buxom girl repeated her question.

"One of them?" Gallier sat down and took a generous gulp of Hanson's mild.

"A poofter!" Kate smirked and her naive embarrassment struck again.

"Only on Tuesdays..." Gallier joked and the chubby blonde snorted as she giggled. "Nah... Not my cup of tea bab, but it ay none of my business what folks get up too..." Gallier lied again, he was strictly heterosexual but as a police officer, he made it very much his business to find out what other people were up to. He winked at Kate and then placed his hand firmly upon her knee. "So you know all about Cedric Tanner then?"

"Just the same as what most people know..." She smiled and her eyes were wide, completely oblivious to the fact that she was being manipulated as part of Gallier's personal vendetta against the Black Country drug lord.

"Oh yeah? And what's that?" The policeman encouraged the young woman to take a generous gulp of her drink. "Ar'll get yer another Babycham in a minute..."

"Am yow trying to get me tipsy?" She suddenly realised that she did not even know her male companion's name. "What is your name?"

27

"Reg… But yow can call me Reggie…" He smiled flirtatiously and wondered how far he could push his questions about Tanner before arousing suspicion. *But then, looking at her, she was far from an intellectual and he could probably ask away as much as he wanted!*

"Like Reggie Kray?" The randomness of her question surprised him.

"What do yow know about Reggie Kray?" He laughed as he continued to retain a subtle visual on Tanner's table.

"He's a villain ay he? Down in London… Him and his brother am always in the papers. Yow even look a bit like Reggie Kray…" Kate took another gulp of her drink and gazed into Gallier's eyes. He had never been compared to the gangster before and he was surprised by her observation. He was roughly the same age as the Kray twins, had the same colour hair and was of a similar build, but for him that was as far as the resemblance went…

"What about him over there?" Gallier nodded towards the table where Tanner and his boys were sat.

"Cedric Tanner?" She really was not the brightest…

"Yeah… Ain't he a bit of a villain?" Gallier retained his flirtatiousness and smiled as he tried to portray an aura of naivety.

"Of course he is… He's the one who sells all the drugs ay he…"

"I don't know…" Gallier lied as his false smile was beginning to make his face ache.

"Yeah…" She crossed her chubby thighs and fluttered her eye lashes. "You see that young bloke sat next to him? The good looking one in the nice suit."

"The chap smokin' the fag?"

"Yeah him… He sells pills in all the pubs and youth clubs where the kids gew…" Gallier was surprised by her knowledge and felt annoyed with himself for having significantly less knowledge of the number one gangster locally than some 'air head' he had just met in the pub.

"What's his name?"

"They call him Doctor George... Ar dow think he really is a doctor... He just sells drugs..." She downed her Babycham and looked at Gallier expectantly for her next drink. Her friend Gemma was still sat nearby with another man and as her mini skirt rose further up her thigh whilst in full view of the policeman, Gallier continued to wish that he was talking to the more attractive of the pair... *Oh well, he had found out some valuable information and the night was young.*

He returned from the bar with yet more beer for himself and a second Babycham for Kate. As he got closer to the table, he figured that the alcohol was beginning to take effect as suddenly she didn't look quite so bad... *She was busty, blonde, caked in makeup and her skirt was short... So what if she looked a bit like a pig!*

"Here you go bab... Get that daahn yer..." He handed her the drink and then thought briefly of Lucy, the girl from the previous night... He certainly did not feel bad for flirting with another woman, it wasn't as if he had officially begun any kind of relationship with Lucy, but he did like her and secretly he did hope that she herself was not out on the town that night! Flirting with men as he was with Kate! *This was just work...* "So... This Doctor George fella, do yow buy gear off him?" He watched as she took a gulp of her drink and once again he tried to fix her with a flirtatious and charming gaze.

"Oh no Reggie... Ar'm a good girl..." She giggled and snorted again and Gallier forced another fake smile as he continued to wish that he was with either Lucy or the nearby Gemma instead...

"I bet you are..." Gallier raised his eyebrows lasciviously and then cast his eyes around the bar. *He had to make the most of a bad situation.* "So how do you know he sells pills?"

"Everyone knows!" She shook her head in disbelief. "My brother's friend Colin buys pills off him and he tecks um' when he goes to see the groups at the plaza in Dudley..." She was completely oblivious to the fact that she was talking to a police officer and Reggie Gallier nodded with a professional interest. He was aware that drugs were being abused by many of the youngsters who were watching the latest bands at

29

the Plaza and what Kate was saying 'tied in' with the knowledge and intelligence he already had. *When he was a youngster in the 50s, he was more than happy with a night filled with Chuck Berry and Elvis records, a belly full of beer and a good scrap at the end of the night! He had been a 'Teddy boy' and the youth of today's obsession with peace, love, flower power and all those 'loopy' drugs was beyond him...*

An hour and a half passed and Gallier bought several more drinks as he continued to discretely eyeball Cedric Tanner's party. He was running out of 'small talk' to occupy his female companion and when the man allegedly known as Doctor George got up and left the room, Gallier immediately rose to his feet.

"I'm just poppin' to the lavatory bab... I'll be back in a minute." He tapped Kate on the knee and then swiftly followed Doctor George into a narrow hallway that separated the bar from the lounge. The younger man went into the men's toilet and unzipped his flies as he stood at the urinal.

"Are you the one they call Doctor George?" Gallier was relieved to see that the toilets were empty apart from himself and the supposed drug dealer.

"Who wants to know?" The young man replied smugly and before he could utter another word, Gallier smashed his face off the brick wall above the urinal and then dragged him backwards into an open cubicle as Doctor George was stunned from the impact. He tried to struggle but Reggie Gallier punched him in the guts with such force that he fell down onto his knees in agony.

"So then Doctor George..." The policeman locked the cubicle door and then turned to look down at the drug dealer who was on his knees before him. "I bet it ain't the first time yow bin down on your knees in a toilet cubicle!" Gallier couldn't resist the smart comment and Doctor George gasped to gain his breath so that he could talk.

"Do you know who I am? Do you know who I work for?"

"I know exactly who you work for..." Gallier gave the villain a look of disgust and then hit him with a slap that cast Doctor George backwards into the toilet. "I wanna know where Tanner stashes his gear... Where's the distribution point?"

"Yow'm a copper!" Doctor George could not help but feel a sense of relief. *A copper would just give him a kicking... A rival gangster would bury him and he had heard that another Black Country crime figure, William 'Billy' Mucklow was due to be released from prison soon...* "Fuck off pig!" George sniggered as he spoke and Gallier responded by shoving his head violently into the toilet bowl. First, he flushed the chain and then wedged the Doctor's head between the toilet bowl and the seat. It was certainly not the freshest of toilets and it stank of stale urine and faeces.

"I said, where does Tanner stash his drugs?"

"Fuck off pig!" George remained defiant and even began to make grunting pig like noises. Gallier had heard it all before, but he had a venomous hatred towards drug dealers, especially those that were affiliated with Cedric Tanner! He summoned up all of his strength, aggression and hatred and proceeded to smash the toilet seat back and fourth into Doctor George's face until suddenly it shattered under the sheer force. The drug dealer's face was battered and covered in blood and Gallier could see that a couple of teeth had become lose.

"So are you going to tell me?" Gallier lent against the side of the cubicle and looked down as the crook tried to talk through the blood that was gurgling inside of his throat.

"I ain't tellin' you nothing copper..." The younger man's defiance was almost impressive and Gallier smiled.

"Well... I know that yower name is Doctor George and that yow sell pills to kids outside the Plaza in Dudley... What do yow think your mate Cedric Tanner would say if half a dozen hairy arsed coppers dragged him into Dudley Police station?" Gallier paused and now it was his turn to laugh smugly. "Then I walk into Tanner's cell and tell him all about my new informant... The guy that sells pills outside the Plaza... The fella they call Doctor George..." Gallier paused again and for the first time a look of fear came over the drug dealers face.

"Fuck off! I ain't no grass!"

"Maybe... Maybe not... But our mutual friend Mr Tanner ain't gunna know that when I fit him up for supplying drugs..."

"Where's your evidence copper?" Doctor George was becoming increasingly agitated by the second as Gallier began to laugh even harder.

"It ay ever stopped me in the past..." Gallier shrugged and stroked the slight stubble on his chin as he pretended to be deep in thought. He was toying with the villain as a cat toys with its prey... *He loved it...* "Besides, yow'm right... It would never make it to court... But what would happen then? Tanner would be released and he would be back on the street... Who do you think the first person he's gunna come looking for is?" Gallier suddenly stopped laughing and his eyes became deathly serious.

"You rotten bastard... You absolute filth..." Tears from the pain of his injuries and from his frustration began to fill Doctor George's eyes.

"I reckon Tanner would have you buried in concrete under that new motorway they'm building..." Between 1967 and 1970, the stretch of road north of junction four of the M5 motorway at Bromsgrove was constructed alongside Frankly Services and ran from Lydiate Ash at Bromsgrove through to the M6 near to West Bromwich and Wednesbury, cutting straight through the eastern edge of the Black Country. "Or he'll teck you over to Bartley Green reservoir and drop yer into the water wearing a pair of concrete boots!" There was no hint of humour left in Gallier's voice and Doctor George knew full well that what the policeman was saying was correct.

"What do you want?" The young villain sat up on the floor of the toilet cubicle and spat blood onto the ground.

"What I just said.. I wanna know where Tanner stashes his gear... If you tell me now, you'll never see me again and ar won't tell Tanner that yow grassed him up..."

"Why should ar trust yow? Yow'm a copper..."

"You can't...But it seems to me as it is the only option aer kid..." Gallier shrugged again and pulled out a note pad and pencil from his jacket pocket. "But just know this kid, if yow give me a false address or lead me on a wild goose chase, yow better start prayin' that I find you before Cedric Tanner does!" The Black Country policeman held the notepad against the cubicle door and then raised his pencil to the page. "Now... Tell me that address..."

Chapter 4

Dudley Borough Police Force first opened its new Police Station on the 22nd of October 1941 with an official ceremony conducted by Viscount Cobham. The architects were local, Webb and Gray of Dudley and the construction cost a total of £50,000 which in 1941 was a considerable sum of money. It stood in Priory Street, Dudley and featured a curved frontal appearance with two lion statues at the main entrance of the building. Above the grand main opening were two imposing statues of a 17th century nightwatchman and a 1940s Policeman complete with a large Dudley coat of arms that stood at the very top of the building.

By November 1967, Dudley Borough Police Force had now become amalgamated into West Midlands Constabulary after a restructure in April 1966, but the imposing building on Priory Street, Dudley remained an important Police station and Reggie Gallier's primary place of work. On the ground floor, a main reception stood which led through into a series of small corridors that featured several cells and interview rooms. The offices were upstairs and on the morning of Monday the 27th of November, Reggie Gallier trudged through the station with the aim of speaking to his senior officer.

It had been an interesting and eventful weekend. He had acquired a new love interest on the Friday night in Lucy and then attended a victorious football match for his beloved Baggies and 'bagged' some valuable intelligence on the loathsome Cedric Tanner on the Saturday. He had quite a spring in his step and not even the slight hangover from Sunday afternoon's beer drinking session could but a dampener on things. The only downside of the weekend was that he had agreed to meet the chubby blonde Kate again, but it was the least he could do after she had provided him with such invaluable information. *She may even have more intel? He would just have to make sure that he was never spotted with Kate by Lucy!*

At the top of the stairs, a large office lay in front of him that was littered with several desks that belonged to the various members of CID. One of those desks was his own, but instead of making himself a cup of tea (he rarely made his own tea when there were pretty female plods around to do it for him) and sit down at his work station, he continued to the rear of the room where a light brown coloured door led into a small office that belonged to his senior officer. He took a deep breath and then knocked softly on the oak door. Since his childhood and especially since his time spent in the army, Reggie Gallier had detested any form of authority and it was part of the reason as to why he had never and would never rise above the rank of Sergeant. By embracing the higher ranks, this would mean accepting the concept of authority and this was something that Gallier simply could not bring himself to do. An inner arrogance that was deeply rooted in an historic lack of self-esteem and confidence would not allow himself to be looked down upon by anyone, no matter what their social standing or professional rank. However, this inner turmoil in relation to those that were supposedly better than him, gave him a strange and curious apprehension and borderline fear... *He simply could not allow himself to be humiliated by his superiors...* Orders were orders and everyone had to follow them, but the slightest hint of anyone humiliating him or promoting their own self-importance at his expense filled him with a constant dread... He certainly did not fear his senior officers, but his own feelings of inadequacy and humiliation would taunt him in his most personal of hours and he could not allow the events of the day to add to this torture. When he lay awake at night, constantly replaying events in his mind that had become more and more exaggerated and detrimental with each repetition, he would become angry for having let himself become weak, taunted, belittled... Above anything, he could not stand his own questioning, feelings of inadequacy and self-loathing...

"Come in..." Detective Inspector Fowler was not much older than Reggie Gallier. Ten years at most. Somewhat surprisingly, he was not an authoritative man. He had risen to the rank of DI because he had been fortunate enough to have been in the 'right place at the right time' and more vitally, he had a distinct talent for 'kissing backsides' and 'licking boots' as Gallier thought of it.. As a Police officer, Fowler had been weak and had come far off the successes of other coppers, including Detective Sergeant Reggie Gallier. His voice was soft and his gaze lame.

"Good morning Sir..." Gallier smiled and waited for his senior officer's permission to sit down. In London, it was popular for members of the Metropolitan Police to call their senior officers 'Guv' or 'Guvnor', but in the Midlands and throughout the rest of Britain, the more traditional term of 'Sir' was still very much the order of the day.

"Reg... Sit down..." Fowler gestured smugly towards a wooden chair that sat opposite his own chair at a large mahogany desk that featured a leatherette top. Several filing cabinets stood in a corner of the drafty room but apart from that the space was relatively sparse. "You had a lucky win on Saturday!" The DI referred to the events of the weekend's football match and Gallier suddenly remembered that his senior officer was for some reason a supporter of Tottenham Hotspur, the team that Albion had beaten. He had always wondered why Fowler supported a team that was not local, but then he remembered that it was something to do with Fowler's father being from North London... *Fucking Cockneys!*

"Thanks Sir... I've got some 'shit hot' info on a known local villain and I'd like your permission to act on it..." In order to obtain a warrant for the search of the property where Tanner's drugs were supposedly stashed, Gallier first needed the approval of an officer with the rank of Inspector or higher. He would then have to type out several copies by hand on his imperial typewriter so that one copy could be left with the approving magistrate, one at the Police Station and then one at the property that was to be raided. Gallier hated this red tape and bull shit, the typewriter made the tips of his fingers ache and he always ended up using masses of tip-ex to correct his errors!

"Ok..." Fowler seemed a little confused. "I know you Reg and since when have you needed my permission to make an arrest?"

36

"It's a bit more complicated than that Sir… I need a warrant to search a property and I will need boots on the ground to help make it happen."

"Surely you're capable of getting a few plods to come with you?" Fowler was genuinely surprised. "Am I talking to the same Reggie Gallier? In the past your biggest problem was storming in without backup or the correct authorisation!" The senior officer grinned sheepishly. Gallier and some of the other hardened CID officers made him nervous. He was very much aware that they were significantly tougher and more street wise than he was and he lived in a constant fear that one day he would be 'found out' for being the weak minded, people pleasing, career chasing fraud that he was. Gallier lent forwards and reduced his voice to a whisper. *Cedric Tanner had far too many coppers on his pay roll and he simply did not know who he could trust.*

"The face I'm after is Mr Big himself…" Gallier reduced the volume of his voice even further. "Cedric Tanner…" He studied Fowler's eyes for a reaction and the DI did not fail to reveal Gallier's worst expectations.

"What!" Fowler's fear was somewhat disappointing. Reggie Gallier did not rate the man as a senior Policeman, he was weak and had very little in the way of detection skills, but he had not suspected him to be on Tanner's pay roll. He was disappointed, but ultimately not surprised. "You can't just go after a man like Cedric Tanner!" Fowler's greying hair appeared to turn significantly greyer in just a few short seconds. "Tell me Gallier, exactly what 'hot information' do you have?"

"I know where he stashes his gear…" As soon as he opened his mouth, Gallier regretted his words… *He had now informed his enemy of his knowledge…* He was immediately livid with himself… *He should have known better!*

"Right… I see…" Fowler's eyes searched the room nervously, fearful to look into the younger detective's eyes. "And what do you intend to do about it Gallier?"

"I would suggest that we get a warrant to search the location and seize the drugs and whatever faces we can get our hands on... Give me half an hour in the cells with the bastards and I will get them singing like Tom fuckin' Jones Sir..." Gallier's eyes were deadly serious and Fowler shuddered at his Sergeant's efficiency in such interrogative situations. "It will help us to build a case against the big man..." DS Gallier was still not quite convinced as to whether or not Fowler was on Tanner's payroll. *Maybe he was just scared?*

"And where is this supposed drug storage unit?"

"Sorry but I cannot give up that information at this point Sir..." Gallier sat back in his chair and fixed his senior officer with an intimidating glare.

"Damn it man! Why won't you turn over your information to a senior officer!" As Fowler became further agitated, Reggie Gallier became further fearful and suspicious that the man was in fact on Cedric Tanner's payroll. Gallier looked away, smiled and then changed the subject entirely.

"That's a nice Humber Imperial you've got parked outside Sir... It is a very nice car... Especially on a humble Police officer's wage..." The DS stopped smiling and then grunted sarcastically as he glared at Fowler again and silently dared the man to react.

"What are you suggesting Reg?" The Detective Inspector knew exactly what Gallier was referring to and he suddenly calmed nervously. He simply could not look at the Detective Sergeant and Gallier could almost smell his fear.

"I'm just saying that you have a nice car Sir..." Gallier considered lighting himself a cigarette but decided against it. "So can I get a warrant for this Sir?"

"Er..." Fowler fidgeted uncomfortably as he tried to think of an answer. "Leave it with me Reg... For now I want you to go with plod and look into some recent vehicle thefts in Dudley..."

"But surely bringing down the biggest drug dealer this side of London would be more of a priority Sir?" Gallier narrowed his eyebrows suspiciously.

"I will decide what is and what is not a priority Gallier! Now get out of my office and get on with it..." Fowler was far from confident in his attempts to be assertive. Gallier remained rooted to the spot for several seconds before finally standing up. *Intimidation was his middle name...*

"Ok Sir... You're the boss... Whatever you think is best..."

Gallier's intuition and gut judgement proved accurate. He sat behind the wheel of an unmarked CID squad car, a brown 1964 Austin Westminster and waited discreetly as Fowler emerged out onto the station's car park and climbed into his own luxurious Humber Imperial. The luxury car was a rebadged version of the Coventry manufacturer's famous Super Snipe model and was aimed at the nation's upper middle classes. Certainly not a car for middle ranking Policemen...

Where the fuck is he off to then? Gallier spoke aloud to himself as he shook his head with a mixture of suspicion and sheer disappointment. It was DC Graham Ward's birthday and the Detective Constable had booked out the Westminster so that he could go and pick up the cakes! The whole station would be disappointed that the car's keys were missing, but Gallier had much more important issues upon his mind. Besides, *he preferred Pork scratchun's to cakes!* As the Humber moved off, Reggie Gallier put the Austin into gear and proceeded to follow his senior officer from a safe distance.

Following a fellow Police officer without being detected was far more difficult than 'tailing' a regular member of the public. But Reggie Gallier was an expert at keeping out of the sight of the target car. He turned the in-car Police radio unit as quiet as it would go and focused his attention solely on Fowler's Humber. His hypothesis was that Fowler had probably made telephone contact with Tanner from the Station and had now arranged a meeting. *That would explain the twenty-five-minute delay between him (Gallier) speaking to the Inspector and Fowler actually getting into his car... Of course, he could still be wrong? He hoped that he was wrong... Maybe Fowler was popping out for a fried breakfast somewhere?* But his cynical and hardened intuition told him that he was not wrong. *Detective Inspector Fowler was on Tanner's payroll and it sickened him to the core...*

Gallier's fears were all but confirmed when Fowler's Humber Imperial led him down the long driveway that led to the Crooked House pub in nearby Himley. The pub was originally built in 1765 as a farmhouse but during the early 19th century, land subsidence in the area caused by the many old mines caused the building to lean to one side giving it a somewhat lopsided appearance. At around this time, the farmhouse was converted into a pub and was christened the Siden House. It was later renamed the Glynne Arms in honour of a local landowner by the name of Sir Stephen Glynne who owned the land upon which the pub was built. The building was later marked for demolition during the 1940s as it was considered to be unsafe, however, Wolverhampton and Dudley breweries bought the pub and they constructed buttresses and girders that helped to make the building structurally safe. The pub was renamed the Crooked House and it soon became something of a local legend as many customers were drawn to the premises in order to see the famous optical illusions where marbles and glasses would appear to roll up hill!

As Gallier pulled the Austin up at a safe distance and walked to the edge of the carpark, the pub's history was far from his mind. Trilby hats were by no means fashionable for men of his age in 1967, but as he approached the car park of the pub on foot, he wore a large grey overcoat and a black trilby in order to try and conceal his identity. He dodged stealthily between cars and was not surprised to see that Fowler's Humber was now parked alongside Cedric Tanner's Jag. He got as close he dared to and then ducked between an old Vauxhall Velox and an even older Ford Prefect. Slowly and as carefully as possible, he protruded his head from around the side of the Velox and then quickly identified the unmistakable features of Cedric Tanner who was stood at the rear of his Jaguar and speaking directly to Inspector Fowler. Reg Gallier was not close enough to make out any of what was being said and he was half tempted to approach both men who were present and challenge them over their allegiances. He thought better of it... *For now...* He noticed that Tanner looked particularly angry and the gangster raised his voice several times as he pointed intimidatingly into Fowler's face. Frustratingly, the voice was still somewhat muffled and Gallier could still not make out a word of what was being said. *Fowler was clearly warning Tanner that one of his officers had discovered the whereabouts of the drug distribution unit...* Of course, Gallier had no way of knowing this for sure, but it was highly likely... He looked at his watch and realised that he had minimal time to act before Tanner moved all of his drugs and then all would be lost... He made his way stealthily and quickly back towards the Austin and then re-checked his notebook for the address 'Doctor' George had given him the other night... The race was on!

Chapter 5

The address that 'Doctor' George had provided was in a small industrial region on the far border of Tipton on the road towards Oldbury. Close to Dudley and the hillside town of Tividale, the premises still carried a Tipton address and when Gallier pulled up nearby he was relieved to see that there were no signs of Cedric Tanner's Jag. It had been just a few short miles from the Crooked House in Himley to the site of Tanner's supposed drug storage unit, but the traffic had not been great and the journey had taken longer than Reggie Gallier had anticipated. He was very aware that he did not have a search warrant so he had no legal methods of searching the property for drugs, however, he also knew full well that he could apprehend and search any individual that happened to be leaving the building. In this eventuality, if the individual was found to be in possession of illegal drugs, Gallier would then be able to prove a link and a justifiable reason for entering the drug store without a warrant... *Fuck DI Fowler!* His senior officer's actions sickened him and as he parked the brown Austin nearby, he looked around hopefully for signs of human activity.

The rest of the locality had appeared to be bustling and busy but Tanner's unit was concealed behind an array of autumnal trees and was situated in a quiet corner of the estate that was desolate and undisturbed. The building itself was Victorian and the sound of heavy hammers and blast furnaces from miles around were deafening, but like most Black Country folk, Reggie Galler was more than used to it. As a child, Gallier had fully expected to eventually follow his forefathers into the kind of heavy industry that had become a natural ascension for youngsters in the area in which he lived, but his National Service and natural abilities in the Military Police had led him into a very different means of employment. His parents had neither approved or disapproved, though he was very aware that his two younger brothers and his three sisters had looked upon his career choice with a certain suspicion and disdain.

Like many working-class people in the mid twentieth century, they had a certain respect for officers of the law, but this was also coupled with a level of distrust and fear. Not necessarily for the honest Bobby on the beat who kept the streets safe and helped old ladies to cross the roads, but for the smartly dressed Detectives who were always on the lookout for new informants whom they could keep in the pockets of their freshly pressed, off the shelf Burton suits. The men that stunk of a mixture of Old Spice cologne, blended Scotch whisky and Park Drive cigarettes. DS Reggie Gallier was certainly one of the latter and conversations amongst his brothers and brother in laws would always fade to silence upon his entrance into their vicinity, as if they always expected him to be looking to 'fit them up' for some kind of imaginary crime. He would never admit it, not even to himself, but it was very much an 'us and them' attitude that had seen him mostly excluded from his own family and subconsciously, it hurt him deeply. Ultimately, his family were jealous of his career successes. They did not go to work wearing shiny shoes and new suits and even though his wages were relatively humble, they were still superior to those of his siblings and their other halves. However, he had no guilt... He still lived at his parents address in Tipton, but it was he who paid the rent to the council each month! Of course, his mother and father had wondered why their eldest son had not yet found himself a wife and moved out, but on the other hand they also had their concerns as to who would pay the rent once their son had finally fled the nest!

He lit himself a cigarette and peered over the large steering wheel at the gloomy looking Victorian building. *Were there really thousands of pounds worth of illegal drugs stashed in there?* He thought about how he would put 'Doctor' George's face through the nearest window if he found out that he had been lied to and then a bizarre thought entered his mind which seemed to grow less bizarre and more appealing the more he thought about it. *If Tanner had so much money tied up in the gear stashed inside that decrepit old warehouse and he (Gallier) could not get a search warrant, surely the most disruptive thing to Cedric Tanner would be to set the place on fire? Burn it to the ground with the drugs inside thus taking the gear off the streets and striking a significant blow upon the Black Country drug lord...* Gallier smiled to himself and appreciated the idea as it stood in theory and then began to think seriously about the actual logistics of the task and he came to his senses... *He didn't have the slightest idea about how to commit effective arson and by the time he had gone away and returned later that night with the relevant resources, Tanner would have probably removed all of his product upon the advice of DI Fowler...* He shrugged and put the cigarette to his lips and inhaled deeply. *It was a good idea and the sense of justice would have been almost poetic, but alas, it was not to be...*

After a few minutes Gallier flicked his cigarette butt out of the window of the Austin Westminster and began to grow increasingly concerned about the likely arrival of Cedric Tanner and DI Fowler who would surely be along to authorise the removal of the drugs. Suddenly, an idea entered his mind and he got out of the car and strolled purposefully towards an old metal door that stood at the front of the warehouse. The windows were protected by sinister looking metal bars and instead of peering inside he hammered loudly on the main door with the side of his right foot. Just a few seconds later, he heard footsteps from the other side and then the sound of several padlocks being undone before the door began to open slightly. A large chain prevented the door from opening fully but Gallier could just about make out the features of a tall, long-haired man who wore an Afghan coat and a pair of elaborate sun glasses.

"Hey man, what do you want? This is private property..." The man stunk of marijuana and Gallier felt a rush of excitement and adrenaline as he detected a hippie-type weakness and gullibility to the individual that stood before him.

"Hello... Ar was wondering if yow could give me a hand aer kid? Ar'm a travelling salesman but my motor woe start..." Gallier pointed back towards the Austin that was just a few yards away. "I was wondering if yow could give me a push whilst I try ter jump start it?"

"That's a big heavy car man... You can't park there..." The hippie was surprisingly trusting and did not doubt that Gallier was anything other than a lost salesman, but he was fully aware that his boss would not like a stranger being parked outside of his premises attracting all sorts of unwelcome attention. *It was in his interest to get it shifted...*

"I know I cor park there mate... If yow prefer ar can push the motor if yow try and start it for me?" Gallier was sincere and convincing and the hippie sighed and unlocked the chain.

"Man, you gotta get out of here as quickly as you can ok?" The longhaired man emerged out of the building and Gallier hoped and prayed that he was stupid enough to be carrying some form of substances upon his person. *He would need this as a means of legally justifying a raid on the building, but then again, if the hippie was clean, he could always fit him up by placing some of the gear from inside about his person... But then, if 'Doctor' George was wrong then he would be totally fucked, but his intuition told him that he was on to something. This was quite clearly a drug distribution unit, hence the presence of the long-haired stupid bastard...*

As the hippie approached the Westminster, Gallier suddenly pulled out his warrant card and his voice became assertive.

"Ok Goldilocks, lets see what's inside yer jacket..." Gallier held his badge up so that the hippie could see it and the long-haired man suddenly panicked... *He had been had, hook line and sinker...*

"Fuck you copper!" The hippie swung his right hand as if to plant a punch on the side of Reggie Gallier's face, but the Detective saw it coming. He quickly blocked the fist and then headbutted the other man hard on the end of his nose. Blood exploded across his face and Gallier swiftly followed up with an intense knee to the groin before grabbing the man by the hair and smashing his face down onto the bonnet of the Austin.

"Now empty yer pockets you stinky, long-haired piece of shit..." Gallier seized another substantial piece of the suspect's hair and then raised his face up as if he was about to smash it back through the bonnet of the Westminster when two cars suddenly appeared... He recognised them both straight away and his heart instantly began to sink...

Detective Inspector Fowler and Cedric Tanner had also made their way to Tanner's premises after their meeting on the car park of the Crooked House. Fowler had suspected that Gallier would try something and he had not been wrong.

"Let him go Gallier..." Fowler got out of the Humber and tried his hardest to sound authoritative in front of Cedric Tanner.

"Sir..." Gallier bit into his bottom lip in sheer frustration. "I have reason to suspect that this man is carrying illegal substances..."

"I said let him go Gallier..." The Inspector walked closer to his colleague and was slightly fearful as to how Gallier would react.

"But we are Police officers Sir... Is it not our job to detect crime and arrest villains?" Detective Sergeant Gallier's voice was steeped in sarcasm.

"It's a fucking order Reg so just do it!" Fowler was red faced and a grinning Cedric Tanner suddenly appeared at the DI's side.

"Hello Mr Gallier... We meet again..." Tanner recognised the Detective from several nights previously at the Doughty Arms in Tipton. "It doesn't pay for you to interfere in my affairs Sergeant..." Tanner was highly patronising and Gallier was seriously tempted to wipe the smug grin from off of his face with the back of his hand.

"It doesn't pay to break the law... Or interfere with kids..." Gallier gazed at his Inspector as he made his last remark... *Was Fowler even aware that he was protecting a man who was not only a drug dealer but also a sick kiddie fiddler?* He gave Fowler a look of disgust and then averted his gaze back to Tanner who now looked annoyed. The gangster composed himself and then became smug again.

"Well... I know your name and rank Sergeant... It will be quite easy for me to find out where you live... Where your family lives..."

"What's that supposed to mean?" Gallier slung the hippie to the ground and then squared up to Cedric Tanner.

"Think of it whatever you will... But it does not pay for you to interfere in my business Detective Gallier... I am sure that you have a lovely wife, maybe even some succulent young children at home? Ageing parents maybe..." Tanner had already done his homework on Gallier and even though he knew that the Detective was not married, he knew that Gallier still lived at home with his parents on the Lost City estate... Gallier foolishly ignored the threat.

"Fuck you Tanner... I'm gunna have you... One of these days I'm gunna fuckin' have you..." Gallier pushed his face intimidatingly close to that of the drug dealer. He was several inches taller and his presence was threatening, but Cedric Tanner did not bat an eye lid.

"Inspector Fowler, please but a collar on your dog and take him home... Before he gets bitten..." Tanner turned away from the men and then walked purposefully towards the old warehouse.

"Look Reg... I know how it looks but..." As soon as Tanner was out of earshot Fowler tried to explain but Gallier cut him dead.

"I don't want to fucking know Sir... I'm about to arrest this man..." Gallier went to grab the hippie who had now risen to his feet and was walking sheepishly behind Cedric Tanner.

"Reg, if you do that, you will only make things worse for yourself. Tanner will only say that you planted the stuff on him and it will be your word against his..."

"What about your word Inspector?" Gallier searched Fowler's eyes for a hint of remorse but the Inspector looked away.

"Think about the safety of your family Reg... Cedric Tanner is a nasty piece of work believe me..."

"I thought that it was our job to lock up nasty pieces of work?" Gallier knew that the battle was lost and he began to trudge back towards the Austin Cambridge. "Will that be all?" He paused for a second and then added a sarcastic utterance of "Sir" to his question.

"Look Reg, you know how it works surely... Don't look at me like that..." Fowler suddenly tried to sound friendly and regretful but Gallier was not interested.

"No Sir... No I do not know how it fucking works Sir..." He swung the car door open and then climbed in before slamming it shut. *He needed a drink...*

Chapter 6

"So how come you're not married either?" Her question came out of nowhere and took Reggie Gallier by surprise. "You asked me the same question the other night remember and ar told you that I used to be married to a fella that was violent... It puts some blokes off, the fact that I have been married before, but it can't have put you off because you have asked to see me again..." Her smile was infectious and Gallier had been pleased when Lucy had agreed to meet him again for a drink in Cradley Heath.

"Maybe ar just wanted a beer..." He laughed and took a swig of his drink.

"Seriously Reg, I told you about me and my past... What about you? Most fellas am married with kids by the time they'm thirty years old..." Her eyes narrowed slightly and Gallier felt flattered that her interest in him was genuine. He shrugged and then looked down at his pint glass.

"I ay gunna lie to you bab, there have been a fair few wenches, but ultimately you could say that I am married to my job... It ay nine til five and it ay something you can just switch off from when you come home at night. Some coppers can do that, but with me, I'm always thinking about it..." He looked up from his beer and she could see the honesty in his eyes.

"So you're just thinking about work when you're here with me?" She stroked his chin seductively, she really did like him and his aloof nature was almost like something of a challenge.

"Now I didn't say that did I?" He placed his hand upon her exposed knee and smiled.

"So you haven't thought about work once since we have been sat here tonight in this pub?"

"Of course not..." Gallier lied. It had been a couple of days since his run in with Inspector Fowler and Cedric Tanner and he was still seething with rage. Fowler had been avoiding him and that had suited the Sargeant in some ways but his annoyance and frustration at Cedric Tanner and his drug dealing antics continued to eat away at him. As he sat in the Bell Hotel in St Anne's Road, Cradley Heath, he kept a discreet vigil for drug dealing activity as he simultaneously continued in his quest to try and impress the voluptuous and alluring Lucy. He had been eager to see her again, but his desire for her was equalled by his desire to bring Cedric Tanner to justice. He had chosen the Bell in Cradley Heath as it was a popular music venue where local *'long hairs'* would try and emulate their idols the Beatles and the Stones for the entertainment of local youngsters. Of course, this certainly was not his thing and Lucy had been surprised at his selection of venue for their second date, but Gallier figured that it may be an opportunity for him to spot more drug dealing activity. In his mind, drugs went hand in hand with 'hippies' and this was the perfect place to find it. It was also convenient as it was close to Lucy's home in Blackheath and *maybe she could fill him in on some local information in the same way that Kate had done so over in Tipton.* If he had of thought about it deeply enough, he might have felt guilty for simply using the women for information, but the pursuit of truth and justice was something that he held in high regard and to Reg Gallier, anything that was required in its achievement was deemed to be acceptable and worthwhile.

"Its good that you take your work seriously... It means that I can sleep safely at night in my bed..." She took a sip of her gin and tonic and Gallier smiled lasciviously.

"Maybe I should inspect it? Your bed... Just to check that is a safe place away from nasty villains!"

"Lets see about that one!" She nearly spat her drink out across the table as she exploded into a fit of giggles and Gallier could tell that he was onto a winner. He looked around at the long haired *'undesirables'*

49

around them and he remained surprised that he had still not witnessed anything that vaguely resembled drug dealing.

"Well the offer is there Lucy… Yow cor be too careful these days with all these druggies about!" He maintained his humorous tone and then decided to drop a 'probing' statement. "Looking around this pub, I would expect that you get a few issues with drugs around here?"

"What do you mean?" She didn't change her light-hearted tone of voice and Gallier was pleased that she had not cottoned on to the fact that he was asking a work related question.

"Well it just seems the sort of place where you might find the odd drug pusher?" Gallier lowered his voice and once again looked suspiciously around them at the younger customers inside the pub.

"Do you not know who owns this place Reg?" Lucy was genuinely surprised that Gallier did not appear to know.

"No… Who?"

"Eddie Fennel…" She lowered her voice to an almost whisper and Gallier knew straight away who she was referring to. Fennel was a local businessman with a tough reputation who was linked closely with a crime boss by the name of Billy Mucklow… *But this was not on Gallier's patch and for all he knew Mucklow was still very much in prison, as was his protégé Dickie Hickman and Mucklow's cousin, Harry Scriven who had supposedly fled to Spain… Could this have any link to Cedric Tanner?*

"I know the name… Is he a drug dealer?"

"No… Everyone knows that Fennel woe allow drugs in his venues and he literally controls this town…" Lucy suddenly began to twig that she was possibly being questioned as part of some kind of investigation and she was not impressed. "I thought you said that you weren't thinking about work?"

"No I'm not… Sorry… I was just joking about the bed thing bab!" He laughed again and demonstrated enough pseudo calm and confidence to make her smile again. "So tell me Lucy, is your bed really a safe place? Or do you need me to just check?"

"It's safe! Yow don't need to worry about that Reggie..." She smiled and shook her head jokingly. Gallier smiled back and made a mental note of the name Eddie Fennel... *Cedric Tanner literally controlled the drug trade in the Black Country and Wolverhampton so how was this Eddie Fennel able to prevent him (Tanner) from selling drugs in Cradley Heath? Maybe Fennel knew something that he did not? Maybe this Eddie Fennel could be of some kind of assistance to him?* He shrugged to himself and then diverted his attention back to the delectable Lucy... *It looked as though he may be in for a good night!*

The town of Cradley Heath was originally an area of Heathland near to the old Anglo-Saxon settlement of Cradley. With the industrial revolution and the emergence of the Black Country, the community of Cradley Heath began to evolve and in 1833 a landmark was attained when the region gained its own Baptist Church. A notable and historically important feature of this Church was that it had the distinction of being Britain's first religious establishment to have an Afro-Caribbean Minister by the name of Rev. George Cosens in 1837. Chain making became closely associated with the area and during the industrial revolution and beyond, Cradley Heath and the nearby town of Netherton became known as the Chain making capital of the entire world. In 1910, the chains that featured on the infamous cruise ship Titanic were built at the Noah Hingley works in Netherton and heavy industry, smog and pollution were a quintessential feature of the locality.

The local police station was situated in nearby Old Hill and stood near to Halesowen Road in the central area of the town. Reggie Gallier's close friend Tony Giles was based there as a Detective Constable and on the morning after Gallier's second date with Lucy at the Bell Hotel in Cradley Heath, Giles was sat in a large communal office inside the station and drinking a cup of tea. He was hoping for a quiet and peaceful day so that he could catch up on paperwork and as he dipped a McVities Rich Tea biscuit into his milky tea he was certainly not expecting any visitors.

"Morning aer kid..." Surprisingly, Giles's friend Reg Gallier suddenly appeared in the room and Giles almost let his biscuit become too 'soggy' and disintegrate into his tea as he thought about as to why his colleague from another division was present at his place of work.

"Hello Reg... What am yow doing over this way mate?" Giles stopped the biscuit from slopping into his drink and he quickly ate it.

"I need to ask you about summet mukka... Shall we gew for a walk outside?" There were relatively few colleagues in the office, but Gallier was suspicious of everyone and anyone and he nodded towards the main doors as he spoke.

"Er, ok Reg... Dow yow want a cupp'a tay? Its bloody code out there!" Giles looked sadly at his tea that he would prefer to finish in the warm!

"No mate... Ar just had one... Come on, I ay got that long..." Gallier was supposed to be looking into a recent spate of car thefts in Dudley so he only had limited time in which he could conduct his own personal investigations into Cedric Tanner, but thankfully Fowler was still avoiding him and this had cut him a little bit of slack.

The duo emerged out onto Halesowen Road and walked towards the Church of the Holy Trinity which stood nearby on the main High Street as a landmark. Gallier offered his colleague a cigarette as he placed one into his own mouth and they both lit up.

"So what's gewin' on Reg and why cor yer ask me in the office? Is this about that wench Lucy ar set yer up with?"

"No Tony... Nothing to do with her... What do you know about Eddie Fennel?" Gallier asked the question and Tony Giles nearly choked on his own cigarette smoke.

"Fuckin' hell Reg, Fennel is like fuckin' Royalty raahnd here mate... You know like the fuckin' Kray twins in the East End of London, Fennel is like the local boss, Mr Big..." Although Giles and Gallier worked for the same force and their areas and stations were not that far apart, 1960s Police areas were like little individual kingdoms where information was seldom shared between neighbouring colleagues.

Everyone had their own 'manor' and quite often, higher ranking officers did not approve of Detectives from rival stations 'poking' their noses in!

"He's a drug dealer?"

"Definitely not Reg... Quite the opposite actually... Fennel is connected to the Mucklow family (not to be confused with the famous and reputable builders from the Halesowen area), surely you have heard of them?" Giles was surprised.

"Of course I have Tony... Billy Mucklow was like the Black Country Al Capone until he went to jail in the '50s, his old mon, Willie Mucklow was the same before him too, but that's just before our time mate..." Gallier exhaled smoke into the cold autumnal air and watched the traffic as it moved along the High Street towards Haden Hill. "In the mid '50s ar was in Germany kickin' the crap out of pissed up squaddies in Hamburg! So tell me about this Fennel chap..."

"Like ar said, he is Mr Big around here now Reg... Since old man Mucklow retired and his son Billy got sent down, Fennel has taken over... He's got a background in extortion, long firm fraud, torture, violence, illegal boxing and the fuckin' rest..."

"Sounds like a lovely bloke..." Gallier grunted sarcastically. "If you know so much about him, why is he not in jail?"

"Because he makes far too much money for people who are higher up the food chain than us Reg! Just like ode Billy Mucklow, he knows exactly who to pay off so that he can do whatever the fuck he wants..." Tony Giles took a long hard drag of his cigarette and then shrugged. "But in all honesty Reg, Eddie Fennel is actually quite a decent bloke by all accounts..."

"Am yow avin' a fuckin laugh?" Gallier was surprised by Giles' remarks.

"He's an old school villain Reg... Lives by a code of honour and respect and all that bollocks... He's some kind of War hero too from the Second World War, the locals love him... He keeps the streets safe for old grannies and he hates drugs. There are no drugs in this town mate and that's the god's honest truth Reg..." Tony Giles was surprised at his own words and he wondered what Gallier would think of his somewhat strange opinion.

"That's what ar want to know about Tony... I heard that Fennel woe allow drugs on his turf, so how does a 'small time' local gangster like Eddie Fennel stand up to a villain like Cedric Tanner? What has Fennel got on Tanner?"

"For fucks sake Reg!" Giles groaned as he exhaled more cigarette smoke. "Yow'm still bangin' on about Cedric fuckin' Tanner! Yow'm gunna end up under the new fuckin' motorway if you carry on like this Reg..."

"So do you reckon that we should all just sit back and let scum like Tanner teck over?" Gallier was beginning to become irritated by his friend. *Surely his old friend Tony Giles was not bent as well!*

"No Reg... Not at all, but we gotta be realistic ay we? What can we do?" Giles looked to Gallier for reassurance but his colleague looked suspicious and annoyed.

"Where can I find this Eddie Fennel? I want a word with him... He might be able to help me in my enquiries..." Gallier's facial expression was deadly serious and Giles shook his head disapprovingly and with concern.

"He drinks in the Neptune on Powke Lane... Do you know it?"

"Yes..." Gallier appeared to regain a friendlier tone towards his friend. "Its just daahn the road from here... Thanks Tony, just do me a favour and keep all this to yerself... Yer dow know who yer can trust aer kid..."

"Just be careful Reg... Be very careful..."

Chapter 7

The Neptune public house stood adjacent to the Dudley No 2 Canal in the town of Rowley Regis. In reality, it was probably closer to the High Street of Old Hill or Cradley Heath, but officially the building was just over the bridge from Powke Lane cemetery and came under Rowley Regis.

At the end of their shift, most coppers liked nothing more than to go home to their families or enjoy a relaxing pint in the Police club bar, but Reggie Gallier was no ordinary copper. After a day collecting statements on the Dudley vehicle thefts with a junior aide, Gallier was now ready to start what he believed to be 'worthwhile' police work. An aide to CID was a regular police officer who had been recognised as being particularly skilled in the art of detecting crime. They were subsequently recommended for plain clothes CID work and before they could become full Detectives, they first became 'aides' who worked alongside regular Detectives and would have their positions reviewed on a regular basis to determine whether they would eventually be promoted to full Detective or shipped back into uniform. Gallier had no time for it... He recognised the importance of supporting and training junior colleagues, but this was not what he had signed up for. *All he wanted was to kick the shit out of 'bad guys' and then lock them up so that they could no longer harm innocents...* His (Gallier's) shift was now over and his intention was to go and see Lucy again at her home in Blackheath, but first he had an important task to fulfil.

He parked the Ford Zephyr on the car park of the Neptune pub and walked around towards the main entrance. As he walked he noticed a flash looking Jaguar mkII parked on a patch of ground opposite the pub. *That must be Fennel's car* he thought to himself as he pulled open the heavy door to the building and climbed up a rather steep step. Inside, it was a typically old-fashioned boozer. The floor was covered in red tiles and an old mahogany bar lay directly in front of him with small circular tables dotted around. Bench seats were positioned under the windows opposite the bar and Gallier noticed several men dressed in work overalls sat around, sipping their beer, chatting openly and playing cards. Immediately he felt over dressed in his suit and overcoat, but the locals paid him no interest and he was not made to feel uncomfortable. A middle-aged and significantly overweight barmaid waited eagerly behind the counter and she greeted Gallier with a smile as he approached the bar.

"What can ar get yer Sweetheart?" She was missing some of her front teeth but Gallier's gut feeling was that she was friendly.

"Pint of bitter please bab..." Gallier nodded to the Banks's Bitter pump and the barmaid pulled down a straight glass from the top of the bar.

"Is this ok for yer me Darlin?" She held the glass up for his inspection and Gallier nodded. Some people were particular over what type of glass their beer was served in. Some drinkers preferred a tall straight glass with a bulge near the top whilst others preferred the more traditional 'jug' shape with a handle. Reg Gallier really didn't care... *It still tasted the same!*

"Yes thank you..." Gallier nodded and waited in anticipation for his first beer of the day. She poured it accurately with a skill that the Detective could tell had been honed over many years working behind a bar. Her fingernails were filled with dirt and he made a mental note that he would not be sampling any of the beef cobs!

"I ay sid yer in here before... Am yow local?" She placed the perfectly poured pint in front of him and began to make small talk.

"I don't think ar've been in here before... Ar'm from Tipton bab..." Engaging in small talk was an integral part of his job. Talking to people, chatting, getting them to trust him enabled him to find things out...

"Not too far away then... What brings yer over this way?"

"Mar wench... I'm seeing a lady from over this way at the moment." Gallier was not lying as Lucy lived not far up the hill of Powke Lane in Blackheath.

"Oh right, yow should bring her in here sometime... She'd be more than welcome. I know its mostly chaps in here, but yer can bring wenches in here too..." The barmaid was clearly trying to 'drum up' more business for the pub and Gallier smiled and took a long drink of his beer.

"That's bostin... I will have to bring her down..." Gallier placed his beer glass back onto the counter and his facial expression suddenly became more serious. "You might be able to help me out with something actually bab..." He pushed himself closer to the bar and reduced the volume of his voice. "I'm looking for a chap by the name of Eddie Fennel?" He watched as the expression on her face changed. "I heard that he drinks in here?"

"Is that right..." She looked him up and down as she examined his suit, shoes and watch. "If you're here lookin' for Mr Fennel then that means that yow must be one of two things... A gangster... Or a copper..." She continued to scrutinise him. "You look as though yow could quite easily be either, but judging by the fact that your suit is cheap and your watch is not gold... Yow'm a copper..."

"Is Fennel here?" Gallier had done enough small talk. He had no desire to try and convince the barmaid that he was anything other than a law man.

"I will let him know that you are here, but its up to Mr Fennel as to whether or not he will see you..." Her respect for Eddie Fennel was plain to see and her previously friendly and welcoming attitude towards the newcomer in the pub had ceased to exist.

"Much appreciated..." Gallier lent forwards against the bar and lit himself a cigarette as the large barmaid disappeared off to the left into what looked like a small corridor and a possible back room. He expected to be called through to the rear quarters of the pub, but instead, much to his surprise, the barmaid reappeared with a bald-headed man whom Gallier estimated to be of about ten to fifteen years older than himself.

"You asked to see me… Ar'm sorry but ar dow have a fuckin' clue who yow am mate…" Fennel was of a stocky build with a wide face and eyes that were disturbingly intense. Instantly, Reg Gallier got an overwhelming sense that this man was dangerous and was capable of extreme violence, but something else, his gut instinct, told him that this man was not all bad, well at least not in the same vein as Cedric Tanner.

"My name is Reg… Detective Sergeant Reg Gallier…" Gallier exhaled smoke confidently into the already smoky atmosphere of the old barroom.

"Hello Mr Gallier…" Fennel was relaxed and confident and Gallier could not quite tell if he liked or detested the man. "What yow drinkin' aer kid?" The crook pointed to Gallier's half empty pint glass. "Lager? Mar mate Bill always used to get good lager beer from Europe. Not like the Harp shit we get in this country… Good quality beer…" Lager was not a common drink in Britain in the late 1960s and Gallier wondered what on earth Fennel was going on about. "Do you like lager Mr Gallier? Do you know Bill?" The villain gave Gallier an arrogant stare, as though he was toying with the Detective. "Do you know my friend Billy Mucklow?" Gallier suddenly realised that Fennel was talking in some kind of code. *'Friends of Bill' were clearly 'bent' coppers who had previously been on the pay roll of the highly respected former gang boss Billy Mucklow.*

"No… I'm ok with bitter thank you Mr Fennel…" Gallier drained his glass and Fennel promptly bought him another beer.

"So you're not a friend of Bill?" Fennel suddenly became suspicious of the policeman.

"I've never met the man…" Gallier took a drink of his fresh beer. "Thanks for the drink Mr Fennel…"

"My pleasure…" Fennel took out his cigarettes and Gallier courteously lit it for him. "So what can I do for yer? There's only two reasons why coppers come to see me... They either want to arrest me, or they want payin'... Which one is it?"

"Neither..." Gallier gave the gangster an honest look and Fennel became even more suspicious. "Ar was hoping that yow could help me with my enquiries..."

"I ay no fuckin' grass mate..." Fennel appeared offended. "And dow get no ideas about tryin' to bully me into grassin' cus ar'll knock you into fuckin' next week aer kid! Copper or no copper!" The slightly older man looked a fierce and formidable opponent and Reg Gallier had no reason to challenge him at this point.

"I'm investigating the activities of a face by the name of Cedric Tanner..." Upon Gallier's mention of the name Tanner, a look of sudden and intensely deep hatred came over Eddie Fennel's eyes.

"Bull shit... Nobody investigates that bastard because he's bought all the coppers out..." Fennel 'downed' his own beer in one swift motion before ordering another.

"I can assure you Mr Fennel that nobody has bought me out..." Gallier spoke with an assertiveness and authority that impressed the mighty Eddie Fennel. It pleased him to see that there were still honest cops around who were not open to the highest bidder... Even though most of the time he often was the highest bidder!

"Well, good luck to yer Mr Gallier... Cedric Tanner is a nasty bastard and I genuinely hope that yow nail that piece of shit..." Fennel's words were venomous but then he suddenly paused, as if an intriguing thought had just entered his cunning, criminal mind. "Were you ever in the military Mr Gallier?" Fennel's question came out of the blue and was completely random. Gallier nodded.

"Yes... Ar was in Hamburg... 1954... National Service..." Gallier answered the question but Fennel seemed to find the answer slightly amusing.

"So you didn't fight in the War?"

"I ay that old Mr Fennel..." Gallier almost sounded apologetic.

"Ar did… Ar fought with the Royal Worcestershires… First Battalion… '39 ter '41 ar fought the Italians in Africa… They called us the Desert Rats, then in'41 the Germans turned up and kicked our arses… We surrendered at Tobruk in June 1942, but me and Billy Mucklow managed to escape and meck it back to England just in time for the Normandy Invasion… We landed in Normandy in Summer '44 and then fought across Europe until we finally got into Germany…" Fennel stared blankly into his beer as if he was staring back in time at dark memories and experiences that were burned into the fabric of his mind and Gallier could not help but feel a deep respect for the man… "Do yow know how many men ar killed Mr Gallier?"

"No…" Gallier shook his head. He was impressed by Fennel's War stories but somewhat confused as to their relevance to Cedric Tanner and his investigation. *Was Fennel just nuts? Another violent 'head case' who had struggled to readjust from a brutal military career and the horrors of his past?* The gangster's face was red and swollen and his eyes were puffy and 'lived in' suggesting an over reliance on alcohol.

"Neither do fuckin' I…" Fennel laughed as he shook his head, not knowing whether to feel pride or guilt… "Fucking thousands aer kid… Kill or be killed, them or me and ar was fuckin' good at it… Billy Mucklow taught me…"

"It was a War Mr Fennel… You did what you had to do…" Gallier could not believe that he was offering words of comfort to a known villain…

"That's the point though Mr Gallier… Me and men like Bill Mucklow did what we needed to do, but for what?" Fennel suddenly slammed his beer glass down on the counter and gazed into Gallier's eyes with an intensity that was particularly uncomfortable. Unphased, Gallier matched the intensity and a mutual respect passed between the two men who stood on opposing sides of the law.

"For our freedom…" Gallier was confident in his reply and he took another drink of beer.

"For a country that is being taken over by dirty drug pushin' bastards like Cedric Tanner?" Again, Fennel spat Tanner's name with contempt. "Thousands of young minds being turned into mush by drugs so that that dirty kiddie fiddlin' scum Tanner can get rich..."

"This is exactly why I am here Mr Fennel... I wanna see Tanner nailed as much as you do and ar thought that yow might be able to help me..."

"Ar'm sorry Mr Gallier, but ar dow help coppers... Like ar said, I ay no grass..." Tanner was resolute and the criminal code never failed to confuse Gallier.

"I heard that Tanner does not sell drugs in your manor Mr Fennel?" Gallier tried a different approach, *maybe flattery would work?*

"That's right..." Fennel flicked ash into a glass ashtray that stood on the mahogany bar.

"Why not? How do you keep him out? I mean, with all respect to yourself Mr Fennel, you are no match for Tanner's organisation, so what is the secret? What do you have on Tanner?"

"I have friends in high places Mr Gallier... The Mucklow family and their associates in London..."

"But surely the Mucklows ay nothing now? The ode mon is retired, Bill Mucklow and Dick Hickman am in jail and Harry Scriven is out in Spain..."

"Maybe yow could help me Mr Gallier..." Fennel's tone of voice suddenly changed and Gallier had the feeling that he was being toyed with.

"Look Fennel, am ar missing summet here? Ar was asking yow for help!" The Detective was beginning to get frustrated and further confused.

"Well you are right... Cedric Tanner does not sell drugs in my territory... So how do I stop him from spreading his muck around here?"

"That is exactly what I just asked you!" Gallier took a deep breath and clenched his teeth. The War veteran was clearly very intelligent and he could not work out just exactly what the man was trying to achieve.

"I have friends in London who are very influential in the criminal world Mr Gallier. They have connections with Billy Mucklow and they are helping to look after his interests whilst Bill is inside. They have been helping me to keep a 'lid' on Tanner but unfortunately they have problems of their own with a copper by the name of Nipper Read. As a result they have not been able to back me up as well as they have been in the past..."

"You're talking about the Krays aren't you?" Gallier asked the question but Fennel ignored it.

"Tanner knows that if he tries to sell his gear on mar turf I will break his fuckin' neck, regardless of who has the biggest organisation... Ar dow give a fuck mate... Ar will kill him and he knows it, so he is trying to be smart..."

"What do you mean? Smart?"

"Tanner's got this copper, an Inspector working for him... Where did yow say yow was from again?"

"I didn't..." Gallier took another drink and cast his eyes around the room at the other drinkers who were all minding their own business.

"The wench behind the bar told me that yow was from over Tipton way..." Fennel exhaled smoke and Gallier silently cursed himself for being so open with the barmaid about where he had come from. "This Inspector is from over your way... Dudley..." Fennel waited for a reaction but Gallier gave nothing away.

"What is your point Mr Fennel? Tanner is from over that way himself..."

"Tanner's from Wolverhampton... His whole stinkin' family come out of Wolverhampton.... My point Mr Gallier is that Tanner is trying to get me out of the way so that he can expand his operations and he is using this bent Inspector to try and do it..." Fennel lent in closer and lowered his voice as Gallier figured that the crooked Inspector to which Fennel was referring to was probably DI Fowler. "This Inspector has got a file on me with evidence linking me to a load of historic Long Firm frauds... I go to court next month and it looks like ar'm gewin' down… With me out of the way and with my associates in London busy with Nipper Read, Tanner will be free to expand his operation…"

"Why are you telling me this?" Gallier extinguished his cigarette and shrugged.

"Because if yow work in Dudley nick, you could get hold of that file against me and then there will be no evidence to convict!" Fennel smiled and it now became clear to DS Gallier… The villain had been toying with him and Fennel clearly had his own agenda. "I would of course show my gratitude for such a favour of course…" Fennel pulled out the top of his brown wallet as if to suggest a bung.

"I hope yow ay trying to bribe a police officer Mr Fennel? I already told you that I wasn't bent…"

"Ok… I respect that, but just think of all the good you would be doing? If ar gew down then that will be more poor families and kids that will have their lives ruined by Tanner's drugs…" Fennel had a point but Gallier refused to give into him straight away.

"Did you do it?" Gallier's gaze remained intense.

"Do what?"

"The Long Firm frauds? The evidence in the file, did you actually commit the crimes?" Gallier could tell from Fennel's smirk that the man was guilty but the gangster said nothing. "And how do I know that yow ay just bull shitting me to get yourself off the hook?"

"You ask anyone… Cedric Tanner's pushers do not sell drugs anywhere near here… That's all thanks to me…Tell you what…" Fennel took one last long inhale of his cigarette before extinguishing it in the ashtray next to Reggie Gallier's. "If yow get me that file. Then I will give you the name of the crooked Inspector…" Fennel spoke with a smug confidence and Gallier had all but forgotten the gangster's impressive War heroics that they had previously discussed. *He already suspected that the bent Inspector was Fowler, but he did not know for sure… Maybe there were others?*

"I will be in touch Mr Fennel… But yow keep yer dirty fuckin' money… Ar dow want a penny of it…" Gallier drained his second pint and then turned as if to leave. *Fennel was the desperate one, he needed him (Gallier) more than he needed Fennel...*

"So are you going to help me Sergeant?" Fennel did not exactly sound desperate, but Gallier could tell that the villain was anxious to attain his help. Gallier shrugged and then turned back to face the famous Eddie Fennel.

"Goodnight Mr Fennel... I will be in touch..."

Chapter 8

Gallier looked at his reflection in a cracked mirror as he stood in the stinking toilets of the Doughty Arms Public house in Tipton. The mirror had not been cracked when he was there the previous week hammering 'Doctor' George's head between the toilet seat and the pan and he wondered if he had in fact inflicted the damage upon the mirror by smashing the drug dealer's face into it, but as he recalled the memory more vividly, he remembered that he had not. *After all, this was Tipton and there had probably been some other form of altercation!*

As he gazed at himself, he noticed that his face was red, distorted and swollen through alcohol abuse and considerably large, black bags hung revealingly underneath his eyes. *He probably should cut down on the fags and booze, but what for?* His masculine pride was stinging slightly as he had been making particularly promising progress with Lucy up until that night when she had announced that she would be unable to see him that evening due to a 'busy day at work.' *Things had been going so well and he had seen her the two previous nights in a row!* Feeling slightly 'put out', he had dragged himself to the Doughty Arms in his hometown and after a busy week was now wandering about the prospect of meeting up with Kate again! The plump, young Tipton woman had given him some useful information on Tanner and a childish arrogance within him felt the need to 'punish' Lucy by having some fun with the relatively unattractive Kate. *It would certainly make him feel better about being stood up! Though he would have to hope that Lucy would never find out…* As he made his way from out of the toilets and through to the bar, little did he know that an even better proposition than Kate was just around the corner…

She was almost doll-like with a maturity in her eyes that confirmed that she was certainly no adolescent and Gallier recognised her instantly.

"Gemma isn't it?" Gallier approached the woman as she sat near to the bar with an unremarkable female companion he had not seen before.

"Er yes..." At first, the brunette whom Gallier had met briefly the previous week with her friend Kate did not recognise the policeman, but on her second glance she remembered him as the man she had tried to 'set up' with Kate.

"We met briefly last weekend bab..." Gallier smiled as he took out his cigarettes. He offered both Gemma and her acquaintance one but they both declined.

"Yes... You had a drink with my friend Katie... I'm sorry but she ay out tonight..." She tossed her eyebrows flirtatiously and then grinned seductively. *The mysterious man was a good few years older than her and he looked a little rough around the edges. He was slightly overweight and his eyes looked tired, but there was something about him that appealed to her. An almost toxic masculinity that was strong and powerful, yet reassuring and safe...*

"Maybe it ay Kate ar was hoping to see..." Gallier smiled as he lit his cigarette and Gemma's female friend rolled her eyes with irritancy.

"I'll be over there..." The disgruntled woman sighed... "Come over when you're done flirting..." She was not impressed with Gemma's antics but in reality she was sick and tired of Gemma always being the one who got all of the male attention! She stood up and trudged over to the other side of the room where a mix of male and female acquaintances were smoking and drinking.

"Your friend doesn't have to go on account of me!" Gallier lied... He was glad to get Gemma to himself.

"Oh its ok... She's a miserable cow anyway..." Gemma giggled as she continued to flirt.

"Can I get you a drink?" Gallier had still not ordered from the bar and he studied the petite and attractive woman as he spoke. *Just like Kate the previous week, Maybe she would have more knowledge about Doctor George?*

"G and T please..." She answered quickly before sitting back in her chair and crossing her slim and slender legs.

"I'll be right back…" Gallier headed straight to the bar where he was eventually served. He bought a large Gin and Tonic for the lady and a pint of Banks's Bitter for himself before returning to the table at which Gemma was sat. Two local men had spotted the pretty girl sitting on her own and had tried to make a move, but Gallier quickly jumped back in. He placed the drinks down on the table and then gave them both an intimidating glare.

"Oh sorry Mr Gallier, we day know that she was with you…" The first man recognised Gallier as being a tough local copper and he quickly made his excuses for himself and his friend. Gallier thought that he knew them from somewhere. *They were probably local scallywags, street punks who nicked lead from Church roofs and siphoned petrol from cars.* He knew Tipton as well as anyone, but he was proud of his working-class Black Country roots.

"Its ok aer kid…" The policeman adopted a friendly tone before abruptly adding. "Now fuck off…" The two men smiled nervously and then backed away sheepishly as Gallier sat down next to Gemma.

"Wow… Do you work for Cedric Tanner or something?" Gemma could not hide that she was impressed and Gallier tried his hardest not to react to her comment. She had spent her entire school days as a good girl, an academic, a boffin who studied hard and had not fraternised with boys, but as she grew older she had discovered that boys did actually like her and a mischievous streak inside was intent on making up for all of the fun that she had missed in high school.

"No I most certainly do not work for Cedric Tanner… What mecks yer think that?"

"Well yow look like the sort of bloke who might work for a crook like Mr Tanner and them two fellas looked pretty scared of you…" She took a generous drink of her gin and tonic and her words gave Gallier an idea for later that evening.

"What do you know about Tanner then?" The Detective could not resist the opportunity to try and find more dirt on the loathsome gangster.

"I know that he is dangerous and I know not to talk to coppers like you about him…" She suddenly oozed a confidence that was beyond her relatively young age. *She was not as naive as she looked.*

"What mecks yow think that ar'm a copper?" Gallier was surprised.

"The way yow suddenly jumped down my throat with questions about Cedric Tanner… And when you scared off them two fellas just… Ar like a man in uniform…" She teased him with a cheeky smile and Gallier was quite smitten. *Lucy was his main love interest, but this young brunette was mesmerising.*

"I ay got no uniform bab…" He was torn. *The lady clearly had a 'thing' for policemen and he could either use this to his advantage to win favour with her or deny it in a quest to try and remain under cover…*

"But ar bet yow have a big truncheon and a pair of handcuffs?" She lent forwards and ran her hands up the inside of his leg. Her breasts were not big but he found her hard to resist… *Fuck being undercover!*

"Wouldn't yow like to know…" He touched her hand and looked deeply into her brown eyes. *Was he being set up? Was she another whore on Tanner's pay roll? Did he care?* She giggled again and purposefully held onto his gaze. "So do you have plans for later on this evening?" The Policeman went straight for the 'kill' and Gemma continued to giggle sheepishly like a naughty schoolgirl.

"Well I really should go back to my friend over there…" She looked back to her friend who had walked away a few minutes previously and then bit into her lower lip as she turned back to face Reggie Gallier. "But maybe if you are still here come closing time, perhaps we could go on to somewhere else?"

"Maybe…" Gallier nodded enthusiastically and then checked his watch. "I have to pop out for a bit first…" It was barely seven o'clock on a Friday evening and the night was young. "Perhaps I will see you back here at kicking out time?"

"Maybe..." She shrugged her petite and delicate shoulders and Gallier still could not tell if she was teasing him or if she was genuinely interested...

A Black Country Mick Jagger wannabe gyrated on a small stage as four adolescent young men struggled through a barely adequate rendition of 'Satisfaction' by the Rolling Stones. A crowd of adoring young girls stood staring and danced as Reg Gallier sipped a beer and stood at the main bar. The Bell Hotel on St Annes Road, Cradley Heath was one of Eddie Fennel's venues and Gallier had been given an idea by Gemma earlier that night in the Doughty Arms. She had informed him that he 'looked like the sort of guy who would work for Cedric Tanner' and he thought that he would put this to the test and use it to help him discover more about the intriguing character that was Eddie Fennel. Following his drink with the gangster the previous evening he had been in two minds about whether or not he should help the man. *It went against the grain for him to act illegally and get Fennel off the hook for crimes that he had committed, however, the alternative was to allow Tanner to extend his empire, grow more powerful and introduce a fresh batch of young innocents to a world of drugs and most probably knowing Cedric Tanner, seedy prostitution... He hated the thought of letting Fennel get away with fraud and racketeering, but he hated Cedric Tanner a damn sight more!* Before he made any decisions, he would have to find out more about Fennel and see if he was in fact true to his word...

"Hello mate..." Gallier had moved over to a huge, imposing doorman who stood near to the main entrance of the pub. The bouncer wore a long black Crombie overcoat and had no neck.

"Can I help you Sir?" The doorman was not exactly rude, but his tone and manner was not the friendliest.

"Who runs this place?" Gallier already knew full well that Eddie Fennel ran the pub. He was not the licensee or the owner, but he ran a protection racket in the area and the owners paid Fennel well. The doorman also worked for Eddie Fennel and therefore he pretty much controlled what went in and out of the premises...

"Who wants ter know?" The doorman grunted.

"My name's Reg... Reg Daniels..." Gallier lied convincingly. "Ar've got a bit of business yower gaffer might be interested in..."

"What kind of business?" The doorman did not make eye contact and Gallier moved a little closer and lowered his voice as low as the loud rock music would allow.

"You get a lot of kids in this pub mate... The sort of kids that would be interested in the sort of gear my organisations sells..."

"You mean drugs?" The bouncer turned to face Gallier and he did not look impressed.

"Keep yer voice down ay mate! Yow never know when there might be a copper about!" Gallier almost smiled at the irony of his comment. "Don't worry, I dow work for Tanner... Ar got me own organisation ay I... I know that Mr Fennel ay exactly a friend of Tanner..." The Detective figured that a little 'name dropping' might help him.

"Yow dow know a fuckin' thing about Mr Fennel pal and if yow knew what was good for yer, yow would teck my advice and fuck off!" The doorman became threatening and Gallier found the reaction encouraging.

"Do you know who yow'm fuckin' talking to mate?" The Policeman squared up to the large bouncer. "If yow tell me to fuck off again aer kid ar'm gunna knock yower fuckin' block off! Now get Fennel down here right now... Ar wanna talk to the organ grinder not the monkey!"

"Ar thought ar told yow ter fuck off!" The bear like bouncer was not intimidated by Gallier's words but before he could speak another word, the burly detective smashed him in the mouth with a solid right hook that sent him tumbling back into the doorway.

"Ar fuckin' told yer day I!" Gallier played the part perfectly and just as he had hoped, two other tough looking bouncers emerged out of nowhere and grabbed him. The first bouncer then regained his composure and stepped forwards.

"Yow med a big mistake pal!" The doorman went to strike Gallier back in vengeance but then he suddenly stopped himself... "No... Ar'm gunna let Mr Fennel teck care of you... Ar warned yer and now yow'm gunna find out!"

"Find out what?" Gallier snarled but put up no real effort to try and free himself from the grip of the doorman's colleagues.

"Eddie Fennel dow have drugs in his pubs Pal... Everyone knows that... The last bastard who tried to sell gear in here got his bollocks toasted in Fennel's lock up!" The doorman replied and the other two sniggered at the memory. *It was exactly what Gallier was hoping to hear... It was looking as though Fennel was true to his words and he did not allow drugs to be sold upon his turf.*

"Bull shit..." Gallier kept up his defiant act... "You get Fennel down here and he can tell me that his fuckin' self!"

"Yow really ay scared are you?" The doorman was surprised but his smug attitude suggested that he was relishing the prospect of his employer Eddie Fennel torturing this supposed drug dealer. "Teck this stupid bastard out the back and keep him there until Eddie gets here... Ar'm gunna run up the 'Nep' and get Eddie down here... Then this flash wanker will get what's coming to him!" The doorman now seemed to find the situation quite humorous despite his bruised face and he quickly disappeared out of the front door to find his employer. The band had continued to play throughout and Gallier glanced at the two men either side of him. *Would they try to rough him up whilst they waited for Fennel to arrive?*

"You can let go of me now lads... I ay gewin' fuckin' nowhere... Ar wanna speak to this Eddie Fennel..." Gallier yanked himself free and went for his cigarettes.

"Fennel's gunna wipe the fuckin' floor with yer!" The younger of the two henchmen spoke and the older one gestured towards a door that Gallier figured led out to some kind of back room.

"Come with us... You will get your chance to speak with Mr Fennel in a minute, but he's right... Eddie Fennel will not tolerate fellas pickin' fights with his boys and he definitely woe have drug pushers around here!" The older man, whom Gallier estimated was just a little older than himself, put his hand on his back and led the way as the three of them moved through the pub to the back room.

At first, it was pitch black and Gallier was expecting a sudden and violent strike to come out of the darkness, but instead, a small, inadequate light flickered on and the Detective could see an old wooden table with four wooden chairs placed around the outside.

"Sit daahn!" The older henchman pushed Gallier towards the table and the policeman sat down peacefully.

"How abouts a fuckin' drink whilst ar'm a' waiting lads?" Gallier exuded a cocky arrogance and the two men were gobsmacked.

"I dow think yow realise just how much bother yow'm in mate..." The younger thug shook his head.

"Tell Eddie to bring a bottle of Johnnie Walker Black and two glasses..." Gallier smirked and the two men laughed... *Fennel was gunna sort this joker out good and proper...*

"Hello Eddie... Remember me?" The Black Country villain emerged into the back room alongside the doorman with the bruised face.

"Is this some kind of fuckin' joke?" Fennel was not impressed. "Ar thought yow said that he was some filthy drug pusher?"

"He is boss... He wants to sell gear in this pub..." The bruised bouncer protested and Gallier smugly pulled out his Police warrant card.

"Sorry boys... Ar just wanted to check that Mr Fennel here was as anti-drugs as he said he is... Now run along and fetch that bottle of Scotch and two glasses... Ar want a private word with yower boss..."

Chapter 9

Gallier woke up particularly early and it immediately occurred to him that he was far too old to be behaving in such a manner. He was 32 years of age and nestled closely in the single bed beside him was a young lady who was barely into her early twenties. Posters of the Beatles and the 'Stones adorned her pink walls and a disturbingly not so old dolls house stood in a corner of the small bedroom. As she slept, naked and peacefully in his arms she looked angelic and he could not help but feel a slight sense of guilt. In reality, Gemma had seduced him and she had used him just as much as he had her, but he was a police officer and was vastly approaching middle age... *He should not be behaving like this...* It was a Saturday morning and he thought of Lucy. He was due to see her again that night, however he felt no guilt with regards to his number one love interest. *After all, she had opted out of spending time with him the previous night!* He was desperate for a smoke and he checked his watch only to see that it was just 7AM. He was not one for lying in and he wondered as to what time the sleeping beauty in his arms would awake? He had been vastly intoxicated when they had returned to Gemma's home in Robert Road off Owen Street in Tipton. He could not remember much more, but he could remember that they had had to be quiet on returning back on account of Gemma's parents and he suddenly became embarrassingly aware that he was possibly closer in age to Gemma's parents than he was to her! For a second he thought of how he would react if he was Gemma's father and he caught a 'middle aged' man in his daughter's bed! He certainly did not feel afraid, but it would be particularly harsh if he had to 'batter' some poor old bloke who was quite rightly angry at some 'hairy arsed copper' copping off with his little girl!

Gemma stirred and he stroked her face in the hope that it would awaken her. Her pretty brown eyes fluttered open and she was so fragile and innocent that he simply could not regret the night that he had just spent with her. He felt like a sleazy old man, but ultimately, she had been a more than willing participant and she was a considerable number of years older than the age of legal consent!

"Good morning Princess…" He immediately shuddered at the corniness of his line but her smile was warm and infectious. She yawned, stretched her slender frame and then broke wind loudly before erupting into a fit of giggles. *Delightful* he thought to himself and then he realised that he preferred his women to be a little more mature… "I better be off now bab… Maybe we could have a drink together sometime?" He climbed out of the bed and began to pull his grey suit from off the cold wooden floor. *If he ever was to see her again then he would have to be careful in case Lucy found out!*

"That would be nice…" She sat upright in bed and watched as he got dressed. "But please promise me yow will be quiet as you leave the house?" She bit into her lower lip nervously. "My dad would gew mad if he caught you in here, Copper or no Copper!" It was not the first time that she had 'snuck' a lad back home after a night of drinking, but Gallier was certainly the most 'mature' of such men. She liked him and she genuinely hoped that the Detective would be true to his word and see her again. After stuffing his tie into his jacket pocket and slipping on his winklepickers, Gallier raised her chin affectionately and planted a kiss on the brow of her head and she gazed up at him lovingly… *She certainly was cute, how could he not see her again?*

Gallier's Zephyr was parked further down Robert Road near to the Tibbington Estate. As he walked from Gemma's parent's house he sucked on a cigarette and appreciated the early morning air as he watched the sun begin to slowly rise and cast menacing shadows across the buildings of the imposing Locarno Road Primary School that stood in front of him. The car was perfectly intact and just as he had parked it and as he opened the driver's door he felt particularly proud of how he had managed to parallel park the big Ford between a Morris Minor and an Austin A35 whilst being particularly inebriated at the time. He pulled himself down into the seat and then wound down the driver's window so that he could savour the sweet flavour of the early morning Black Country air. There was no home game for the Baggies that day and he could quite quickly get his dreaded 'task' over and done with at Dudley Police Station before slipping back home to his parents' house for a few hours 'kip' before driving over to Blackheath to see Lucy. If it all went to plan, he would go for a few drinks with Lucy in the Shoulder of Mutton and then he would get to 'stay over' at Lucy's place. *It would not be the first time he had 'bedded' two separate women within the space of 24 hours! But then again, if things went to plan, he would also have to schedule a quick meeting with Eddie Fennel at some point during the day.* They had literally drunk a full bottle of Johnny Walker the night before and both men had been impressed by the other's drinking prowess.

The lower sections of Dudley Police Station were overwhelmed with drunks and brawlers from the previous night's festivities, but Gallier did not pay them much attention as he quickly passed them towards the upper regions of the station. As far as he knew, there was no reason for CID to be in the office and he figured that most of them would be at home sleeping off their hangovers. It was 8AM on a Saturday morning and as he went into the deserted office his first port of call was to make himself a cup of tea. He smoked yet another cigarette as he watched the kettle boil and then he thought about where he might find the file Eddie Fennel was so desperate to get hold of. *If it was so important to Tanner, then chances were it would be in Fowler's office...* He grinned smugly to himself as he relished the prospect of routing through the crooked Inspector's possessions.

Gallier knocked on the Inspector's door and after a good thirty seconds, he was quite satisfied that the room was empty so he entered carefully. There was nobody to be seen in the upper regions of CID, but he was taking a massive risk and would have to be discrete. In his mind, he had already worked out a cover story just in case he was disturbed. *He had reason to suspect that DI Fowler was a corrupt officer and he was looking for evidence to support his suspicions…* This was not actually far from the truth. *He knew that Fowler was bent and if this paid off and got Fennel off the hook, the gangster would give up the name of the crooked policeman whom DS Gallier already knew to be Fowler.* Even if Fowler himself caught him in the act he could use exactly the same story. *It would be quite amusing to watch the crooked bastard squirm!* He went straight to Fowler's desk and opened the top drawer. Thankfully it was not under lock and key and the first thing he pulled out was a three quarters full bottle of Grants blended Scotch Whisky. He quickly checked his surroundings and then shut the door so as not to arouse suspicion if anyone were to enter the main CID office before taking a long swig of the Scotch. It was not his favourite brand of whisky but the fact that he was taking a 'free drink' from his recently much despised senior officer was quite a thrill. He screwed the bottle shut and placed it down on the desktop before proceeding to sort through the contents of the drawer. At first he found nothing of any interest until then at the bottom of the drawer he found a small metal key that looked as though it might fit the large metal filing cabinet in the corner of the room. *The cabinet would not usually be locked, but if it contained valuable files that Fowler was keeping on behalf of Cedric Tanner it would make sense for the crooked Inspector to keep them under lock and key…* Gallier placed the contents of the drawer, including the Scotch, carefully back in exactly as he had found it and then crept slowly over towards the filing cabinet. He was very much aware that the lower quarters of the station were very busy and as there had been no major incidents to amuse CID the previous night, the 'plod' downstairs would not have any reason to hear movement in the offices above. *If they did hear him, it would be highly likely that one of them would come up to investigate!*

Unsurprisingly, the key fitted the cabinet lock perfectly and Gallier pulled it open to reveal a list of familiar villain's files that Fowler had been collecting for Tanner. As he flicked through, the Detective Sergeant made a mental note of the 'famous' names. Men who were serious crime figures locally whom it would be advantageous for Tanner if they were to be sent down. *With Fowler building up evidence on these* criminals, it would be easy for Tanner to take over 'turf' without any gang wars... All he had to do was feed Fowler the evidence and the Inspector would take out the competition! If it wasn't so crooked and conductive to drug dealing activity, Reggie Gallier would have actually been quite impressed. But what was particularly intriguing and valuable to the DS was the newfound knowledge that the 'great' gangster Cedric Tanner was in fact some kind of super grass! *It clearly worked two ways... Fowler got to bolster his record with high profile villains like Eddie Fennel and Tanner got fresh territory in which to sell drugs...* Eventually, Gallier stumbled upon a file that simply read: Fennel, Edward... He pulled it out and carefully examined its contents... *Eddie Fennel had been busy... He certainly was a villain and the information inside the file revealed a very detailed picture of Long Firm fraud, Protection rackets, illegal gambling, unlicensed boxing and general violence and thuggery...* Gallier closed his eyes and took a deep breath... His own actions sickened him to the core... *Here he was, a good honest copper, scrapping around to steal evidence so that he could get a rotten gangster like Eddie Fennel off the hook!* Once again, he reassured himself that this was the only option and he consoled his moral compass further by telling himself that eventually he would use all of this knowledge to bring Fowler and Tanner's empire and arrangements crashing down around them. *It would take time to build up a case and Eddie Fennel and some of the other non-drug dealing villains may prove to be quite an asset...* He pushed the file into his jacket pocket and then returned the key to Fowler's drawer before taking another generous swig of the Scotch... *Now he would have to go back to see Eddie Fennel again...*

Gallier used the information in Fennel's file to locate the villain's home address on Furlong Lane near Colley Gate in Cradley. He parked the Ford Zephyr outside and surveyed the plush detached dwelling in front of him. Before Fennel had began life as a gangster working for the infamous Mucklow family, he had been a highly decorated War hero before working in a humble fruit and veg shop in Cradley Heath... He had certainly come a long way and not for the first time in his career,

Gallier thought about whoever had invented the phrase 'Crime doesn't pay' was either very drunk when they had said it or was just a *bloody liar! Still, no amount of money would make him (Gallier) become a slippery, toerag villain and* Gallier continued to feel a sense of guilt and apprehension as he walked up the driveway towards Fennel's front door. A Lotus Sports car and a red Jaguar MK.II adorned the driveway and Gallier shook his head in disgust and frustration... *His father had worked hard the entirety of his honest life, but all he had to show for it was a rented council house on the Lost City and a decrepit old side valve Ford... Life was not fair...* He hammered heavily on the front door and was pleasantly surprised when a particularly attractive blonde woman opened the door. In fact, 'particularly attractive' was not an accurate way of describing the beauty... She was downright stunning...

"Hello, can I help you?" Her voice featured a silky-smooth Irish accent and Gallier figured that she must be Fennel's wife. He had studied the Black Country criminal's files and they had revealed that Fennel had spent a substantial amount of time in Dublin and that his ancestry was half Irish and the other half related to the Mucklow crime dynasty.

"Hi... I'm looking for Eddie? Is he in?" Gallier could not help but flash her a cheeky smile as he responded but he got the feeling that she had far more expensive tastes!

"And your name is please?" She was slick, professional in an almost secretarial way. An act that had been honed over many years of 'playing' the part of her husband's secretary during many successful and lucrative long firm frauds. The famous London villains, the Richardson brothers, Charlie and Eddie, and to a lesser extent the Kray twins had also found much success in long firm frauds throughout the late 1950s and 1960s. The process involved setting up a legitimate company that bought goods on a mass scale and then promptly paid for their purchase. The next step, once credit had been acquired was to order a massive delivery of lucrative goods that would never be paid for. The company would disappear overnight, the goods would be sold off at a knock down price and the villains would pocket one hundred percent of the income. It was a tried and tested form of villainy and just like the Richardson's and his associates the Kray twins, Eddie Fennel was a master of it.

"Just tell him its Reggie... He'll know who I am..."

"Mr Kray?" Fennel's wife narrowed her eyes suspiciously. *She had seen Reggie Kray in the newspapers many times and she was quite sure that the man at her front door was not the famous London villain.*

"Err no... Just tell him that it's a different Reggie..." Gallier almost laughed but was relieved to see the man himself, Eddie Fennel appear at the door.

"Oh its ok Teresa bab... He's a friend of mine... Let him in..." Fennel greeted the policeman with a friendly smile and Gallier found it particularly uncomfortable to be met with such warmth by a notorious local crime figure. He was used to criminals spitting at him and calling him a pig... *He liked that.* He liked that he pissed them off and he liked that it gave him the opportunity to arrest them with a generous degree of obscene police brutality...

"No its ok Mr Fennel... I won't come in..." Gallier looked around for signs of a tail or a surveillance team. *The last thing he needed was to be spotted handing over the file to Fennel...* When he was satisfied that he was not being watched, he swiftly and discretely removed the file from out of his jacket pocket and placed it in Fennel's hands. The villain took it enthusiastically before looking sideways to his wife.

"Do us a favour Teresa, gew and get us a cuppa tay will yer?"

"What did yer last feckin' slave die of!" Fennel's wife gave her husband a sultry smile and Gallier could not help but discretely admire her figure as she disappeared back inside the house.

"Thanks Reg... I owe yer one aer kid..." Fennel was an old school Black Country tough guy. His face was wide and his fists were like shovels with red knuckles that were worn from over use. His gratitude was genuine but Gallier didn't want it..

"Just keep that bastard Tanner out of yer pubs ok..." Gallier spoke assertively and Fennel nodded. "Now just one more thing Eddie..."

"What's that?" Fennel looked up again... *He was not gunna be in the pocket of any copper!*

"Yow told me that you were gunna give me the name of Tanner's crooked Inspector..."

"Yes..." Fennel grunted. "Of course... I ay about to protect no crooked copper from anyone..." The gangster smiled. "His name is Fowler... That's all I know..."

"Thanks..." Gallier nodded awkwardly and pulled a cigarette out of his pocket as Fennel closed the front door. *Eddie Fennel had given him nothing more than he already knew, but he had discovered more about Tanner and Fowler's cosy little arrangement and now that he knew where to look he could begin to build up some kind of evidence in his own time...*

Chapter 10

It was early December and signs of the festive season were beginning to appear within the locality. Reggie Gallier did not care much for Christmas. He was not married and he had no children of his own so to him, all Christmas represented was a time when he had to clean up the streets after a spike in rowdy drunks, fights and extreme domestic violence. It was a period when tensions were increased through alcohol consumption and the holiday meant that the inebriated working classes were confined closely to spend extended amounts of time in each other's company. This would often lead to violence and disputes and Gallier had many a troubling memory of dealing with brutal murders, assaults and neglect of children that had been burned into his mind over his extensive police career. He was almost hardened to it, but each year the bright decorative lights and festive atmosphere never failed to stir past professional memories that he would rather have forgotten.

There was a year when he had to deal with an out of work factory worker on Christmas day... The individual had drank through so much money (that he did not possess) that his heartbroken wife had confronted him about his consumption whilst they had not been able to provide a solitary Christmas gift for their six children... The man had then proceeded to beat her to death in front of their screaming offspring whilst a humble Christmas meal lay uneaten... With the mother dead and the father in prison, Gallier never did find out just what did happen to those poor young children. Another year, a young girl from Brierley Hill had been raped and strangled to death on Christmas Eve as she had walked home from work to share gifts with her grandparents. Then, how could he ever forget the year when he dealt with the case of a new-born baby boy who was found dead in a frozen council house whilst it's parents lay drunk and unconscious at a friends house nearby... Sadly, he held many such memories and the thought of adding to them as Christmas rolled around each year was not something he remotely looked forward to.

"It will soon be here..." Inspector Fowler looked out of the windows of the CID Austin Westminster but DS Gallier did not speak as he drove the car and kept his eyes trained firmly on the road ahead of them. Gallier absolutely detested the Inspector and he could not think why his senior officer had requested for Gallier to accompany him on a seemingly routine arrest. It was late on a Wednesday afternoon and Gallier had been hoping to 'knock off' on time so that he could go and see Lucy in Blackheath, but Fowler had randomly appeared at his desk and requested his presence on the arrest. The Detective Sergeant had no questions. He could barely bring himself to look at the crooked Inspector let alone speak to him. Since their altercation outside of Tanner's storage unit in Tipton, there had been a particularly awkward and frosty atmosphere between the pair and Gallier was overtly suspicious as to why he had been selected for this job. They were driving to an address on the Wren's Nest estate in Dudley and due to the lateness of the day and the time of year, the sky was growing rapidly darker outside. "You can't ignore me forever Gallier... At some point you will have to open your fucking mouth!" Fowler was getting frustrated, but he was apprehensive of what the notoriously 'tough' Sergeant might do to him.

"I don't know what you're talking about Sir..." Gallier sneered his reply, his eyes still fixed firmly on the road ahead.

"Finally! You can speak to me..." Fowler sounded relieved. "You know how it is Reg... Like ar tried to tell yer before, we all have to take a little 'drink' from time to time..." The term 'drink' had originated in the Metropolitan Police in London and basically meant a brown envelope that was filled with cash... In other words a blatant bribe...

"No Sir... I do not know how it fucking is Sir..." Gallier spoke through gritted teeth as the Inspector relaxed back in his seat.

"That's not what I heard Reg... I know what happened..." The Inspector looked out of the window at the intermittent Christmas lights as the Austin drove through some of the toughest parts of Dudley. Many of the houses were not decorated, people could not afford such luxuries as Christmas lights in their homes, especially this early in December, but a few of them were lit up.

"What do you mean?" Gallier was intrigued by the comment and he actually broke his defiance and looked over at the Inspector who was sat alongside him in the passenger seat. "You know what happened?"

"You're skating on thin fucking ice Gallier..."

"What the fuck are you going on about?"

"Eddie fucking Fennel..." The inspector left a deliberate pause. "Do you know what I'm referring to now Reg?"

"No..." Gallier diverted his eyes back to the road and gave nothing away.

"I wasn't born yesterday Reg... You even nicked some of my Scotch as well... I get it, just stop giving me this 'holier that thou' bull shit when you are just as bad as I am!" Fowler shook his head. "But fucking hell Reg, your antics have caused a lot of shit mate... You know these villains, they have all their codes and stuff and once you do a favour for a rival gangster you become fair game... Do you know what I'm saying Reg?"

"Fuck you Sir... I ay the same as yow and ar can assure you that anything that I may or may not have done, I did not receive any payment for it whatsoever!" Gallier took a deep breath. "Maybe it just suits me to see that bastard Tanner being unable to expand his empire of filth..."

"Is that right?" Fowler grunted, hardly surprised. *Gallier wasn't a crooked copper, but his obsession with Cedric Tanner was dangerous...* "Well this is exactly what I need to speak to you about Reg... Tanner knows that it was you who got Fennel off the hook and like I said, now that you have committed allegiance to a rival firm, we gotta meck it up to him... I'm trying to do you a fucking favour mate!"

"Ar dow need no fucking favours from you... Besides, what you're saying is bull shit..." Gallier began to wonder how long he could try and deny his blatant involvement in retrieving the evidence against Eddie Fennel.

"Look Reg, one of Fennel's goons was fucking livid... He said that yow give him a slap over in Cradley Heath in some pub..." Fowler spoke as if he was making a statement, not asking a question and Gallier remembered clearly the disgruntled doorman he had punched in the Bell. "This bouncer told one of Tanner's boys that you were well in with Fennel... Enjoying cosy bottles of Scotch together..."

"Ar can drink with whomever ar choose... Sir..."

"Maybe so... But when you are spotted socialising with a criminal face and then miraculously his criminal file goes missing from my office a few hours later, it doesn't teck a genius to work it out does it?" Fowler was frustrated but he didn't show it. "I managed to talk Tanner down but now he reckons that we, or should I say you, owe him!"

"Oh yeah? Well yes ar do fuckin' owe him... I owe him a one way fuckin' ticket to porridge the filthy bastard..." Gallier shook his head in anger and Fowler could tell that he was getting nowhere trying to reason with the detective.

"Pull up over here... The chap we'm here to nick lives in number 47..." They were deep into the notorious Wren's Nest estate and Fowler pointed towards an ordinary looking council house with a well-presented front garden.

"Who are we here to see?" Now Gallier had questions, *were they pulling folks at the request of Cedric Tanner?*

"Never you mind... Just do as I say..." Fowler got out of the car and Gallier was tempted to drive off, but ultimately Inspector Fowler was still his senior officer and for now at least he would go along for the ride. *He never knew what he might find out next!*

The garden was well cared for and Gallier could see that whoever lived at the address had taken the time and pride to make their garden nice. *Hardly what he would expect from a vicious villain..* Callously, Inspector Fowler spotted a porcelain garden gnome and he blatantly and unapologetically smashed it with his right foot. Gallier said nothing. He stood behind Fowler and waited eagerly to see what would happen next.

"If anyone tries to leg it, grab um!" Giving orders to fellow officers did not come easy to Fowler and his tone of voice was almost apologetic. He knocked hard on the front door of the house and very soon a middle aged and friendly looking Afro Caribbean lady opened the door.

"Hello gentlemen... How may I help you?" The black woman had a beaming smile and Gallier had an overwhelming sense that she was a good person.

"Where's your Leroy then Mrs White?" Fowler spat sarcastic laughter at the mention of the woman's surname. "A bit ironic that ay it? Don't you think?" Fowler's racism was representative of many Police officers at the time, but Gallier had no time for it. *There were good people and there were bad people...* He had no political agenda and the colour of a person's skin was irrelevant... *If they were bad, then they deserved a kickin!* Fowler pulled his warrant card from out of his pocket and literally shoved it into Mrs White's face. Moments later he had appeared weak and unassertive when addressing an overtly masculine colleague, but when addressing a female, ethnic minority he suddenly became quite the bully.... It certainly did not impress Reggie Gallier.

"But my Leroy is a good boy Sir... He not done anything wrong?" The woman protested in vain but Fowler shoved his way into the house in search of her son and Gallier was confident that the Inspector did not have a warrant.

"I'll be the judge of that, now where is he?" Fowler pushed deeper into a small hallway and a young black male of around 19 years of age suddenly appeared on the stairs. The young man looked as confused and as surprised as his mother and he made no attempt to escape. "Ahh, there you are..." Fowler grunted and then turned to face Gallier. "Cuff him..."

"But what for? I ain't done nothing wrong?" Leroy White protested and Gallier hesitated. Usually he would follow his duty and obey a senior officer without question, but recent events had caused him to question everything that Fowler did...

"Leroy White, I am arresting you on suspicion of theft... You do not have to say anything, but it may harm your defence if you do not mention when questioned, something which you later rely on in court... Anything you do say may be given in evidence." Fowler had an impressive arrest record, it was the only way to gain promotion and he was used to reciting the obligatory caution. White's mother became emotional and Gallier felt torn, but for now he would go along with his orders and hand cuff the man.

"But I ain't done nothing man!" White protested again as DS Gallier produced the hand cuffs from out of his pocket and approached him. "This ain't fair I ain't done nothing!" White became upset and somewhat uncompliant and Gallier reluctantly pushed his wrist into a goose lock hold and then cuffed him as the lad cried out.

"Take him out to the car Sergeant... I have a few questions for this young man that he can answer back at the station..." Fowler turned upon his heel and gave Leroy White's mother a look of pure racial hatred before marching out to the car, closely followed by DS Gallier and their captive Leroy White. White's mother was an honest, law abiding Christian and she could not help but feel total shame and embarrassment as she noticed that several of her neighbours had gathered outside to watch the spectacle. For Fowler and Gallier it was all routine...

After several hours of the captive Leroy White sitting alone in a cold, damp and dark police cell, Inspector Fowler finally decided that he was ready to speak to him. The young man was scared and alone and this was exactly what Fowler had been trying to achieve. DS Gallier and the DI had waited silently in an interview room until eventually, a burly Custody Sergeant led the prisoner in. White was sat down at a small table in front of the two detectives and the Custody Sergeant left without a word. Gallier could tell that the youngster was scared out of his wits and he wanted to have no part in it, but then he figured that it would be better for Leroy White and for his own investigations against Tanner and Fowler if he stayed in. DS Gallier got up out of his chair, lent against the exposed brick wall and then lit a cigarette as Fowler sat and eyeballed the young Afro Caribbean boy.

"Please Sir, please tell me what all this is about?" White was visibly upset and Fowler sniggered, enjoying his torment.

"I will tell you what all this is about young man... I am going to ask you some questions and you are going to tell me exactly what I want to hear... If you do not do that Mr White then I am going to have my colleague, that big bastard over there Sergeant Gallier, bounce you around the walls and beat you black and blue!" Fowler sneered his sarcastic laughter yet again. "Well, beat you blue anyway... You'm black enough as it is!" As the DI spoke, White looked up at Gallier nervously but the DS said nothing as he smoked his cigarette and looked on. *He should have met up with Lucy hours ago!*

"Ok..." White was genuinely innocent and was prepared to answer all questions honestly. Fowler continued to laugh and then slowly produced a small pouch from his pocket. Carefully and paying extra care not to touch the object with his fingers, the Inspector revealed an expensive looking, gold Rolex watch that Gallier figured would be worth many hundreds of pounds.

"Do you know what this is Leroy?" Fowler held the watch up so that White could see it, still being extra careful not to actually touch the watch himself.

"It's a watch Sir..." White answered and Fowler yet again exploded into a fit of laughter.

"He's much cleverer than he fuckin' looks ain't he this one..." The remark was another racial slur and Gallier ignored it. The Inspector suddenly raised his arms up in a mock monkey gesture and began to make ape-like noises... The poor boy looked terrified and Gallier felt genuine pity. *Fowler was an utter bastard...* Once DI Fowler had completed his offensive spectacle, his face suddenly became deadly serious again and he suddenly and without warning slung the watch at Leroy's chest with force. The expensive timepiece rebounded off the young man's torso and fell to the floor near his chair. "Pick it up!" Fowler barked the command and Leroy White lowered himself to retrieve the Rolex from the ground when Gallier sprung into action and kicked the watch across the floor so that it was out of the young man's reach. Gallier had seen this trick used several times before and had even made use of it himself, but only when he had been quite sure that the interviewee was completely guilty of the crime! *Well at least in his mind this had been the case!*

"Don't pick it up..." Gallier's voice was assertive and commanding and Leroy White sat back upright in his chair. DS Gallier knew full well that as soon as the man touched the watch, his fingerprints would be all over it, an innocent man would go down for a crime he had not committed and Inspector Fowler would have another statistic to add to his arrest list. Unfortunately, this had been all too common, especially in London where crooked police officers had furthered their careers by 'fitting up' innocents. Often, it was the most vulnerable that were picked upon... Supposed 'unsavoury' individuals who did not appeal to the mostly white, middle-aged juries of the 1960s... Young black males and those from the working classes were prime targets, but on this occasion, Reggie Gallier was not prepared to stand back and let it happen. *But what was going on? Was this just a random arrest to add to Fowler's record? Why had he (Gallier) been specifically asked to help and did this have anything to do with public enemy number one? Cedric Tanner...*

"Oh dear..." Inspector Fowler adopted another patronising tone. "It appears that Sergeant Gallier here is not in the best of moods... Best not to upset him ay?" Fowler did not look at Gallier. "Now Mr White, tell me exactly how you stole that watch and then me and Mr Gallier here can get off down the pub... We know that you are going to tell us eventually so please do not waste our time... It will save you much..." Fowler paused as he searched for the appropriate word. "Discomfort..."

"I know who that watch belongs to but I did not steal it Sir..."

"Don't waste my time Leroy... I want to know how you stole it and then we can sort out the paperwork for your confession..." Fowler was beginning to grow impatient.

"No tell us... Who does that watch belong to Leroy?" DS Gallier was further intrigued and he exhaled cigarette smoke as he spoke.

"Mr Tanner Sir..." White sounded as genuine as ever and Gallier took another deep inhale of his cigarette in anticipation at the mention of the name... "That is Mr Tanner's watch and I believe that he is trying to set me up Sir..."

"Bull shit you thieving little bastard!" More than a hint of anger was creeping into Fowler's voice.

"No its true... Mr Tanner has a girl that works for him, a white girl... A prostitute..." Leroy White said the word prostitute quietly, he had been brought up to be a good Christian and he knew that his mother would not approve. "Me and her, well, we have fallen in love and Mr Tanner does not like it..." White shook his head and looked sadly at the table as Gallier thought of the young lady he had spotted in the Doughty Arms with Tanner a few weeks previously. *Maybe it was the same girl and Tanner was pissed off because he had been saving her for himself or the highest bidder when Leroy got in there first!* Gallier almost smiled as he hoped that this genuinely was the case...

"You lying piece of shit!" Fowler was fuming and he moved his chair closer to the young man threateningly. "How dare you speak so disrespectfully of such an upstanding member of the community like Mr Tanner..." Fowler's expression turned to pure hatred. "It ain't right that your kind come over here to this good clean country and then throw accusations around like that!" The DI stood up. "Now are you going to confess to the crime and pick that fucking watch up or am I gunna have to leave you in the cell all night whilst I ask some of Mr Tanner's associates to go and 'visit' your lonely old mother..."

"No Sir, please!" A look of pure terror came over Leroy White's face and Reggie Gallier had seen enough.

"That's it Fowler... Sir!" Gallier paced over to where the watch lay on the floor. He picked it up slowly with his right hand and then held it to the light so that he could inspect it closely. *It certainly looked genuine and very expensive.* "Nice watch..." He kept it in his right hand and then smashed it twice off the bare brick wall with such force that its inner workings and glass exploded all over the floor. Knowing who the watch belonged to, he found the action particularly satisfying and he placed the remnants of the Rolex into his inner jacket pocket. "It appears that there is insufficient evidence for us to hold you any longer Mr White..." Gallier placed a friendly hand on the younger man's shoulder and then beckoned White to his feet. "Go and wait by the door Leroy... I will take you down to the Custody Sergeant in a minute and we will get yow signed out aer kid..."

Feeling confused, Leroy White walked over to the door as Gallier turned to face Fowler who was red faced and cross armed.

"You tell Tanner, that if he wants his fuckin' watch back, he knows where he can find it!" The Detective Sergeant patted the broken Rolex in his jacket pocket and glared at his crooked colleague...

"You really don't know what you are getting yourself into Reg..." Fowler shook his head. "I tried to help you... I've tried to help you make things up to Tanner for what you did for Eddie Fennel, but you just won't have it will you? Maybe you should think about the safety of your family... Or that nice new wench you've been spotted with from over Blackheath way..." Fowler did not dare to look Gallier in the eyes as he made his last comment and the Sergeant resisted the urge to smash his senior officer's head in there and then...

Chapter 11

The American vocal duo, The Righteous Brothers had a top twenty hit in the U.K. in 1965 with a cover of the famous old love song Unchained Melody and as Reg Gallier drove his Ford Zephyr up Powke Lane near Blackheath, the song played on the radio. It was certainly not one of Gallier's favourite records, *but at least it wasn't another bloody novelty Christmas song!* At the top of the hill and just past the Old Bush pub he came to a crossroads where he turned right down a narrow road that was filled with Victorian, terraced houses. Lucy lived down there near to the top of Waterfall Lane and after finally getting out of work he had driven over from the Police station in Dudley to see his love interest. He came to Lucy's house on Highfield Road and was straight away frustrated to see that a dark coloured Morris 1300 was parked outside of her front door. *Lucy did not own a car, to his knowledge she did not even drive!* He slowed the Zephyr right down to a crawl and looked up and down the tight road for a place to park. Not everyone owned a car, but by the time he had got out of the police station, everyone that did own a car had now returned home from work which meant that he would have to park further up the street away from Lucy's house. Eventually he found a space and he quickly and efficiently reverse parked the Zephyr before hurrying up and getting out of the vehicle. Some people liked to moan and complain about strangers parking outside of their homes and after the evening Gallier had endured at work he simply did not have the energy or the patience for any kind of conflict. He locked his car and did not look at the houses. He had already noticed the net curtains 'twitching' and he was very much aware that he was being watched. In fact, he had 'stayed over' at Lucy's house a few times that past week and each time he had been forced to endure the 'walk of shame.' Lucy had lived in the house originally with her ex husband and now that she was a single woman in her early thirties living alone, she was often the 'talk of the street' whenever a new man had started turning up at her house and remained there for the whole night!

It was very dark and icy cold and the orange glow of the old streetlights illuminated the rows of terraced houses as Gallier walked closer to Lucy's place. On account of his profession and his natural disposition, Gallier was a particularly suspicious and untrusting individual and he could not help but think about who the Morris parked outside Lucy's might belong to... In his mind, he fabricated an elaborate scenario where Lucy was lay inside with another man! *Surely he had no right to feel such jealousy and mistrust after his own shenanigans with Gemma, the young girl from his hometown of Tipton?* Suddenly, the front door of Lucy's house flung open and Gallier could hear raised voices. He could make out Lucy's voice and she sounded agitated and annoyed so he quickened his pace.

"Oi! What's gewin' on?" As the police officer drew level with the house he noticed a slender man in his thirties unlocking the front door of the Morris. The man had been inside of the house with Lucy and Gallier could tell that something was not right.

"Ooh, this must be yer new lover boy ay Lucy?" The man's voice was steeped in a patronising sarcasm and not for the first time that evening Gallier resisted the urge to commit violence.

"Who the fuck are you?" The DS went to grab the man by the scruff of the neck but he stopped himself, *he did not want Lucy to see him for the vicious thug that he really was.*

"Reg, this is my ex-husband Stan... The one that I told you about before..." Lucy spoke nervously. *She did not want her new boyfriend to misinterpret the presence of her ex!*

"The bastard that likes to beat on women?" Gallier remembered that Lucy had previously mentioned about how she hated men trying to 'play the hero' and protect her from her ex so he continued to exercise restraint. The other man, Stan, spat a fake and smug laughter.

"Well, the only problem is we'm still married ay we!" The wiry man exploded into a mocking laughter as he opened up the front door of his car and got inside. "You know what you need to do if you want me to sign them divorce papers!" The door slammed shut and the small car exploded into life before shooting off aggressively up the street.

"What was all that about?" Gallier looked at Lucy questioningly. She looked good in her short skirt and knee-high boots and he could not help but wonder further about the purpose of Stan's visit and why the man had made such a strange announcement about them still being married.

"You better come inside Reg... I have enough folks in this street gossiping about me as it is!" She gestured for him to come inside and he followed her in. "Do yow want a cuppa-tay bab?"

"No... I figured that we would gew and have a drink in the pub..." He always wanted to go to the pub and at first this had excited her. It got her out of the house and he could afford it, but *he certainly did like to drink a lot!* "Now what was going on outside? That idiot said that yow two am still married?" Gallier's question interrupted her thought process.

"I chucked him out over eighteen months ago Reg..." She looked down sadly and Gallier could tell that something was wrong. "He is trying to take me for all that he can... I want a divorce but he won't sign the papers unless I pay him £200... That's nearly six months wages Reg!" A tear appeared in her eye as she spoke.

"Why? Is that his half of the house or something?" The policeman questioned her in a professional manner and he instantly regretted the cold tone of his voice.

"No! The house is rented... I owe him nothing... In fact, it was me that paid for most of that stupid car that he is driving around in!" She was seething with annoyance and she certainly did not appreciate Gallier's seemingly unsupportive manner.

"I see..." Gallier adopted an apologetic and more understanding tone. "Maybe I could have a word with him?"

"I told you before Reg, ar dow need no bloody knight in shinning armour to fight my ex-husband for me!" Lucy was defiant and Gallier could tell that she had issues with allowing men to sort out her battles for her. She was fiercely independent and had clearly been a victim at some point in her life which had given her a tenacious desire for it not to happen again.

"So where does he work? What does he do?" Gallier gave her a reassuring and affectionate cuddle before returning the topic of conversation to the smug man he had just met.

"What? So you can go round there and sort him out? For god's sake Reg! How many times do I have to tell you that I can sort things out for myself!" Her frustration was mounting. *She really liked Gallier but to her, the whole 'tough guy' act was not attractive. Her ex Stan had always played the tough guy... He drank too much and he got into fights, then he would punch her too... The last thing she needed was more of the same!*

"Look Lucy, I'm a policeman, I'm here to look after decent people, to help the public... It is not my purpose to go around beating folks up!" He lied... In Gallier's mind, beating up villains and low lives was an integral part of his job and he enjoyed it... "Maybe I could just speak to him and reason with him?"

"Look Reg, I know you're only trying to help and I appreciate it, I really do... But lets just gew and have that drink ay? I like spending time with you... It helps me to forget about this rubbish with Stan so please just drop it ok?" She gave him a flirtatious smile and then kissed him passionately. He smiled and stroked her face affectionately.

"Ok bab... Lets gew and get a drink..."

DS Gallier knew that the two biggest employers in Blackheath were the Thomas William Lench works and the electrical engineering business of British Thomson-Houston and the next morning, after a big breakfast at Lucy's he decided to drop in on these business premises in the hope that he might locate the Morris that he had encountered the night before. He had remained true to his word with Lucy the previous night and had discontinued any questioning about her ex-husband, however, at one point during the evening after she had enjoyed several G and Ts she had let it slip that she had originally moved to Blackheath from nearby Halesowen to be nearer to her husband's work... Of course, Gallier had consumed a fair few drinks himself at this point, but the information went straight into his mind and the next day he had not only retained this knowledge but also the registration number of Stan's dark coloured Morris... *So now he knew that the man worked nearby and he knew the registration details of his car!*

The BTH electrical firm changed in 1960 and by 1967 it was known as AEI, Associated, Electrical, Industries. It stood in Cakemore Road near to some old railway sidings and as Gallier drove the Zephyr carefully through the works car park he smoked a cigarette. He would be late for work himself, but after the further altercation with DI Fowler the previous evening, he did not care, besides, he would easily be able to claim that he was working on a case of some sort in order to explain his absence.

"Bingo!" Gallier spoke aloud to himself as he spotted Lucy's ex-husband's car in the works car park. He pulled up the Ford Zephyr immediately behind it and then proceeded to get out and walk towards the offices. It was all a welcome distraction from DI Fowler and Cedric Tanner who had plagued his thoughts as of late and he had all but forgotten of Fowler's warnings the previous evening... *He would not be bullied by Cedric Tanner!"*

"Excuse me madame..." Gallier walked into an office and was immediately met by an ageing secretary who sat at a front desk. He shot her a friendly smile and produced his warrant card for her to inspect. "I was wondering if you could fetch me one of your employees? I have his car registration, it is parked outside on your car park... I believe that the man's name is Stan..."

"Oh!" The woman was surprised and slightly afraid by the presence of a plain clothed police officer at her desk. "Good morning officer... I do hope that he has not done anything wrong?"

"I'm afraid that I cannot say madame... Here is the registration number of his car... It's a dark blue Morris..." Gallier forwarded her a piece of paper upon which he had written the registration. "Could you please find him? It is of the upmost urgency…"

"I will try Sergeant, but you must understand that we have a lot of employees working here… I will pass this onto one of our floor managers and see if he can locate the gentleman in question… Are you quite sure that this vehicle is parked outside on our car park?"

"Yes Madame… It will be most helpful to the police madame if you can locate this individual as quickly as possible… Time is of the essence…" Gallier was already going to be late for work!

"Of course Sergeant… I will do my very best…" The middle-aged woman smiled at the ruggedly handsome policeman… *He had quite a way with women!*

"Thank you madame… Please tell the man to come outside to the car… It is essential that I keep an eye on it…" Gallier lied again and then watched as the woman made her way through a side door and went out into what he assumed to be the factory works area.

"You?" Lucy's ex-husband Stan made his way towards his blue Morris on the car park and was surprised to be met by his wife's new boyfriend whom he had met the other night. Gallier stood casually and was smoking yet another cigarette. "They told me that there was a copper outside to see me?"

"They were not wrong Stanley…" Gallier produced his warrant card from his pocket again and Stan looked at it.

"Well it dow surprise me… Yer need to be a copper ter keep that saft wench Lucy in order!" Stan was about the same age as Gallier but of a smaller build. The policeman ignored the comment about Lucy… *After all he had not been married to the woman, maybe Stan was right?*

"So you think that it is acceptable for blokes to knock wenches about then?" Gallier extinguished his cigarette on the floor and trod it into the ground with his right shoe.

"Fuck off copper… Ar got work to do…" Stan wasn't impressed and had no intention of answering the question.

"What about extortion?" The DS physically moved to block the factory worker from escaping. "What about extorting money out of your ex-wife because she is trying to escape you?"

"That ay none of your fuckin' business! Besides, what do you wanna do? Marry her yourself?" Stan's reply caught Gallier by surprise. *He had certainly not thought about that! He had only been seeing Lucy for a few weeks!*

"Tonight, when you finish work, your gunna gew home and sign that paperwork for a divorce..." The policeman ignored Stan's *ridiculous* question.

"Piss off... This is between me and mar wife..."

"Ok... Have it your way..." Gallier suddenly smiled. "The reason I asked for you to come to see me outside here by your vehicle Sir is because of your defective rear light..." The Detective adopted a patronising and very official sounding policeman' tone and the factory worker became confused.

"There ay nuthin' bloody wrong with it!" Stan protested and Gallier took a step closer to the car.

"Look... Its bosted..." Gallier smiled again before kicking the rear light of the Morris with force and the whole light and chrome trim came away.

"You bastard! Yow cor do that!"

"Oh yes I fucking can!" Gallier grabbed the man by the scruff of his neck and then pulled his face into his. "Now you take this as a warning... If you do not sign that letter, I will come back here tomorrow and fine you for the broken light... Then I will do the same thing every fucking day until you sign that form... Do you understand me?"

"That ain't fair! This ay right!" Stan tried to protest again.

"Maybe it ain't right? But what's worse? What I'm doing to you, or you battering wenches and extorting money out of em?"

"Ok... Fine..." Stan looked at the floor... There was very little he could do...

"That's a good lad..." Patronisingly, Gallier pinched the man's cheek and tugged it in such a way that it confirmed his small victory, but what he did not know was that another much more dangerous and infinitely more powerful man was waiting to see him...

Chapter 12

"Good afternoon Sergeant... How good of you to join us in work today!" Gallier found DI Fowler's seething sarcasm somewhat surprising. In fact, after the events of the previous evening he was surprised that his senior officer was even speaking to him at all.

"Morning Sarge." Phil Hobbs, a junior Detective or an aide to CID as he was officially known greeted Gallier and the DS nodded a friendly acknowledgement. *He wasn't that late, besides, what was coming into work half an hour late compared with what Fowler was up to?* "Are we off to look into that spate of burglaries in Sedgley today Sarge?" Phil the aide was eager to impress in CID and was keen to make the switch from uniform permanent.

"Sounds like a plan to me aer kid..." Gallier filled up an old kettle and put it to boil. "Let me have a cuppa' tay and a fake and then ar'll be with yer... Go and fetch the car keys off the latch and book the motor out in my name for the morning..."

"Too late Sarge, DS Jenkins has already took it..." The junior Detective grimaced as he waited for Gallier's reaction.

"That fat, little Welsh bastard!" Gallier half laughed. DS Jenkins was a colleague who he actually quite liked, but the pair enjoyed a friendly banter in their day-to-day work. "We will have to teck one of those little mini vans then..." He shook his head and sighed as he spoke. *He hated the little vans. He struggled to fit in them and they gave him a bad back and knees for days afterwards.*

"That will not be necessary Gentlemen..." Inspector Fowler was still in the vicinity and he had other plans for the two men. "PC Hobbs, I want you to stay here... I've got a mountain of paperwork that needs filling. It should keep you busy for a few hours..." Fowler did not look at the men as he spoke and therefore he did not see the annoyance and disappointment on Phil Hobbs face.

"Ok Sir…" The aide to CID nodded and waited for further instructions.

"Go and wait in my office Hobbs… I will come and show you in a minute…" Fowler nodded back towards his office at the end of the room and Hobbs' usual enthusiasm appeared to lag slightly as he trudged over to the door. "You can never be too careful who you trust around important police files!" Fowler's comment was an obvious reference to Gallier's recent antics with Eddie Fennel's file but the DS ignored it.

"I will go on my own then…" Gallier stood up to go and fetch the keys to the mini van and then Fowler interrupted him again.

"No Reg… I want you to go and meet somebody… A new snout…" Fowler still did not make eye contact with the detective Sergeant. "This fella reckons he can give us inside information on that gang who are stealing all the cars at the moment…"

"Don't you want to speak to him yourself?" Gallier was finding it particularly difficult to even speak to Fowler… *The man was scum…* He was also highly suspicious of the request, especially when he considered the events of the previous evening.

"Not yet… I want you to sound him out, listen to what he has to say and then let me know how it goes…" Apart from not making eye contact, Fowler was speaking as if the events of the previous evening had not occurred and to Reg Gallier, something definitely did not seem right. *Was it a set up? A meeting with Tanner and his goons? He certainly was not afraid of the drug dealing gangster and his loathsome thugs…*

"Where have I gorra meet him?" Gallier decided to go along with the request. *If it was a meeting with Tanner then it would be an opportunity to try and find out more…*

"Tipton… I know that it is your neck of the woods Reg, that's why I chose you for the job…"

"Where abouts in Tipton?"

"Victoria Park, by the Cenotaph…"

Victoria Park opened on the 29th of July 1901 and was named after the British monarch Queen Victoria who had died seven months previously. The park was constructed after local residents had started a petition in 1893 for the building of a new leisure area. Six years later, in 1899, construction began and the park was built in Randalls Lane in the Tipton Green area of the town. Not long after the opening of the park, Randalls Lane was renamed as Victoria Road where subsequent houses were constructed in the early to mid-phase of the twentieth century. In 1921, a Cenotaph was erected at the park in memory of the Tipton men who had lost their lives during the First World War. Subsequently, in 1945, the names of those who had perished during the Second World War were also added.

To visit the park with the supposed intention of meeting the new snout, Gallier had opted to take his own personal car. This was certainly not usual practice, however, if he was being set up by DI Fowler, Tanner's thugs would be expecting him to be in one of CID's pool cars: the Austin Westminster or an Austin mini van. Gallier figured that by turning up discretely in his own Ford Zephyr, he could sneak into the park 'unannounced' and see what was going on before anyone was alerted to his presence. He parked the car on Victoria Road and then paced purposefully towards the lake and then walked a little closer to the Cenotaph. It was a cold and windy day and the grey skies meant that visibility was not at its best, but as he got closer to the war memorial, he could not see anyone else in the immediate vicinity. He checked his watch. It was 10:30am, the time at which it had been arranged for him to meet the new contact… He lit a cigarette and then turned his back to the cold wind. He was not at the Cenotaph, but from his position near to it he would be able to keep a visual…

"Hello Reggie…" A familiar voice sounded from behind him and Gallier recognised it straight away…

"Tanner…" Gallier turned around slowly and was surprised to see that the short and stout gang boss was alone.

"I believe you have something that belongs to me Sergeant…" Tanner held his right hand outstretched for the Rolex and Gallier smirked.

"Here you go… But I'm afraid that it's a bit fuckin' fucked!" Gallier pulled out the obliterated watch from his jacket pocket and tossed it into Tanner's hand. He enjoyed the moment but the sight of the destroyed time piece did not appear to have any effect on Cedric Tanner whatsoever.

"Oh yes… So it is…" Tanner took the watch and slung it through the air so that it landed in the Victoria Park Lake. Even in its broken state, the gold alone would have been worth a substantial amount, but as it hit the water and quietly sank to the bottom, Cedric Tanner did not seem to care… "Easy come… Easy go…" The villain shrugged and then smirked. "I didn't think that you cared for money Mr Gallier… I thought that you was one of those special breed of coppers that could not be bought… A true servant of the public… A fucking do gooder…" Tanner laughed. "But it appears that I was wrong?"

"What the fuck are you talking about Tanner?"

"It appears that you are just another bent, dirty copper Mr Gallier… Maybe it is time you stopped trying to kid yourself that you are one of the good guys and make some real money ay?" Tanner oozed confidence. His eyes were as black as coal and his smile was odious and unnerving.

"I dow teck bungs from gangsters… Believe me Tanner, I ay nothing like that prick Fowler…" Gallier knew exactly what Tanner was about to bring up.

"What about our mutual friend Mr Fennel?" As Tanner spoke, Gallier thought that he looked like the devil personified… "I could tell yer a few fuckin' stories about that man believe me Sergeant… Do you wanna know something about Eddie Fennel Mr Gallier? The man that you represent…"

"Ar dow represent nobody!" Gallier grunted but Tanner took no notice.

"Fennel took a young man that works for me to a lock up garage on the Brickhouse estate in Rowley Regis... He cut half his fuckin' face off and then stuck a battery charger on his testicles and fried his bollocks... Nice guy ay he Mr Fennel?"

"Is that right?" Gallier was quite amused. The statement did not surprise him. He had already got the impression that Fennel was a dangerous man who was capable of extreme violence... *So what?* "If Eddie Fennel likes to torture drug dealing scum like you then perhaps they should give him a fuckin' medal!" Gallier took a step closer to Tanner. "And for your information, I didn't teck a penny from Fennel... Not a fucking penny... I got him off the hook so that I could stop you from expanding your empire of filth across the Black Country... That was the only fucking payment I needed..." Gallier fixed Tanner with such intimidation that the mobster was impressed... It gave him quite a thrill... *Reggie Gallier would make a very good gangster...*

"That's the problem Mr Gallier... You don't want money... I tried to give you the opportunity to redeem yourself with that stupid kid Leroy White, but you just will not listen will you Reg..." Tanner shrugged again and looked out across the lake.

"I don't want anything from you Tanner..." The detective took another intimidating step closer to his enemy. "I will not rest until you are rotting in prison... You have my word on that..." Gallier spoke through gritted teeth and Tanner began to laugh.

"Ok Mr Gallier, as you will not respond to conventional means, I am afraid I will have to resort to alternative tactics..." Tanner continued to gaze out over the lake and he lit himself an expensive cigar. "I hear that you have a new lady friend who lives in Blackheath? It would be so sad if something truly awful was to happen to her... Then there is your ageing parents on the Moat Farm estate... There are some really sick people around these days Reg and you just cannot be there all of the time to keep your loved ones safe can you?"

"Fuck off Tanner! Yow ay gunna bully me! I'm gunna fuckin' have you! Believe me..." Gallier was not fazed by Tanner's threats, but the villain suddenly turned and faced him full on. An intensity appeared in Cedric Tanner's eyes and an expression filled his features that could have been that of the devil himself.

"I heard that your sister had a little boy a couple of years ago..." Tanner's comment caught Gallier completely by surprise and the detective was visibly shaken.

"What?"

"You have a young nephew Mr Gallier... What, two, three years old?" Tanner left a pause so that the sickening reality of his potential threat could begin to sink into Reggie Gallier's mind. "I like little boys Mr Gallier... Just ask my stepson Michael... Yes I really like little boys and I know that your young nephew lives on the Lost City too doesn't he? Maybe I should pay him a visit sometime... Yes... Nice and tender..." A sickening spittle of sexual anticipation flew from Tanner's tongue and as his perversive excitement began to grow, Reggie Gallier completely lost his cool. He punched Tanner in the stomach two times with such force that the despicable, paedophilic villain fell to his knees and struggled for breath. Gallier then grabbed his right arm and pushed him into a hard lock before forcing the man's face into the hard, grassy ground.

"You sick fuck! You lay a finger on my family and I'll bury you alive you bastard!" Gallier screamed in anger as he pushed Tanner's face further into the grass. He took hold of the gangster's little finger and then wrenched it forcibly and aggressively until he felt the satisfying sensation of the bone cracking which caused Tanner to utter a slight groan at the pain. "You see that fucking grass Tanner?" The policeman continued to hold Tanner's face in the grass. "I know how you and all the other fucking bastards in your business hate grasses! You fucking hate grasses don't you!" Gallier proceeded to rant like a psychotic lunatic. "Well guess what Cedric, I want you to fucking eat it! Eat that fucking grass scum!" Gallier screamed in Tanner's ear, but the villain, his eyes pouring with tears from the pain proceeded to laugh hysterically... Gallier responded by wrapping his knuckles across Tanner's eye sockets several times with the uncontrollable ferocity of a wild animal before going back to the fingers. He wrenched another finger forwards, causing it to break and then placed Tanner's broken little finger into his mouth. He bit down hard and continued to apply firm pressure as his mouth filled with crimson fluid that tasted of metal. "I said eat the fucking grass!" This time, the villain opened his mouth and took a bite of the cold green grass that was on the floor before him. "Swallow it! Swallow it!" Gallier continued to rage and Tanner laughed perversely and defiantly as he followed his instructions. Coming to his senses, after Tanner had swallowed a satisfactory portion of the grass from the floor of Victoria Park, Gallier eventually stood up... "I mean it Tanner, if you harm a hair on the back of anyone in my family's head, I will fucking bury you!" As Gallier began to cool down, his breathing laboured and causing condensation to rise into the atmosphere, Cedric Tanner finally rose to his feet. His hand was bleeding and his face was red from the blows he had received.

"I tried to warn you Gallier... I tried to give you the opportunity..." Tanner's confidence had not gone and Gallier was at a loss as to what to do next... *He had maximised his aggression levels and he had severely hurt Tanner, but what else could he do?* There and then, he knew full well that the only way to protect an unsuspecting member of his family was to physically murder the man... But he could not do it, and oh how he would spend the rest of his life regretting not taking this decisive action... *Ultimately, he was too weak...*

"Get out of my sight..." Gallier growled the command and Tanner continued to grin... His camel-coloured overcoat was covered in fresh mud and blood and his trousers were ruined, but Cedric Tanner was far from broken...

Chapter 13

The rest of the working day passed with little incident and Gallier resumed his routine investigations into relatively 'small-time' crime. He made a point of avoiding DI Fowler and as soon as the end of his shift came around, he was out of the door and on his way back to his parent's home in Tipton. He had spent the previous night at Lucy's and he was more than due a hot bath and a fresh set of clothes, especially after the altercation with Cedric Tanner in Victoria Park. *The close contact with the despicable man made him feel physically unclean!*

Reg Gallier had been born and brought up on the Moat Farm Estate (also known the Lost City) in a small council house on Windsor Road. The family home was near to the junction of Palethorpe Road and despite the estate's fierce reputation, Gallier felt safe and happy there. It was all he had ever known as a child growing up and even though some of his neighbours and family acquaintances knew the nature of his line of work, he had never felt threatened or in any danger. It was his home and like so many Black Country men and women, he was proud of it! His father had recently retired and whilst his mother still worked as a part time cleaner at nearby Glebefields Primary School, Gallier's intention was to take his 'ode mon' out for a quick pint before his mother got home from work and he had his bath and ventured back over to Lucy's place.

As he entered the estate from St Mark's Road, a carelessly and aggressively driven, white, Ford transit van almost crashed into him and as Gallier steered his Zephyr out of the way and sounded his horn angrily, the Transit was soon out of sight as it sped off.

"Fucking lunatic!" Gallier spoke out loud and even though nobody other than himself could hear the insult, it at least made him feel slightly less annoyed. He made a mental note of the van's registration number and then carried on. His father would be at home waiting and as Gallier pulled up outside of the house, there were plenty of parking spaces in which he could park his car. Many of the working men that lived on the estate had no need for a car and it was an unnecessary expense that few of them could afford. They could walk to their place of work in the many nearby factories and they could walk to the local public houses. Where else did they need to go?

As soon as he had climbed out of the Ford Zephyr, Gallier could tell that something was far from right. The tatty old front door that led into his parent's home was half open and a sinking feeling began to come over the detective... *What had Tanner done? It was all his own fault...* He quickened his pace as he hurried up the short pathway and then pushed open the front door.

"Dad?" He called out in vain, but there was no response... "Dad? Where am yer?" With haste and concern, the detective Sergeant hurried through to the kitchen at the rear of the house and he was truly horrified by his findings. "Dad! What happened?" The old man was slumped, semi-unconscious over the tiled floor, his face and arms were covered in severe bruising and his blood decorated the room. Gallier's father tried to speak, but his face had been so severely beaten that his teeth were broken and his mouth was swollen. Gallier leant down and cradled his father's head. Later he would regret his actions, but his policeman's instinct was to try and procure a 'name' from the victim before telephoning for help. "Who did this to you Dad? Who did this?" Gallier knew full well that this was the work of Cedric Tanner's organisation, but first and foremost, he wanted the individuals who had inflicted this horrific beating. The old man's head moved and he tried to speak again.

"Net... Netts..." The broken ramblings made little sense to Reggie Gallier and as his father passed out with the pain, he knew that he had to get him to a hospital and fast. With difficulty, he dragged the dead weight of his unconscious father out of the house and upon sight of a neighbour who was passing by, he accosted the man to join in and help. Together, the two men managed to get Gallier's father into the back of the Ford Zephyr and after a quick 'thanks' to the neighbour, Gallier started the car and set off at full speed towards the Dudley Guest Hospital on Tipton Road...

A thousand memories swept through Gallier's mind as he sat and gazed upon his father's corpse... In front of him, his mother wept as she nestled her head between her dead husband's heavy arms and Gallier knew that for her especially, life would never be the same again ... His siblings sat and wept too, his youngest sister sobbed uncontrollably and the Detective was relieved that his one brother was at least trying to comfort her... *He could not... This was his fault... What would his family think of him if they knew that this was his fault? He had underestimated the evil of Cedric Tanner and his poor, old, innocent father had paid the price...*

It was not long after arriving at the hospital that the old man had suffered a severe cardiac arrest as a result of his intense injuries and Gallier's father had never again regained consciousness... The detective Sergeant could not take his eyes from off his father's face... He could not leave that room knowing that it would be the very last time that he would see his much loved Dad... No matter how much the detective wanted and willed it to happen, the corpse did not move... *He longed for it to suddenly twitch, for his father's eyes to open and then him greet them all with some humorous comment as he had done so many times in the past... This time it would not be happening... It would never happen again...* As he lay there he looked peaceful, but his brutal death had been far from peaceful. The bruises and swelling made the whole situation so much worse for all of the family and apart from Reggie Gallier, not one person inside of the room could understand for one second why this had happened to their kin...

"Just why?" One of Gallier's brothers finally broke the sound of uninterrupted sobbing and the policeman could not look him in the eye... "Was anything taken? Mom and Dad ay got nuthin' worth teckin! Why did this happen?"

"He was a good man... He day get into fights or anything like that... Who would want to do this?" Gallier's sister finally gained the composure to speak but for once, Reg Gallier said nothing as he continued to stare at his Dad in disbelief... *He was gone... Just like that...*

Gone, finished, ceased to exist… How could he go from chatting with his son the previous morning to simply not being there? Gallier had seen countless dead bodies… It was his work and he was used to it, *but this was so different… This was not work, it was so personal and he simply could not come to terms with it, he could not accept it, he would not accept it…* He looked away, took a deep breath and then shut his eyes, as if trying to wake himself up from a bad dream… But he could not… *This was real!* He opened his eyes and then returned them to the sight of his poor father… *The proud Black Country man would have hated the pity, but he was gone… He ceased to exist and Gallier knew that he would never be able to fully accept it…*

"Yow'm the copper… What do you think? Or am yer just gunna sit there and say fuck all?" Gallier's brother had never approved of Gallier's choice of career and his use of bad language in front of his mother and sisters was out of character. The DS opened his mouth as if to speak, but for once nothing came out… He had no words… The tough talking, ultra assertive, hard nosed copper had nothing…

"Who do you think did this Reggie?" His sister's hand touched his arm and her voice was distraught and pleading.

"I… I have no idea…" Gallier stuttered as he lied… He needed a cigarette, but he could not move.

"So why has this happened? Why do us tax payers pay your bloody wages for you to sit there and say you have no idea?" Gallier's brother was seething, but his words had no effect on the detective… *It was natural for his brother to be angry… Of course he was gunna be angry! He deserved anger… This was all his fault…*

"Leave it!" Gallier's mother suddenly raised her head and scolded her children… "Your father's lying here dead and he ay ever coming back, so stop arguing about it!" The sound of the sobbing woman's voice caused them all to remain silent and as she continued to weep uncontrollably, the grief pouring from out of her, Reggie Gallier continued to feel a deepening sense of guilt… He took another deep breath and tried to think about the situation logically, *but there was no logic…* A rising and ferocious anger began to rise inside of him… *His father had not deserved to die and there would need to be vengeance... Not an arrest, or a trial, or a prison sentence... No long investigations, no waiting around, no gathering of evidence, no legal justice... Just cold hard vengeance...*

Before getting up to leave for the last time, Gallier took one final look at his old man as his weeping mother clung to his body hopelessly... The image would remain with him for the rest of his life... He looked down at his suit and hands and suddenly realised that they were covered in blood from when he had carried his dad out to the car... *His hands were covered in his father's blood... It was quite symbolic, it was his fault... His own father's blood was on his hands and somebody would have to pay the price...*

Chapter 14

Gallier checked his watch as he left the hospital. It was half past eight in the evening and he knew that there was a possibility that Fowler would still be at the station. Inside the hospital, Gallier had left his mother and siblings. He was confident that they would take care of each other and since joining the police force he had been something of an outsider within his own family… This did not mean that he was any less affected by his father's death than they were, but his underestimation of Cedric Tanner had been the root cause of the tragedy *and he had to make things right…*

Detective Inspector Fowler sat alone at his desk and sipped on a large cup of Scotch whisky. It was well passed 'going home' time, but he like to be alone in his office at night. His crooked and dishonest methods of policing were suspected and frowned upon by some of his colleagues and deep down even he knew that the way in which he conducted himself was morally wrong. As a result, he had grown to feel paranoid and this state of paranoia clawed at his very existence. When the office was quiet, there were no suspicions, no stares and to Fowler, most importantly, there was no Reggie Gallier… Most of the other officers 'understood' the importance of forging a mutual 'alliance' with the local underworld, even if they did not take 'drinks' themselves, but to Gallier *it was always black and white…* A pile of paperwork sat on Fowler's desk and the Inspector regarded it with eyes of annoyance. *The money he was making from Cedric Tanner, surely he should be paying some nice young WPC to do paperwork for him!* But his doing it himself was imperative… *He could not allow any 'loose ends' to be detected by junior officers! Especially the likes of Reggie Gallier who were obviously snooping around and out to get him!* He looked at a large, simple clock on the wall. *His wife would be wandering as to his where abouts… She would suspect him of having an affair, which of course he was…*

Earlier that evening, Fowler had received a phone call from a rather agitated Cedric Tanner. Gallier's antics at Victoria Park that morning severely humiliated and angered the gangster and Tanner was baying for blood. He had informed the Inspector of his plans for vengeance and in return he (Fowler) was to see to it that there would be no repercussions on Tanner's organisation from the police. He had not agreed with Tanner's plans. He knew exactly just how stubborn and resilient DS Gallier was and he knew full well that Tanner's approach would only make matters worse, but ultimately, *what could he do? What could Gallier do? Sooner or later the detective Sergeant would get himself killed and then it would be his mess to clear up! He would have no choice… He could never be able to go after Tanner for killing a copper, the villain had far too much on him… He would be dragged down for sure, and for a disgraced former policeman in prison, his jail time experience would be considerably less 'comfortable' than it would be for Tanner!* A flicker of excitement suddenly came over Fowler as he remembered that one of his favourite WPCs was on duty that night. WPC Angie Allen was young, relatively attractive and willing to do anything for the prospect of a promotion or favour within the force. This was exactly how Fowler liked them and without delay, he telephoned the front desk.

"Hello Ray?" The desk Sergeant answered the phone and Fowler addressed him by his first name. "It's Inspector Fowler here. Is WPC Allen in the office tonight at all?" The voice on the other end of the phone confirmed that she was and Fowler smiled inwardly as he asked for her to be sent up to his office immediately… *The young WPC would be able to ease his tensions and help him relax…*

"You sent for me Sir?" A few minutes later, there was a knock at the door of DI Fowler's office and the buxom young WPC walked in. Her face was covered in acne but her breasts were full and her thighs were thick and in her tight fitting, recently pressed uniform she looked particularly alluring in a somewhat unorthodox way.

"Yes WPC... Come in and shut the door will you..." Fowler pushed his chair back as he lent backwards, making the lower half of his body readily available. The WPC was good and he quivered in anticipation of the prospect of what he was about to receive. "You're a good girl aren't you Allen..." He eyed her intently and the young girl smiled lasciviously. "You know how to get on in this job don't you..."

"Of course Sir..." She made her way around to the side of his desk chair and without nerves or embarrassment, she got down to her knees and undid Fowler's flies.... She had certainly done this before... He stroked her rosy cheek and then guided her mouth down to his intimate region, smiling wildly as he did so... *Sometimes he really did love his job!*

"Does your mother know you do that WPC Allen?" The office door suddenly flung open and Fowler nearly jumped out of his skin as Detective Sergeant Reggie Gallier appeared in the doorway. The young girl screamed and quickly rose to her feet as Fowler hurried to cover himself up and zip up his trousers.

"What is the meaning of this Gallier? You can't just barge into my office like this!"

"I need to speak with you... It is very urgent..." Gallier was seething with anger, but he managed to hold onto his cool. He held the door open and looked directly at WPC Allen who by now was extremely embarrassed. "Get out..." In ordinary times, Gallier would have been more concerned about getting his own 'turn' with the WPC who had quite a reputation around the station, but right now this could not have been further from his thoughts.

"Do as he says WPC... I will catch up with you later thank you..." Fowler glanced at the floor nervously and the young woman sheepishly left the room. When she was gone, Fowler spoke again, but this time his tone was much more subdued. "I'm sorry you had to see that Reg... You know how it is..." Gallier was sick and tired of hearing his senior officer say 'You know how it is!'

"We cannot speak here Sir..." Reluctantly, Gallier addressed DI Fowler as Sir, it was vitally important that he appeared to be on Fowler's side...

"What do you mean?" Fowler was intrigued and paranoid as ever.

"Lets just say that there have been some significant events today that have led me to reassess my stance on a few things..." Gallier knew that Fowler would be suspicious of his sudden change, so it was vitally important that his act was convincing.

"I see..." Fowler stroked his thin chin and appeared deep in thought. *There was no way that the great Reggie Gallier would change his way of thinking just like that... But just what had Tanner done? Maybe Gallier had come to his senses and decided it was time to protect those that were dear to him?* "So what have you come here to say?"

"Like I said Sir, I would rather not speak here... I know that most of CID have gone home, but you never know who is lurking around... I don't want anyone to hear what I have to say other than yourself... I am not proud of the conclusions I have come to... But I have to do what is best for my family..." Gallier looked at the floor with a mock sadness and defeatism that was significantly out of character.

"So where do you suggest we talk Sergeant?"

"In cell number four... The walls are thick down there and nobody will hear a word we say... I will meet you down there in five minutes..." Gallier gave the Inspector no choice... He turned on his heel and disappeared out of the doorway before Fowler could even begin to reply.

"I'm glad that you finally came to your senses Reg..." Fowler pulled out his cigarettes as the two men stood face to face in cell number four. Gallier said nothing. As Fowler lit his cigarette, the Detective Sergeant walked over to the door and locked them both inside the cell before placing the key back into his pocket. "What are you doing Reg?" It was at that moment that Fowler suddenly realised that he was completely fucked…

"I need to ask you a few questions… Sir…" Gallier approached his senior officer and before Fowler could protest further the burly Sergeant hit him in the chest with a right-hand body punch that winded him instantly. Gallier was surprised that the Inspector had not gone down so he hit him again harder. This time Fowler folded onto his knees as the pain of the blow left him badly winded. He could not speak and as he clutched his stomach, Gallier swiftly and effectively moved behind him, pulled his arms behind his back and cuffed him so that both of his arms were unusable. Gallier had cuffed a thousand men but he was surprised at how easily a fellow policeman had submitted.

"What the fuck?" Fowler finally cried out but Gallier paid him no attention. The DS rigged a rope up into a hook that he had placed in a corner of the room before going up to Fowler's office and then to DI Fowler's horror he looped it over the detective Inspector's neck before beginning to tighten it. "No! Please no!" Fowler began to panic and he struggled frantically but it was no use, he was trapped. He finally realised that it was useless to struggle and he looked Gallier directly in the eye. "What do you want Gallier? Why are you doing this?" Fowler was truly helpless. *He could try and cry for help, but even if they heard him, what would he tell the rescuing officers? Besides, the cell was locked from the inside.* Gallier lit a cigarette and just stood and stared for several seconds before finally speaking.

"You won't be the first senior detective to be found hanging… It's a stressful job… A lot of coppers top themselves…" Gallier blew smoke into the room and almost smirked. "When they look into your dealings a little closer they will soon find out that you were as bent as they come… It must really mess with your head to be a crooked, bent bastard… I'm sure it would be enough to drive anyone to suicide…"

"Please Reg, what do you want?" Fowler was beginning to seriously panic... *Maybe this was what he deserved? But he did not want to die...*

"Tell me about what happened today..." Gallier wanted nothing more than to let the emotion of his father's death pour out of him and inflict a vicious and brutal beating upon the DI, but if he did choose to become judge, juror and executioner and hang the man, the bruises would look suspicious on the autopsy report.

"What? At Victoria Park?" Fowler was not one hundred percent sure of the complete occurrences of the day.

"No... In Windsor Road, Tipton..."

"What about Windsor Road?"

"That's where my parents live... Tell me about what happened there..."

"I don't know what you're talking about Reg..." Fowler lied.

"Then yow ay much fucking good to me alive are yer..." Gallier callously pulled the rope and as it tightened around Fowler's neck, the DI protested.

"Ok, ok... I'll talk..."

"Go on..." Gallier still held the rope in his right hand and the cigarette in his left.

"Tanner was pissed off about what you did to him in Victoria Park... He sent some guys round to the house to rough your family up a bit, just to try and scare you... I told him that it was a bad idea Reg... Honest..."

"Rough my family up a bit?" A ferociously intimidating gaze came upon Gallier's wild eyes and the Sergeant gritted his teeth venomously... "My ode mon's fucking dead! Tanner's men beat him so badly that he keeled over and died of a fucking heart attack!"

"Shit Reg, I didn't know, really I didn't know..." Fowler was telling the truth and Gallier could tell, but in all honesty he didn't really care. "They went too far Reg... Tanner wouldn't have wanted that... He just wanted to get you on side..."

"Who went too far?"

"I don't know... Tanner's goons..." Fowler lied. Tanner had disclosed the names of his associates earlier as he had not wanted them interfered with in any way by the police as a result of the attack. Gallier applied pressure to the noose again and Fowler struggled for breath. "I don't fucking know Reggie, honest..." Gallier pulled the noose even tighter and Fowler choked as he tried to speak. "Ok, fucking ok... It was a couple of Pikeys from Pensnett... Tanner uses them a lot for this kind of thing... Real heavy Paddies..."

"Their names?" Gallier had calmed slightly, but the coldness that now occupied his eyes was if anything more frightening than his previous rage.

"I can't remember Reg, just a couple of 'Snetters...'" The term 'Snetter was a derogatory term for residents of Pensnett who were of gypsy origins.

"What did you say?" The word 'Snetter jogged a recent memory in Gallier's mind.

"A couple of 'Snetters from down Pensnett..." Fowler repeated the sentence as Gallier recalled his father's last words when he had questioned him as to who had carried out the attack. "Net, Netter..." The two words would forever remain in his memory...

"What are their fucking names?" Gallier tightened the rope again and shoved his face close to Fowler's... When the Inspector was finally allowed to breathe again he began to speak reluctantly.

"Bernard Quinn and Tummy Collins..."

"Good..." Gallier took hold of the rope and pondered his next move. More than anything in that moment, he wanted to tighten the rope and ring the Inspector's neck, but that would not solve anything. It would not bring his father back and it would not punish those who were directly responsible for his death. After a few more minutes further of revelling in Fowler's predicament, the DS dropped the rope and removed the noose.

"Fucking hell Reg, I thought you was really gunna fucking do me then!" Fowler was relieved to say the least but he knew that he was not completely out of the woods yet.

"I'm gunna need your help some more… If you want me to keep my mouth shut about you and Tanner, I need you to come with me back up to the office and you're gunna pull out Quinn and Collins' files… I wanna know where they live and what cars they drive…"

"What are you gunna do Reg? I told you not to fuck with Tanner didn't I!" Now that the noose had been removed, Fowler suddenly seemed to possess a renewed confidence.

"It's your choice… You can either get me those files or I can go to the Superintendent and tell him all about your sordid little operation with Tanner? Or maybe you would prefer it if I put you back up there?" Gallier nodded towards the makeshift gallows and Fowler turned away.

"Fine… But don't ever say that I didn't warn you Reg… For fucks sake I went out of my way to try and help you with Tanner… If it wasn't for me he would have resorted to these tactics much sooner…" Fowler continued to speak but Gallier had stopped listening. First and *foremost he would gain vengeance on those who had caused his father's death… He would deal with Cedric Tanner later on…*

Back up in his office, Detective Inspector Fowler poured them both an extremely large Scotch.

"I really am sorry to hear about what happened to your old man Reg…" The 'small talk' was ignored though DI Fowler did actually genuinely mean it. *Deep down, Fowler knew that he was wrong, he was a dodgy cop, but ultimately he was just greedy… Greedy for money and greedy for sex and Cedric Tanner could always help him with both of these vices… Back in his youth, he had joined the force with honest intentions of trying to make a difference, but time had corrupted him and the higher he had risen the more crooked he had grown… It was not something he was proud of, but it was what he had become…*

"Just find me those files..." Gallier downed his whisky in one gulp as he looked at the filing cabinet eagerly. After a few minutes of sifting through paperwork, the DI finally pulled out the documents he was looking for.

"Here... But just remember what I said Reg... Don't do anything stupid..." Fowler took a gulp of his whisky as Gallier snatched the papers from out of his still trembling hands. The room was dark and Gallier took them over to the light of a small table lamp that stood on Fowler's desk. He thumbed the documents eagerly and then noticed something that was of particular interest. The white Ford transit he had nearly crashed into near St Marks Road in Tipton earlier was registered to Tummy Collins... *The two men had obviously been driving so erratically because they were making their get away from the beating of his father...* His blood began to boil and the livid rage proceeded to rise inside of him again... He made a note of the information he required and then turned to face Fowler.

"If you breath a word of this to anyone, or tip off these bastards that I am on to them, I will not only go to the Super with everything I know, but also I will let it be known to Tanner that you grassed up his boys... Cedric Tanner dow like grasses aer kid... So best keep your fucking mouth shut..." Gallier turned away from Fowler and then without as much as a word or a second glance, he left the room. *He had spent more than enough time in the company of the odious, crooked cop... He had to go and find a friend... He had a favour that needed to be called in...*

Chapter 15

Eddie Fennel stood by the side of the canal and sucked on a Hamlet cigar as he watched the water ripple and disappear into the dark two and a half mile abyss that was Netherton tunnel. Nearly forty years previously in 1929, a young policeman by the name of Harry Leslie Stanton was found brutally murdered not far from the spot on which Fennel stood and it was rumoured in local folklore that the tunnel was haunted.

Work began on the construction of the tunnel (the last to be built in Britain) in December 1855 and it was finally opened for use on the twentieth of August 1858, providing a vital waterway link between the Black Country towns of Netherton and Tipton. Several construction workers had been killed during the highly dangerous construction of the tunnel and many locals had heard tales of mysterious footsteps suddenly vanishing halfway down the tunnel and other eerie and somewhat inexplicable noises. As he stood and waited, Eddie Fennel had no thoughts or concerns of such 'nonsense.' It was 8AM on a Saturday morning and the December skies were barely light as Fennel shivered in the cold. He was surprised to see that the canal had not frozen over as it certainly felt cold enough, *but at least it was not raining or snowing.* He checked his watch and he was relieved to see that he was still early. The nature of his appointment was highly suspicious and he was certainly putting a lot of trust into the man that he was due to meet. Eddie Fennel was way out of his comfort zone, but he had carefully considered the appointment meticulously and he had concluded that it was potentially worth the risk.

As he had predicted, at exactly the time arranged, the man he was waiting for suddenly appeared on the banks of the canal, but Fennel did not feel relieved... *He was taking a huge risk, he was dancing with the devil!*

"Thanks for coming Eddie..." Detective Sergeant Reggie Gallier was friendly enough and Fennel truly hoped that the 'Cozzer' did not misinterpret his cooperation for a form of grassin'! Neither man offered to shake hands. They could not be quite sure of just who could be watching and the sight of a top local gangster and a Police Sergeant shaking hands would have been bad for both of their 'professional' reputations.

"That's ok Reg…" Fennel shrugged. "If it helps to get rid of that bastard Tanner then I'm willing to help… But I will not give evidence or be any kind of grass… Just remember that…" The gangster was resolute and Gallier knew that there was no chance of Eddie Fennel ever becoming an informant.

"You got the stuff?" Gallier was abrupt and to the point and Fennel smiled.

"It ay as easy as that Reg… Besides, why would I turn up to meet a copper at a secluded location with pockets full of heroin? Do yow think ar was born yesterday aer kid?"

"So where is it?" Gallier was not impressed.

"You seem to forget that I fucking hate drugs as much as yow do! I need yow to explain just exactly what you need it for again…" Fennel exhaled cigar smoke and waited for an explanation.

"I thought I explained this the other night Eddie…" The two men had met briefly at the Neptune Public House on Powke Lane where Gallier had approached the villain with his plan. "You know how it works as well as ar do… The less details yow know the better…" Gallier considered pulling out one of his own cigarettes but he was eager to get in and out of there as quickly as possible but Eddie Fennel appeared almost amused.

"Yes, but how do I know that this ay some kind of Police sting? A set up?"

"Yow'm just gunna have to trust me Eddie…"

"Trust a copper? Am yow avin' a loff?"

"You seem to forget Eddie that we have already had dealings… I did you the favour with those files remember? Now not only do you owe me for that favour, but also and more importantly for yow, if this does

121

turn out to be some kind of elaborate police sting, then yow also have enough shit on me with those files I took from Fowler's office... Why would I teck that risk?" Gallier appeared to have a point but Fennel was still not convinced.

"Ar wouldn't put it past that slippery bastard Cedric Tanner to try and double cross me... Maybe Tanner set up all this business just to try and trap me and send me down for a longer stretch? Maybe you are in on it too?" Fennel was suspicious of everyone.

"So my ode mon was killed as part of some complicated plan to trick you?" Gallier stared directly and assertively into Fennel's eyes and the villain could tell that the tough cop housed an honesty that made him feel easier.

"I heard about that Reg... Tanner was bang out of order..." Fennel suddenly remembered that he had heard on the 'grapevine' of the killing just a few days earlier. "Everyone knows that hurting civilians is off limits... That's why everyone hates the Tanner's so much... Cedric Tanner has always picked on innocents, people's families, civilians... His father Brian Tanner was exactly the same back in the day..."

"So where is the gear?" Gallier was not interested in listening to a history of local crime figures.

"Look Reg, ar'm sorry about yer Dad and all that, but yow gorra tell me why you need that heroin before I teck yer to it... After all, I've arranged it and I'm paying for it... That is a fuck of a big risk on my part Reg..." Fennel's words were true enough and Gallier got the impression that he would not be getting anywhere if he did not elaborate a little further on his plans.

"Fine... The long and short of it is ar need the gear to get even with the bastards who murdered my dad and in the process link them and the heroin to Tanner..."

"Yow mean yow'm gunna fit Tanner up?" Fennel was very familiar with the methods of many a policeman...

"Does it matter as long as that bastard is inside?" Surely that will suit you too?"

"Do what you need to do Reg... But like ar said before, dow expect me to sign any statements or give evidence in court! I ay no grass..."

"I understand that Eddie... Now teck me to the gear..."

Jenny Hill was a stern-faced prostitute in her early thirties who lived in the Walsall suburb of Pleck. She had received word from her pimp and drug dealer that she would be getting a visit from two men that morning though she knew absolutely nothing about the two men that she was due to meet. Anonymity was absolutely key. All she had been told was that she was to pass on a large quantity of heroin that had been supplied by her pimp and that she was to 'tutor' the men on how to cook and prepare the drug.

As usual she was in a highly intoxicated state through alcohol and various drugs but the prospect of two strange men in her run down, terraced house that was owned by her Jamaican pimp also brought about the possibility for further potential illicit business. *If she could get them both to have sex with her then she could make a few extra 'quid' for her next fix...* With a shaking hand she applied heavy make-up to her once pretty face and she ignored the hungry cries of her neglected young children as she adjusted her micro mini skirt and pulled up her fish net tights. *If there was extra money for drugs to be made from whoring, she would give it her best shot...*

A red Jaguar mkII pulled up outside the house and as she looked out of her filth covered windows, Jenny Hill watched as two 'suited and booted' men got out of the car and she could tell instantly that they were both men of violence...

"Hi boys..." She answered the front door to the two men and straight away she turned on a flirtatious, giggling, schoolgirl charm.

"Are you Jenny?" The older man with a balding head and unnerving, threatening eyes spoke as the younger man looked on suspiciously. Both of them could have been gangsters or coppers, but with some of them she knew she had often come to ask herself the same question, *what was the difference? The older man was clearly better dressed, his shoes were much more expensive… He was clearly the boss…*

"I'm Jenny… I'm all yours…" Jenny shut the door and bolted the latch before pushing herself seductively against Eddie Fennel. The gangster almost 'gagged' at the scent of her breath which was laced with a mixture of alcohol, tobacco, marijuana, vomit and her rotting teeth and gums as Reggie Gallier looked on and felt nothing but pity.

"You have a package for us I believe…" Fennel remained straight to the point. *Even if she had not have been a filth ridden, stinking whore, he loved his Irish wife and he did not fool around with hookers.*

"Yes I do baby, but I thought we could have a bit of fun first?" Jenny Hill was trying her hardest but neither male was interested. She lowered her right hand to Fennel's crotch and flickered her false eyelashes as she pushed her small breasts against his powerful torso.

"Listen slag!" Fennel grabbed her intrusive right hand and then pushed her back against the wall forcefully as he snarled his words. "I ay one for hurtin' wenches… I ay never laid my hand upon a woman in mar life, so do us all a fuckin' favour and keep your bloody hands to yourself ok?"

"Sorry…" Jenny tried to pull away but Fennel's grip was too strong.

"I've paid good money for this gear and extra to have you demonstrate how to use it… Now if yow dow deliver on that contract than ar will have ter teck my anger out on yower pimp… Jackie, is that his name?" Fennel's eyes were truly terrifying and the scared prostitute nodded. "Now if I have to go round and hurt Jackie, and believe me, I will hurt him bad, over something you have done or not done here today, you can be sure that Jackie will be straight around here to make you pay for what I have had to do to him… Do you understand love?"

"Ok fine…" Her eyes were filled with tears and the prostitute nodded again before Fennel let go of his intense grip. She led the two men through a small corridor and out into a pokey kitchen where she grabbed a half empty bottle of gin and took a generous swig. At the sight of it, Gallier tugged at his inner jacket pocket and pulled out a hip flask filled with cheap Scotch. He took a swig himself and then handed it towards Fennel who looked down at his expensive gold Rolex watch.

"It's a bit early ay it aer kid?" Fennel almost smirked and Gallier shrugged as he took another swig and then shoved it back into his pocket. Since his father had died just a few days ago, there was no such thing as 'too early.' The gangster (Fennel) turned away from Gallier and the prostitute sternly. "You can get pissed later love, just show us what you have been paid to do…"

"Ok, ok, just dow complain to Jackie, please, for fuck's sake!" Jenny was particularly concerned about the repercussions from her pimp if Fennel and his accomplice were to complain. She took two packages from out of a damp and soiled kitchen cabinet and placed them both on the counter.

"See what yer think…" Fennel looked at Gallier and then nodded towards the packages that were tapped up with brown Sellotape. "I ay got a fuckin' clue about this shit…" Eddie Fennel had a genuine disdain for drugs. His underworld contacts had been enough to set up the day's proceedings, but his own knowledge of narcotics was limited. Without a word, Gallier took out a pen knife and then pierced a hole into the top of one of the packets. A pure white powder appeared and the policeman placed his right index finger inside before taking it out, smelling it and then tasting it.

"It's good…" Gallier could tell that it was a good pure sample. He had a relatively good knowledge of illegal drugs and had first began to build his experience whilst working in the Military Police in the exotic German port of Hamburg.

"Good… Right then Jenny, show us what you have ter do!" Fennel addressed the prostitute with no respect. Drugs disgusted him. Eagerly, Jenny pulled a metal spoon from out of a kitchen draw and then scooped a careful amount of the white powder up so that all three of them could see. She placed it carefully on the side and then poured a small amount of water from out of the tap into the metal cap of her gin bottle. Without spilling a drop, she added the water to the spoon and then turned to face Fennel as she steadied the spoon in her hand. Gallier watched on eagerly and it occurred to him that previously she had appeared inebriated and unsteady, but now, nervous of the potential risk of spelling a precious ounce of heroin, she was meticulously careful and precise.

"You got a light?" After asking for the cigarette lighter, Jenny quickly returned her eyes to the matter at hand as Fennel handed her a silver-plated cigarette lighter that had once been a gift to him from his former military commanding officer and mentor Billy Mucklow. She placed the light under the spoon and they all continued to watch as the powder proceeded to dissolve until it became a precious liquid. The skeletal prostitute looked at Gallier and her eyes held a pleading desperation. "Do you want to try it Sir?" She held onto his gaze, hoping that he would turn her offer down and allow her to take every drop for herself...

"No..." Gallier shook his head. All he had wanted was to see how it was prepared. *It appeared to be relatively simple...* He had never used drugs, let alone injected one of the most potent and lethal narcotics known to man. "Knock yourself out..." The Policeman turned away with a mixture of pity and disgust as the young mother placed a syringe deep into a vein in her arm and began to 'shoot up.' After just a few moments, she fell back against the wall in total ecstasy and an almost 'death like' and sinister look came over her face as she rolled her eyes heavenwards in a perverse and illicit grin. Fennel grabbed the remainder of the drugs and looked towards Gallier for the next move.

"Happy?" The gangster was just as eager to get out of there as the Policeman.

"Yes... Lets get the fuck ahht of here..." Gallier's words were a relief and both men swiftly began to make their exit, but Eddie Fennel suddenly paused at the bottom of the stairs.

"Hey, mate, yow come here aer kid..." Fennel saw a pathetic and sad looking young boy on the staircase whom he estimated to be of around seven years of age. The child's mother was dead to the world and Fennel felt a mixture of pity and guilt, *but he had not chosen the mother's way of life!* He pulled out a crisp five-pound note from out of his wallet and handed it to the boy. "Here kid, get yerself something nice for Christmas mate... And look after your mother..." Fennel's kindness impressed Reggie Gallier and the Sergeant frowned in confusion. *Weren't the gangsters supposed to be the bad guys? But then, surely the route he was taking made him just as wrong as they were?* After the death of his father, it was as if he no longer cared, all he wanted was revenge...

Chapter 16

The Jaguar MkII was a significantly different drive to Gallier's usual Ford Zephyr. He wore his sharpest pin stripe suit and he had begrudgingly invested in a brand-new camel coloured Crombie overcoat. DS Gallier had borrowed the car courtesy of Eddie Fennel and it was all part of his elaborate plan to gain vengeance for his father's death. His hair was slicked back with even more grease than usual and as he gazed at his reflection in the internal mirror of the Jaguar he thought of the overweight young blonde Katie whom he had met in the Doughty Arms a few weeks previously. Both Katie and her friend Gemma, whom he had enjoyed the pleasure of spending the night with, had informed him that he resembled a bona fide 'gangster' and this misassumption would certainly work in his favour this day as he carefully ran through his meticulous plan to go 'under cover' as he drove Fennel's luxurious car.

As he drove, Gallier looked upon the many houses that were adorned with Christmas lights and decorations. How the ordinary folks of the Black Country were looking forward to and preparing for the forthcoming festivities, but the sentiment of the moment suddenly evoked a terrible and painful melancholy in the Detective... As a young boy, Reggie Gallier had loved Christmas... The lights, the atmosphere. The family, the food, the present... *Father Christmas...* A solid lump appeared in the hardened policeman's throat as he recalled how his loving father would dress up as Santa Claus every December the 24th for the amusement of the young Reginald, his siblings and his young cousins. How Gallier longed to be able to return to such simpler times, such innocence, a time when his father was still alive... It suddenly occurred to him yet again that he would never see his father's smile again, hear his voice or spend time in his company. For some people, such thoughts and fears would arouse tears... Raw grief and a deep knot in the pit of their stomachs, but for Reggie Gallier it evoked a bloodthirsty, hard coldness that would soon come to its fruition...

The Black Country town of Pensnett stood roughly two and a half miles south-west of central Dudley and held a tough and infamous reputation as an area with a high proportion of deprivation and poverty. Like Reg Gallier's hometown of Tipton, most of the local residents were good, honest, proud working-class people, however, the town also had a notorious reputation for tough, troublesome characters and two such men were Bernard Quinn and Tummy Collins... Bernard Quinn was a career criminal. Born in the Irish town of Ruthkeale in West Country Limerick, Quinn had travelled far and wide throughout his 45 years upon this earth before settling in the Black Country area in the late 1950s. His associate, Tummy Collins was of a similar age but had been born into the same Irish traveller community in the Midlands where he, quite ironically for a 'traveller' had remained throughout most of his life. When Quinn had come into the area, Collins saw something of himself in the Irishman and the pair quickly teamed up. They were both stereotypical 'tough guys', fighting, bare knuckle gypsy men, though Tummy Collins, by the narrowest of margins had always 'just about' been the tougher and more assertive of the pair. Initially, their crimes had been of a mostly 'small time' nature. House burglary, car theft and unlicensed gambling. In fact, as with many families from the same background, both Quinn and Collins's wife and children had suffered intolerable prejudices from the ordinary natives of the area, as was often the case with gypsy-traveller families throughout Britain. This prejudice and hardship had only bolstered the two men's negative resentment towards the English natives and when they had eventually started working as general thugs for Cedric Tanner, the Celtic duo had relished the opportunity to act with brutality towards the innocent locals. As a result, the pair quickly became quite a favourite of the drug dealing crime boss and their non-reluctance and willingness to commit extreme violence against innocent, everyday civilians made them highly popular with Tanner's organisation. In Collins and Quinn's minds, their own families had suffered prejudices at the hands of the locals and as a result the two Irishmen were more than happy to inflict savage, brutal vengeance upon those who had treated their own with such hostility.

DS Gallier pulled the red Jaguar MkII onto the Gypsy site near Pensnett as discreetly as possible. He was very aware that as a middle ranking Detective in the local constabulary, it was highly likely that somebody would recognise him so he pulled up the collars of the new Crombie overcoat and wore a pair of dark aviator sunglasses. The records he had procured from Detective Inspector Fowler only gave the address of the site itself and not individual caravans, but Gallier had the registration number of the Ford Transit that belonged to Collins and he had meticulously studied the police 'mug shots' of both Quinn and Collins. Neither of them were by any means good looking. They were both very Irish looking in appearance with dark hair and brown eyes. They were over six foot tall, heavily built and with distorted cauliflower ears that gave away their long history of involvement with bare knuckle fighting. For hours on end, Gallier had stared at the two photographs of the criminals and he had let extremely violent fantasies play out in his mind as he had drank copious amounts of whisky and gazed into the eyes of his father's killers... *He would be able to spot them anywhere...* However, being a seasoned detective, Gallier had left nothing to chance. As part of the preparations he had already observed the gypsy camp and had carried out discrete enquiries through the watching of the site from a safe location nearby with a pair of binoculars. He knew that Quinn and Collins lived with their wives and children in caravans that were conveniently adjacent to each other and he knew that the pair spent much of their days sat between their caravans next to an open fire that raged inside an old metal dustbin whilst drinking Scrumpy cider and smoking roll up cigarettes.

"Hello boys..." Gallier parked the Jag directly in front of Collins and Quinn's caravans and then lit a large cigar as he got out of the car.

He was certainly pulling off the first impression that he had been striving to achieve.

"Who the feck are you?" Bernard Quinn spoke first and then Tummy Collins added.

"What do you feckin' want? Coming here in a posh feckin' motor like that!" Both men spoke with a strange accent that was a peculiar mix of Irish and hardcore Black Country.

"The boss sent me day he…" Gallier flicked ash from his huge cigar onto the ground and spoke with a confidence that was a vital aspect of the deception.

"The boss?" Collins glanced at Gallier suspiciously.

"Yeah… The fuckin' boss… Yow do know who the fuckin' boss is dow yer?" Gallier took a step closer and as he came face to face with the two men that had caused his father's death, he resisted the strong urge to strike out and commit obscene violence… *The time would come…*

"Who are you?" Tummy Collins spoke again as Quinn looked on suspiciously.

"My names Jimmy… I work for Tanner and that's all you need to know mate…" Gallier oozed a 'gangster like' confidence as he exhaled more cigar smoke into the air and studied the two men carefully.

"What does Tanner want?" This time it was Bernard Quinn's turn to speak and Gallier noticed that Quinn's accent was considerably stronger Irish than that off Tummy Collins.

"You'll have to ask him yourself… He just said to tell you well done for the beating of that old boy in Tipton and that he's got more work for yer…" The reference to the death of his father was almost too much, but Gallier managed to keep it together and his stance remained convincing.

"Yeah well, the fat old bastard didn't put up much of a fight!" Quinn found the beating of Gallier's father amusing and Collins joined in as both men began to laugh in unison. "Where does Tanner wanna see us?"

"At the old warehouse in Tipton... You know the one over Tividale way?" Gallier spoke of the building where he had previously hoped to find a stash of drugs a few weeks previously. After the Detective's antics with 'Doctor' George, Tanner moved all of his drug operations to another site and although the Tipton warehouse still belonged to Tanner, it was no longer a narcotics distribution depot for the drug lord.

"I know it..." Tummy Collins still had an element of suspicion in his eyes, *but why should he not trust the flash apparent gangster?* Gypsies did not have telephones in their caravans and all of their dealings and jobs for Tanner had been from direct word of mouth. "Why hasn't Tanner come here his fuckin' self?"

"How the fuck should I know? Ask him..." Gallier shrugged and added an impatient edge to his tone. "Up to you lads... Do you know how many wannabe tough guys wanna work for Cedric Tanner? If yow pair dow want this job, somebody else will... It's just that Tanner told me yow did a good job in Tipton and he knows he can depend on yer..." Gallier was making it up as he went along, but he could tell that the men were falling for it.

"When does he wanna see us?" Bernard Quinn felt quite satisfied that their mysterious visitor was genuine.

"Right now... Yow can follow me there or I can give you a lift in the Jag? I'll drop you back here after..." Gallier nodded towards the car. He was hoping to get out of there as soon as possible before he was recognised by other gypsies who may have known his true identity.

"What's in it for us?" Tummy Collins was still not quite satisfied.

"How should I bloody know?" Gallier's slight impatience was genuine. "That's between you and the big man ay it... But remember this, if yow dow want the work, there are plenty others who do!"

"Hold on a minute..." Quinn grunted his reply as the two Irishmen turned away and had a private word with each other.

"Well hurry up! It's fuckin' freezing ahht here!" Gallier opened up the driver's side of the Jag and climbed in. He fully expected the two gypsies to climb into their own van and follow him, but much to his surprise, after kissing their family's goodbye, the two hoodlums eventually climbed into the rear seats of the Jaguar.

"We will use your feckin' petrol! That way if this turns out to be bull shit we ain't feckin' lost nuthin!" Collins was proud of his shrewd thinking and the two thugs settled into the rear seats of a luxury vehicle that was 'wasted' upon their rudimentary tastes.

"Whatever…" Gallier smiled knowingly. "The boss pays for everything anyway…"

Gallier parked the Jaguar outside the abandoned warehouse property near Tividale. It had been a short but awkward journey that he had spent in the company of his father's killers.

"Where the fuck is Tanner?" The two gypsies spoke in almost unison as Gallier stopped the car and they realised that Tanner's own Jaguar Mk X was not present on the car park.

"He's inside ay he…" Gallier continued to think on his feet. "When you get as much attention from the law as Cedric Tanner does, it dow pay ter leave yer motor out on show… Last thing he wants is the fuckin' pigs to follow his car and then catch him doing a bit of business…" Gallier found his own derogatory comment towards his own kind somewhat amusing. "He probably got one of his drivers to drop him up here…" Gallier got out of the car and the two large Irishmen began to chuckle in amusement.

"Yeah, Tanner has a few different drivers! All of them about eighteen years old and very pretty!" Tummy Collins laughed. "Everybody knows what them lads do!"

"Yeah!" Quinn joined in on the joke. "They'm all fuckin' rent boys!"

"Are you one of Tanner's rent boys Jimmy? You seem a bit old for Cedric's tastes!" Collins shut the car door as the two thugs followed the undercover Policeman across the car park towards the abandoned building.

"I bet you suck Tanner's di..." Before Bernard Quinn could finish his lewd and mocking sentence he noticed that the once bolted and boarded front door was slightly ajar. "Look! Some feckers already in there! Looks like they feckin' broke in to me..."

"I told yer Tanner was already here..." Gallier held the door open for the two gypsies and with a slight reluctance they both stepped into the completely dark corridor.

"I don't feckin' like this Jimmy... I don't like it one bit..." Tummy Collins protested slightly, but his curiosity and greed for money ensured that he continued to make his way through the dark and deserted room.

"If this is some kind of feckin' wind up we'll have your guts for feckin' garters Jimmy!" Bernard Quinn also followed reluctantly, but still neither man looked back as the slight light from the crack in the front door disappeared as it swung shut. The three men walked deeper into the old building and just when Collins was about to question again as to the whereabouts of Cedric Tanner, DS Reggie Gallier finally spoke.

"You're gunna have to answer for the ode chap in Windsor Road fellas..." Gallier's sudden change in tone took the two thugs by surprise.

"What the feck are you on about?" Tummy Collins searched the dark room for the whereabouts of the mysterious man who had led them into the building but he could only gaze at the darkness that filled the area from which the voice sounded.

"What?" Bernard Quinn was equally as confused. "The old man's son is a copper! That's why Tanner wanted us to kick the shite out of him!"

"Yes that's right..." Gallier suddenly flicked a switch and the room filled with an inadequate and shadowy light that just about enabled the two men to make out the detective and the warrant card that he held in his right hand. "My name is Gallier... Detective Sergeant Reg Gallier... That ode mon was my father..." Straight away, the two hoodlums appeared highly amused and they began to laugh.

"So you bring us here, where you are all alone and vulnerable..." Tummy Collins continued to find the situation amusing.

"I don't rate your chances copper!" Bernard Quinn was also highly entertained but before they could utter a further word, a fourth voice cast from out of the shadows of the room caused a shiver of terror to run through Collins and Quinn's villainous spines.

"Well ar fuckin' do..." Eddie Fennel was a known and respected gangster who had a wicked and genuine reputation for brutal torture and gangland violence. The two gypsies slowly turned around to face the kingpin and were immensely disappointed to spot that Fennel was holding a pistol that was aimed directly at them.

"Is that thing feckin' loaded Eddie?" Nervously, Bernard Quinn asked the question.

"What do you think? You know who I am dow yer? Do you think I fuck around lads?" Fennel's tone was mocking and the two men knew that they were now in a serious situation.

"Not like you to work for the law Eddie... I didn't know that you were a grass..." Tummy Collins glanced directly into Fennel's eyes and he saw the troubled soul of a man who had killed hundreds during the Second World War.

"Ar dow work for the law... Ar work for my fuckin' self and everyone knows that Cedric Tanner is my enemy... So by working for that bastard, you also become my enemy..."

"What you gunna do Eddie?" Bernard Quinn was now almost pleading... "Both me and Tum are family men, we've got kids!"

"He ain't gunna do feck all..." Tummy Collins suddenly found an inner confidence. "No copper is gunna stand by and watch a gangland killing... The pig just wants ter question us..."

"Maybe you are right..." Gallier placed the warrant card back into his pocket and then nodded towards two old wooden chairs that stood in the centre of the room. "I have questions for you both about the death of my father... It's Tanner that I want, so if you cooperate, I'm sure that our mutual friend here Mr Fennel might be able to hold onto his famous temper... Please sit down..." Gallier walked towards the two dusty and cobweb covered chairs and reluctantly the two Irishmen followed him.

"We ain't saying feck all copper…" Collins sounded defiant and Gallier smiled.

"Ok… But I am assured that Mr Fennel here has quite a talent for making people talk…"

"I learnt from the best… Billy Mucklow himself…" Fennel uttered the name of a famous and feared Black Country villain who was currently serving time in a London prison and both Quinn and Collins sat down in the dirty wooden chairs.

"Unfortunately we have to do this properly boys…" Whilst Fennel still held the gun at the two men, Gallier pulled two sets of handcuffs from out of his Crombie overcoat and then proceeded to cuff both men to their seats. Upon realisation of what was happening, Bernard Quinn began to protest, but Tummy Collins offered him reassurance.

"I told you not to worry Bernie… This Copper is just trying to scare us… He ain't really gunna hurt us… He knows he can't… Just keep your mouth shut, then the next thing is they will take us into custody down at the station…" Collins had it all worked out. "Then they will have to let us go…"

"Maybe…" Gallier shrugged… A murderous and heartbroken rage burnt inside of him… He wanted nothing more than to inflict a sustained, ultra-violent assault on the two men, but his plan was much more complex than that and he would have to retain his cool. "So tell me about that afternoon? The one when you murdered my father…"

"We didn't feckin' murder anyone…" Bernard Quinn spoke gruffly, fully aware that his accomplice would prefer for them both to keep their mouths shut…

"But my father died?"

"Maybe so… But we didn't kill him… He died later in hospital of a heart attack I heard…" Quinn continued to spout aggressive replies as

136

Collins remained silent. Gallier took a step backwards so that he was not in physical reach of the Irishmen. *He did not trust himself...*

"Either way you are responsible for his death..."

"Look pig, whatever you say, we aint gunna say feck all and we certainly aint gunna say feck all about Tanner... We aint all feckin' grasses like your man Eddie Fennel over here!" Tummy Collins made a sideways glance towards Fennel as he spoke but the Black Country villain said nothing.

"You know what lads?" Gallier left a deliberate and sarcastic pause... "I actually think that you two clowns are probably big enough and tough enough to keep you mouths shut through an interrogation..." Gallier was not lying... The two men were hard travellers and he did not doubt that they could probably withstand a beating as well as anyone. "But in all honesty ar dow really give a fuck..."

"What are you talking about?" Quinn could see a savage and depraved intensity in Galliers's eyes that was not like that of any other copper he had ever seen before.

"Nasty business ay they... Drugs..." Gallier shook his head mockingly as he took two objects from out of his pockets that the two Irishmen could not quite make out.

"What the feck are you doing copper?" This time it was Tummy Collins turn to shout again.

"Drugs are so dangerous... In the wrong hands they are fucking lethal... I mean, me personally, I can drink about fifteen pints of bitter before ar'm totally shit faced, but mar mate Tony can only drink about eight... Everyone has their own levels of tolerance... It's the same with heroin..." On a small makeshift table that stood nearby, Gallier placed a metal ashtray that had been moulded into a shell shape and then he filled it with a substantial amount of powder... "Now if I drank thirty pints of bitter, I doubt it would kill me... In fact, if yow was to buy me the beer and then bet me a fiver that I couldn't drink it, ar reckon that ar could have a damn good crack at drinking the fucking lot..." Gallier continued to ramble on about beer and all three of the other men within the room were quite confused. "But if someone were to force feed me say one hundred pints and then five bottles of scotch on top, well that would be fuckin' dangerous! I doubt I would survive... Death by intoxication... Misadventure..." The policeman continued to speak along similar lines as he took out his cigarette lighter and held it underneath the ashtray which was filled with heroin. Eventually the drug dissolved and mixed with water from a hip flask as Gallier had been shown by Jenny Hill in Pleck, Walsall. He then repeated the process with a second ashtray until he had a massive and surely lethal quantity of liquid heroin. It was not until he produced the two syringes that the gypsies began to realise just exactly what was going to happen to them. At this point they began to thrash around violently as they were cuffed to the two solid old, dusty, oak chairs. Tummy Collins even managed to knock his chair to the floor where he continued to thrash around as he lay face back looking upwards at the dark, high ceiling of the old warehouse.

"Fuck off copper, you can not do this!" Bernard Quinn proceeded to urinate inside his pants as he protested loudly.

"You see boys, ar dow need no statements or shit about Tanner... Cus when we find two of his known associates dead from an overdose of heroin on his (Tanner's) property, even that bent bastard Fowler ay gunna be able to do fuck all... It will go above Fowler's head and guess what? The 'big boy' detectives am gunna come down here... Next thing will be the mighty Cedric Tanner and his lapdog bastard DI Fowler banged up in prison... But unfortunately yow pair of pricks woe be around to witness it..." Gallier chuckled to himself and then proceeded to administer the ridiculously huge and certainly lethal doses of heroin directly into the veins of both men. He had started with Bernard Quinn and then moved on to Tummy Collins. He had received medical training in the army and injecting drugs into veins was relatively straight forward.

As the tiny needle pierced his skin, Bernard Quinn gazed at it helplessly as he felt the slight sting followed by the forcing of fluid into his tight veins. At first he felt nothing and then after a few minutes he entered into the most amazing, euphoric high as the drug began to take effect. The pleasure was immense and it continued to build to a point that he felt no pain, but he knew that he was dying... His vital organs were shutting down and his brain was suffering irreversible damage, but still, all he could feel was pleasure and a mega high. He knew that he would never see his wife and children again and as his brain faded to absolute mush, their images remained in his semi-conscious thoughts until the very end... With Tummy Collins it was very much the same process, but rather than thinking of his children, his final thoughts became obsessed with his own deceased father and a horse that he had once nurtured and loved as child before it was shot and killed by his uncle... *His life had been wasted...*

As both men died and ceased to exist, Reggie Gallier looked on with a grim satisfaction as he gazed relentlessly into their eyes as they took their final breaths... He had not killed people before... *He was a police officer, it was against the law!* But he felt no remorse... *He could not! It was vengeance... It was just...* For a few moments he revelled in the victory... But then very soon the novelty wore off... *His father was still very much dead and the sudden realisation of achieving his goal confirmed to him that no matter what he did, his 'Dad' would not be coming home...*

Chapter 17

It had been two days since the killings of Tummy Collins and Bernard Quinn and DS Gallier was beginning to wonder why he had not heard anything yet. *Surely somebody would have discovered the corpses by now? If it was left much longer they would start to stink! At least it was December… It was cold and this would help to preserve the bodies…. Unless the rats got hold of them!* The old industrial units were filled with vermin and it was highly likely that the fury rodents had already started to feast upon the fresh meat of the deceased. Gallier smiled. *It was sick and it was wrong, but it was vengeance… An eye for an eye and a tooth for a tooth…*

A CID Christmas party had been in full swing at Dudley Police station. DI Fowler had been attempting to pose as 'one of the lads', giving everyone beer and whisky and playfully slapping the shapely backsides of any willing young WPCs in order to gain himself more acceptance and likeability. In reality, just like DS Gallier, most of the team detested the pompous Inspector and they had literally no respect for the man. Reg Gallier enjoyed a beer as much as if not more than any of them, but he simply could not stomach taking part in the festivities. Instead, he sat and contemplated his situation over a pint of bitter, a bag of pork scratchun's and a beef cob in the comfortable lounge area of the Crooked House pub. Technically he was still on duty, but the rest of CID were back at the station getting 'smashed', *so why shouldn't he enjoy a drink amongst more trusted company? Himself…* He took a long drag of his cigarette and then sat back and closed his eyes as he let the flavour of the Park Drive mix with the malty, bitter flavour of the Banks's beer. He had never thought that he would deliberately end another person's life, but his lack of emotion, remorse or guilt was quite puzzling. The only concern that troubled his mind was *when would the bodies of the deceased be discovered?* It was only then that his plan could begin to fall into fruition. *He really so desperately needed to wipe the grin's off of both DI Fowler and the paedophilic, drug dealing scum Cedric Tanner…*

In a corner of the room and beneath a large window, a non-local spoke loudly and excitedly about the phenomena of a marble appearing to roll upwards by itself. It was in fact the famous optical illusion that the Crooked House was notorious for. Those that were local and used the pub as a regular drinking establishment, had seen it many times before and they shook their heads and looked away in irritation. Gallier looked at his watch. *It really was time that he was getting back to the station.* He drained his glass. *They would all be drunk by now... Playing cards and waiting to go home... He would show his face, have a quick whisky then drive over to Lucy's place...* He extinguished his cigarette in the ashtray and then stood up, grabbed his jacket and then made his way towards the exit. The Crooked House always had a habit of making people feel even more drunk than they actually were as a result of it's apparent uneven floor and crooked walls. But it was very rare that Gallier ever felt inebriated. He had a particularly high tolerance for alcohol and the more he continued to indulge in substance abuse (alcohol), the more booze he could consume and not be affected by it. However, there were tell-tale signs... He would sometimes feel breathless, sluggish, tired and a gnawing aching pain on his lower right hand side, underneath his ribcage became more prominent after particularly heavy bouts of drinking. He was very aware that this pain was in fact his liver protesting against his constant abuse, but at least for the time being, it would make very little difference to Gallier's approach to the legal drug. Every morning when he awoke, he would feel a tingling numbness mixed with pain throughout his body and particularly in his extremities. It felt almost electrical, as if his skin was not quite attached to his spine and nerve endings, but by lunchtime, it would be long gone and the detective would eagerly be awaiting the night's alcohol consumption...

The Ford Zephyr started first time, despite the coldness of the month and Gallier had not even had to use much choke to get it going. As he pulled off the carpark and down the long, tight driveway that led from the pub back to the main road, unusually for the detective, Reggie Gallier did not notice that he was in fact being tailed... Before he even reached the end of the driveway and out onto the main road, two cars suddenly appeared close in his rear mirror and at that exact moment he noticed the Police insignia that adorned the trailing Wolseley 6/110 and the blue light on the large black saloon signalled for him to pull over. *Fucking hell! This was the last thing he needed... Young whippersnappers 'shooting fish in a barrel' as they waited for boozy motorists to leave the pub over the festive period.* Luckily he was on his 'own patch' so it was highly likely that the following conversation would be straight forward enough... *Or so he thought!*

"Hello Reg..." The familiar voice belonged to Gallier's Welsh rival DS Jenkins and the arrival of a CID officer at the side of his car immediately caused Gallier concern... *Why was Jenkins not at the party? Had they found out about his involvement in the killing of the two gypsies? Had he been sloppy? Had he been spotted on the day of the murders? Had Fennel ratted him out? He knew that Eddie Fennel was certainly no grass, but grassin' on coppers was not the same...*

"What the fuck do you want Taff?" Gallier kept his cool and responded in good humour with a touch of the light-hearted banter that was present between the two Sergeants.

"I'm sorry mate, but the gaffer said we are to bring you in..." Jenkins was referring to DI Fowler and the Welshman's strong Swansea accent never failed to irritate Gallier.

"Haven't you got some fuckin' sheep rustlers or something to catch Jenkins?" Gallier continued to try and joke and make light of the situation but the short stocky Sergeant remained stoney faced.

"Come on Reg, don't make it fucking difficult... This is awkward enough as it is mate..." Several large police officers, most of whom Gallier recognised, formed behind Jenkins and Gallier knew that he had no choice but to oblige them. *If he were to protest or try and run, he would only confirm his guilt in whatever crime they were picking him up for... He had to retain his cool and stay oblivious.*

"Am I supposed to have done something wrong lads?" Gallier got out of the Ford Zephyr and did not even remotely move or protest when one of Jenkins' accomplices slapped a pair of handcuffs across his wrists. "Are these really necessary? Is this some kind of fuckin' wind up?" As Jenkins began to lead Gallier towards the Wolseley, the Welshman spoke.

"No wind up Reg… Just get in the car and we will take you to the DI. He will explain more then…" DS Jenkins and his surrounding colleagues were completely oblivious as to why they had been tasked with bringing their colleague in. They were simply following orders, but in Gallier's mind he was certainly not aware of this. He began to wonder if they too were also on Tanner's pay roll. In reality, even the two uniformed officers who were driving the Wolseley were unaware. All they knew was that they were following the orders from senior officers.

"Ok fine… Have it your bloody way… But just let me lock my motor up first! You lot better bring me back here after to pick it up too!" Gallier gestured towards his car with his elbow and Jenkins nodded and then signalled for one of his colleagues to take the Zephyr's keys from Gallier's pockets.

"Don't worry Reg… We'll look after it for you…" Jenkins' voice contained a shred of humanity as his colleague locked the Ford and then handed the keys to the Welshman. "Now lets go and find DI Fowler and get this all cleared up…" Jenkins spoke hopefully as he led Gallier to the Wolseley 6/110 and then helped him into the rear seats by easing Gallier's head beneath the roof of the vehicle. The Black Country Sergeant continued to keep his cool but inwardly he began to panic… *He knew full well what happened to convicted coppers once they got in jail and it frustrated him thoroughly to think that it was him and not Fowler potentially facing such a fate… But then really, after his antics with Collins and Quinn, was he even any better than his commanding officer?*

"It appears that the tables have turned Sergeant Gallier…" A semi sober and gloating Detective Inspector Fowler grinned at Gallier as the DS sat handcuffed to a chair and unable to move. Surprisingly, Gallier had not been taken directly to the Police station in Dudley. Instead, he had been taken to the warehouse in Tipton where he had executed

Collins and Quinn just two days previously. He had been led into the same room where at first he had expected nothing but death, but after being sat in the chair and then the emergence of Fowler, he figured that it would not be quite as straight forward. They were definitely in the exact same room where Quinn and Collins had died and Gallier was not surprised to see that the corpses had been removed. *He had been rumbled... He had failed... How foolish he had been...* "You really have insulted my intelligence Reginald... After that stunt in the cells at Dudley nick, and then when you made me dig out those records on Quinn and Collins, did you really think that I would not suspect you of their disappearance?" Fowler laughed as he toyed with the Sergeant...

"I ay got a fuckin' clue what yowm' on about Sir..." Gallier lied and stared at the floor. Not quite sure of which course of action he should take.

"I mean..." Fowler half laughed. "Fucking hell, I admire it Reg... You've got balls mate... Those thieving gypsy bastards killed your old man... Fair play aer kid..." Fowler wasn't even from the Black Country and it annoyed Gallier that the man from Birmingham was trying to mimic his accent.

"Like ar said Sir... Ar dow have a clue what yow'm on about..."

"Oh you will Reg... Believe me you fucking will... When Tanner's blokes come down here and pull your fucking teeth out one by one...You'll be fucking begging me to make them stop..." Fowler lit himself a cigarette and relaxed into his chair that was placed adjacent to Gallier's. They were in fact the same two chairs upon which Quinn and Gallier had sat when they had died. As Gallier tried to shift in his seat, he suddenly realised that the stinking dampness below him was in fact where one of his victims had lost control of his bladder or bowels upon their death. It was not a nice or comfortable thought, but at that time there were much more pressing issues on his mind. "I admire your attempt Reg... You thought that by staging a gangland execution, or drug overdose on my patch, in Cedric Tanner's premises, you would attract attention from the powers that be and then both Tanner and

144

subsequently myself would be investigated more thoroughly... To be honest Reg, it probably could have worked... But for one thing... After the bodies were discovered, Mr Quinn and Mr Collins, the call came straight through to me so I was able to arrange the collection and disposal of the corpses... It is as if they never existed... Fuck me Reg, it aint as if Gypsies have fucking National Insurance numbers now is it mate!" Fowler laughed mockingly.

"Am yow on fuckin' drugs mate?" Gallier was well aware that he had been caught out, but he was still not ready to give away his guilt.

"You're lucky Sergeant..." A serious expression suddenly came over the Inspector's face. "Tanner is not even aware that these unfortunate killings have taken place... Which means, at present, in the eyes of his organisation, you and your family are safe..." Fowler emphasised the word family.

"What about everyone else? What about the poor kids and their families whose lives are endangered all the time by the filth Tanner pedals on the streets? What about the victims who get attacked by drug hungry beggars in desperate need of their next fix? What about my father?"

"That is to be no longer your concern Reg... If not for yourself, you need to think about the safety of your beloved. Your mother... Your brother and Sister... Their children... That lady-friend you have in Black heath... Plus, the young lady you have been fooling around with closer to home in Tipton!"

"Fuck you!" Gallier gritted his teeth and then stopped himself from spitting at Fowler. *He would not demean himself to the level of those he sought to punish!*

"Wind your neck in Reg... I'm the only friend you've fucking got right now..." Fowler paused to try and attain a dramatic emphasis. "Here's the deal... The two gypsies are gone... All evidence has disappeared, but one word to Tanner and he will destroy everything that you hold dear... After what happened with your old man; can you really take the chance?" Fowler lowered his face to Gallier's and the wicked

Inspector's words cut deeply. DS Gallier did blame himself for his father's death, *who was he to let his macho, tough-guy bravado jeopardise the safety of those that were special to him... He was Reggie Gallier, he did not fear anyone... He would happily piss in Cedric Tanner's face and to hell with the consequences... But he simply could not gamble any further with the lives of his family... He had already taken this approach and he had lost... His father had lost...* "I have arranged for you to be transferred over to Cradley Heath... It's not far and you will be working with your old Army pal Tony Giles..." Fowler spoke again and reluctantly, Gallier began to listen... "All I ask in return is that you end this obsession with Tanner and myself... You have already sorted the men that murdered your father... You have your vengeance Sergeant... Now let it go... Let it go!"

"Those men were acting on the orders of Cedric Tanner... Even you know that Fowler!" Gallier spat his reply.

"Tanner never meant for your father to be killed... He was trying to teach you a lesson for what happened in Victoria Park... The Gypsies went too far... You punished them... Now all is even..." Fowler smiled and then opened his hands in a patronising gesture that infuriated Gallier.

"No! All is not fucking even!" Gallier was still livid, but he knew that he was running out of options and had very little choice in what was to happen next. *Maybe it was time he switched stations and moved onto pastures new? He would be closer to Lucy... He could start a new just a few miles away with the woman he loved... No matter what he did, he would not be able to bring his father back... Tanner had won...* The defeatism was the single most painful emotion he had ever had to deal with... *But even though he would happily sacrifice himself for the cause, he could not gamble further with the lives of others....*

"The offer is fair Reg... You will not be a bent copper... You will not be on Tanner's pay roll or anything like that... You will still have your pride intact... All you need to do is accept the transfer and then keep your nose out of our business... The alternative is that Tanner is gunna come down here with his goons tonight, and whilst you are slowly tortured to death, you can rest assured that your family will all be suffering a similar fate… It's up to you Reg…" Fowler chose not to smile… He had once been an honest and legitimate cop and part of his soul felt immense guilt for his despicable actions… *Gallier was a force for good and for that, the crooked Inspector was envious, but ultimately, he liked the finer things in life more… Plus, he was in far too deep now to ever be able to get out…* "Trust me Reg… This transfer is your only option…" As Fowler looked at the floor, Gallier closed his eyes and stopped himself from spouting further hollow and unrealistic aggression and threats… *He really did have no choice… It was over…*

Chapter 18
December 1973

It had not been until the death of his father that Reggie Gallier ever seriously contemplated the concept of the afterlife. Like many children in the 1930s, he had been made to attend Sunday School, but he had never really paid much attention. All he had wanted to do as a young boy was get back outside and play football and boxing with his mates. His father's death had been so sudden and unexpected that it had seriously affected DS Gallier in the knowledge that he simply would not be seeing his dad again. His last memory of his father and what were in fact their last moments together was a rushed 'good morning' and then out the door for work before spending the night at Lucy's place. At the time it had been so mundane, so usual, so everyday that he had not given it as much as a second thought. But since his father had passed, he could not help but wonder if there really was any truth in an afterlife? *Where was his dad? What was he doing? Was he missing his (Gallier's) mother as much as she was missing him?* However, the more he had contemplated the afterlife, the more it had occurred to him that after his vengeful acts upon Tummy Collins and Bernard Quinnn, *surely he would be going to the fiery place down under!*

As he died, the mocking laughter of Cedric Tanner and DI Fowler filled his last moments upon this earth and then his life did not flash before him. One minute he was sat cuffed to the chair in the warehouse and he was awake, the next there was nothing… No pain… Just total darkness, but he was still conscious… He knew that he was dead and after a few moments of black nothingness before him, he wondered if this was in fact the afterlife? A conscious abyss of blackness that would stretch on agonisingly for all eternity… *Maybe this was hell? No devils poking him up the arse with hot pokers, no burning pits of endless pain… Just nothing… For all eternity… Maybe this was worse?*

After a short time, the darkness began to fade and a dull light began to grow slowly brighter. In front of him he could make out two black shapes that looked like mountains and as further light began to appear and manifest into a perfect, bright sunny day, he could see a spectacular vision before him consisting of a deep blue water with two large, dark green mountains placed almost centrally with the open sea to the left. The sun created a haze and within seconds, clouds appeared and descended upon the picturesque sight, almost covering the mountains at their base as their peaks protruded through the clouds like mounds that were surrounded by masses of soft white ice-cream. It suddenly occurred to Reggie Gallier that he was now dead and was a resident of the afterlife. He instantly thought of his father, *would he be seeing him again? Would he get the opportunity to apologise for the mistakes he had made that led to his father's death?* A strange and curious excitement suddenly came over him and straight away he turned to his right where quite a different scene appeared to manifest before him.

He was now near the Church of St Martin and St Paul in Owen Street, Tipton, but curiously, the mountains, cloud covered coastal view was still very much present to his left. A number of dead souls began to drift towards him and he knew that they were the souls of people he had once known, or whose corpses he had been acquainted with professionally in his police investigations. The face of a young girl he had found raped and strangulated in a dustbin caught his attention and then he noticed a great aunt and several of his grandparents. Initially, he felt happy to see them, but frantically, his eager and excited anticipation began to quickly subside into a blind panic. *Where was his father?* He broke out into an intense and heavy sweat and as he proceeded to search aimlessly through the streams of dead people that he no longer recognised, the sheer worry and panic was like that of a parent who had lost a small child in a public place. Each second he became more grief stricken and frantic, willing for his father to suddenly come into view with his signature smile and slight raising of his eye brows as a greeting... Eventually, a soothing voice sounded from somewhere in a different dimension and he felt a calming, sensitive touch upon his forehead.

"Reg, Reg, Reg!" The soft feminine voice called out again and slowly but surely, DS Reggie Galier began to come to his senses.

"Mornin' bab…" With a hint of embarrassment the policeman opened his eyes and the owner of the feminine voice was now cradling him against her naked breasts. "Sorry about that, ar must have been dreaming…" Gallier sat up in the single bed that he was sharing with his lover and looked around the room as sweat drenched his body and poured from his forehead. It was not particularly warm as it was early December and the morning sky was still dark outside, but as of late, every day had faded pretty much into one. As reality came flooding back to him after his vivid dream, it was very much safe to say that DS Gallier was by no means dead…

After that fateful afternoon when DI Fowler had spoken to him whilst he was handcuffed to a chair in the warehouse in Tipton, Gallier had taken what he believed to be the safest option for his family and accepted the transfer to Cradley Heath… Here he had teamed up with his old friend Tony Giles and he had fallen into a life of utter alcoholic decline as the ghosts of his past proceeded to haunt him prominently. He had avoided the topic of Cedric Tanner like the plague and he had kept to Fowler's deal, though this certainly came at a cost as it slowly but surely ate away at his pride, sense of guilt and overall well-being. It was now early December, 1973 and in the six years that had passed, not all had been bad in Gallier's existence. He had eventually married Lucy from Blackheath and the pair had welcomed a baby daughter, Fiona soon after. However, upon this cold dark morning in Tipton, it was not in the arms of his wife in which Reggie Gallier lay…

"Yes Reg, you were shaking ever so bad and yow was muttering something…" Gemma, the woman he had continued to have an adulterous relationship with over the last six years continued to stroke his brow as he settled back alongside her in the little bed. She was now in her late twenties and even though she still lived at her parents home in

Robert Road, Tipton, she was deemed old enough by her mother to do as she pleased and there was no longer a need for the couple to sneak around. "What were you dreaming about Reg?"

"Oh it dow matter... Ar forgot..." Gallier lied.

"Don't tell fibs Reg... Were you dreaming about her?" As Gemma referenced Gallier's wife, a hint of jealous distaste entered into the tone of her voice. She was more than aware that it was she (herself) that was in the wrong for having such relations with a married man, but she could not help who she had fallen in love with and she desperately longed and dreamed of a time when Reggie Gallier would leave his wife for her.

"No not at all..." Gallier sat up again and fumbled for a cigarette.

"You were dreaming about him again weren't you..." She rested a loving hand upon his shoulder as Gallier lit up a cigarette, passed it to her and then repeated the action for himself.

"Who?" Gallier exhaled cigarette smoke into the cold, morning air and looked out of the bedroom window as the dark silhouette of local factories belched pollution into the Black Country atmosphere.

"That drug dealer... Tanner..." She mentioned the name cautiously and then braced herself as Gallier shuddered with anger at the mention of it... "You have to let it gew Reg... Get over it..."

"It wasn't about him actually... It was about my father..." Gallier sighed and then flicked ash into an ashtray on the bed side table. She tried to pull him close to her again but he protested. "Ar dow want yer pity Gemma... I'm fine... I just need to learn to live with it..."

"A lot of people lose their parents Reg... Look at my dad..." Gemma immediately regretted the callousness of her remark. She had not intended for it to have sounded so harsh... But it was true... Her own father had died of cancer just two years previously and he had been even younger than Gallier's father... "Ar'm sorry Reg..."

"No... Don't apologise Gemma... You are right... I accept that my father is gone, but what I really struggle with, what still haunts me to this day is the fact that he died because of me... He died because of me and every day I feel like I want to smash the fuck out of somebody because of

151

that bastard Cedric Tanner..." Just when she had anticipated him to break into a heartbroken sob, Gallier's manner suddenly changed and he was now gritting his teeth in anger as he uttered the name that was never to be mentioned... He had never told her of what he had done to Tummy Collins and Bernard Quinn... He would never speak of that! But he had filled her in on much of his personal life and dealings with Tanner and Fowler and the pretty young brunette had become something of a confidant... He had always known that really it should have been his wife that he had felt so close too, but she had a cold and often harsh exterior that was obsessed with her own career and their daughter... *With his wife Lucy, he had so much to lose... Their daughter, their marriage and the family home... With Gemma it was just easy...*

"What am I to you Reg?" After a long and considered silence, the randomness of Gemma's question took Gallier by surprise. It was completely out of character and context and for once the pretty young woman felt the need to be selfish and ask a question that was purely for her own benefit. Night after night, the drunk Detective would turn up on her doorstep or at the Doughty Arms and each time she would be expected to take him home, have sex and then listen to his inebriated self-pity as he continued to pour whisky after whisky down his throat. She loved him and in a strange way she knew that he felt the same, but ultimately, it had reached a point where she needed answers. *She was 27 years old. Was she supposed to spend the rest of her life waiting for a man that would probably never leave his wife!*

"What do you mean?" A panic appeared in his eyes as he turned around to face her. He knew full well that he had been 'having his cake and eating it' for far too long. *He wasn't even that good looking anymore! He had put on weight and the booze was more than taking its toll... She really could do a lot better!*

"Come on Reg, you have a wife and a kid at home, but you keep turning up around here... You're always pissed out of your skull and you want to fuck me before crying into my arms...Sometimes I feel like a toy to you, a comfort... Like a bottle of fuckin' Bells... How do you really feel about me?" She searched his eyes for answers and he avoided her gaze and looked down at his cigarette sadly. *He loved her, but he had always known that there would come a time when he would have to let her go...*

"I love you Gemma... I really do... But..." Before he could answer fully, she interrupted.

"But not enough to leave your wife and daughter for me..." Tears appeared in her eyes and his sad silence told her all that she needed to know. "Its fine Reg... I wouldn't want your little girl to grow up without a father because of me... I grew up with my dad and now that he is gone I miss him everyday..." Since her own father had died, Gemma had become more attached to her older lover. In a strange way, the big, strong policeman had almost been something of a father figure to her... *It broke her heart, but now it had to end...*

"I can't lose you Gemma..." Gallier finally looked up into her eyes and he knew full well that he was being incredibly selfish.

"You need to go now Reg... Go back to your life and leave me to get on with mine..."

"But what life do I have now Gemma? A wife who is more interested in her own career than me? I don't even have a job anymore... I'm a nobody..." Several weeks previously, Gallier had been suspended from the police force for brutally beating a fellow officer... His own best friend Tony Giles... He could hardly remember what it had all been about, but the one thing he could remember was that it had all happened because of copious amounts of alcohol.

"Reg..." She put her hand on his shoulder and the pair shared a heartfelt and meaningful exchange. "You need to fight... Ever since ar first met yow, yow have been fighting... Dow stop now... You haven't been officially sacked from the police, its about time that you got yer life back on track and left me to get on with mine..."

Chapter 19

When he pulled up outside of the house in Highfield Road, Blackheath where he now lived with Lucy and their daughter, Reggie Gallier was not even certain of what day it was. Since he had been suspended from work and had been drinking more, it was not unusual for him to become disorientated as each day blended into the next. In fact, whilst he was off work it had often just been a case of sitting around clock watching and waiting for the pubs to open. He hadn't even renewed his season ticket at the Albion and as the ghosts of his past played deeper and deeper upon his mind he could feel himself slowly slipping away… In years, he was only in his late thirties, but if he did not turn things around soon, the future would be looking very bleak.

Just a few months previously he had exchanged his old Ford Zephyr for a black Ford Cortina Mk III and after parking it clumsily outside of the house, he got out and tried to open the front door of his home. It was locked and as he put a little more thought into working out what day it was, he came to the conclusion that it was probably Wednesday. Lucy would be out at work and their young daughter would be with the childminder. Thankfully for Gallier, he often stayed at his mother's in Tipton when he went drinking in his home town and he sold this to his wife as him 'keeping the old woman company' as she was now on her own. Lucy had readily bought this excuse and she was so wrapped up in her daughter and her own career that she had not even remotely suspected that her husband was having an affair. *He was just a drunkard who paid little sexual interest in her… Why would he be interested in or sober enough for anyone else?*

Gallier pulled his own house key from out of his pocket and then opened up the front door before walking inside. As usual, the house was spotlessly tidy and he felt a shame and sadness as he noticed some of his little daughter's toys organised into a neat pile on the other side of the room. *What kind of father was he?* He thought about how he had been blessed with a good father himself. An excellent role model to his children and then he considered his own role in his daughter's life. At the current time, he could not even say that he was a good provider for the family... *He had hit rock bottom...* In an adjacent corner, a wooden drinks globe filled with scotch, brandy, Martini and gin attracted him like a magnet, but as he pulled open the lid and lifted out a bottle of Famous Grouse blended Whisky, he suddenly stopped himself. *He had always enjoyed alcoholic drinks, if he carried on like this, he would reach a point where he would have no choice but to stop drinking or die... He needed routine, regularity, work, challenge... He needed to feel needed again...* Just at that moment, there was a loud and sudden knock at the door... Its timing could not have been any better...

"Who could that be?" Gallier placed the bottle back into the drinks cabinet and pushed down the lid before crossing back over to the front door. The house was a Victorian terraced house and the main living room housed a front door with no porch or hallway and it led directly out onto the street.

"Hello Reggie..." The smug grin belonged to a police colleague whom Gallier had very little time for. Detective Sergeant 'Clubber' Clark got his reputation from being a bully, a brute and a very nasty piece of work. Not that Gallier was not all of those things himself, but at least Gallier had always tried to act in the best interests of the people he was paid to protect. Clubber Clark acted in the best interests of himself!

"Clubber? What yow doing here?" Even though Clark was not one of Gallier's favourite colleagues, the suspended detective could not help but feel a glimmer of excitement and relevance at the presence of another police officer.

"I've got some good news for yer mate..." Clark nodded into the house as if he wanted to come inside and Gallier politely stepped aside to make way.

"Come in Clubber... Can ar get yer a cup of tay?"

"Ar'm celebrating aer kid... Ar'd have thought yow of all people would offer me something stronger than that!" Clark continued to grin

155

and Gallier smiled falsely. His head was pounding from the previous night's booze and he had been feeling particularly proud of himself for having put the whisky bottle back and making a 'stand' just moments previously. *It looked like he would be drinking after all!*

"Sorry Clubber... Scotch ok?" Gallier trudged back over to the drinks globe and pulled out two whisky glasses.

"Bostin' mate..." Clark made himself comfortable on the sofa without being invited to sit down and Gallier gritted his teeth and poured the drinks.

"Here..." Gallier handed his colleague the whisky and then poured one for himself... *It smelt good... Maybe he wouldn't mind indulging after all...* "So what are you celebrating then Clubber? And what the fuck has it got to do with me?"

"The ode mon has gone... DI Spencer has finally hung up his badge for good..." Detective Inspector Spencer had been both Gallier and Clark's senior officer at Old Hill Police station and it had been known for a while that the veteran detective's health was failing and that he would soon be leaving. Ironically, both Gallier and Clark as Detective Sergeants had harboured intentions to replace him. For many years, DS Gallier had never thought of himself as being capable of being an Inspector, but after seeing how truly awful DI Fowler had been over in Dudley, it had almost filled him with a desire to do good by trying to rise up the ranks himself so that just maybe he could one day be in a position to go after Fowler and Tanner... *Of course, he should have known that this was never going to happen... He was not management material... He was just a joke to everyone else... A good hardnosed copper, but too stupid to be management...* Clark on the other hand had no honourable intentions, he just wanted more money, influence and power. It was irrelevant now anyway as Gallier had already destroyed any prospects he may have had of promotion. On a work night out at the pub, he had gotten into a pathetically irrelevant quarrel with his own best friend Tony Giles over something mundane. As usual, Gallier had been very drunk and when Giles made a sarcastic reference to Gallier's supposed friendship with the villain Edward

Fennel, Gallier had responded by head butting his colleague, breaking his nose before proceeding to put the boot in! Giles had not wanted to pursue the matter, but DI Spencer had been present and had seen it all and consequently Gallier had been suspended. It had not been the first time that he had let alcohol get the better of him and the Inspector had not been impressed. Equally as sad, as well as being suspended from work, Gallier had not seen his friend, even though they both lived in the same road and a frosty cloud now existed between the two pals who had once been inseparable.

"How come he's gone so quickly?" It was making sense to Gallier now. *Clark was celebrating because he had been promoted to Detective Inspector.*

"Poor old bugger had a heart attack in the office... He's still alive, but has stood down from active duty immediately and permanently..."

"So you came here to tell me that yow've been promoted?" Gallier gulped his scotch and banged his glass down. He really didn't care and was beginning to grow impatient. *This was just another reminder of his own failure, a further kick in the teeth to kick a man whilst he was down...*

"No Reg... Well yes, I am the DI now, but the reason I came here was to ask you to come back to work tomorrow..."

"What?" A glimmer of anticipation sounded in his voice.

"With you out and me gettin' this promotion, good detectives on the street are thin on the ground aer kid... It was Spencer who had the beef over what happened with you and DC Giles. As far as I'm concerned, you just need to come back in, meck things up with Tony and then yow'm back in work and ar've got another experienced copper back on the team." Clubber Clark sipped at his whisky triumphantly as Gallier could not help but feel patronised. Here was his one-time rival giving it the big 'I am' whilst seamlessly trying to slip into the role of Detective Inspector. Not for the first time in his career, Gallier had been overstepped again, but he tried to make himself focus on the positives. *He would be back in work and he would have a reason to get out of bed in the morning!*

"So this suspension shit all goes away just like that?" It was almost insulting that his reason for misery and worry over the previous few weeks was so expendable and irrelevant to everyone other than himself.

"Yow'm a good copper Reg... We've missed yer mate... Meck yer peace with Detective Constable Giles in the morning and then we can all wipe our mouths and move on..."

The next morning and for the first time in weeks, Gallier shaved and put on a suit and tie before gazing at himself in the mirror. The absence of his stubble meant that his swollen, flabby face was on show and he gazed at his double chin and neck fat before noticing that his eyes were red, puffy and with two large black bags underneath. Not only was he suffering from the effects of alcoholism, but he was also being haunted by the events of the past and frequently he would wake up in the middle of the night after vivid dreams whilst suffering intense panic attacks. He slapped on some Brut Cologne and then attempted a half smile. *He had a long way to go, but at least he was trying to make a start at turning his life around.*

He parked the Cortina on the car park of Old Hill police station and noticed straight away that Tony Giles's copper brown Ford Escort Mk1 was also present. *Clubber Clark was right, before he could get back into his work, he would have to make peace with his old friend.* Gallier glanced at his watch and saw that it still only ten to eight in the morning. He knew Tony Giles as well as anyone did and he knew that at this time of day his old army buddy would be sat in the police canteen enjoying a cup of tea, a cigarette and either a bacon sandwich or a full English. Straight away, Gallier made his way towards the canteen and for the first time in the tens of years he had known Tony Giles, he could not help but feel a hint of nerves. It was awkward and he hoped that one day, their friendship could once again be what it always had been, but on that dark, cold December morning, the prospect of such an outcome remained doubtful.

A small, solitary and pathetic looking Christmas tree stood in the police canteen. A selection of gold tinsel and various cheap baubles hung upon it and there were no lights. The decorations were mismatched and had obviously been cobbled together from a collection of local bobbies who had all donated old and unwanted items from their own Christmas trees at home.

"It's a bit early for all this ay it aer kid?" Gallier noticed Tony Giles sat alone at a table eating a fried breakfast (as he had predicted) and the DC gave nothing away as he raised his eyes from his food to see his friend.

"Folks seem to be putting their Christmas trees up earlier and earlier..." Giles eventually replied but by this time he had now diverted his eyes back down to his breakfast.

"Look mate... You know I ay one for this soppy bull shit so ar'm gunna cut straight to the point..." Gallier pulled up a chair opposite DC Giles. "Ar'm sorry about that shit that happened a few weeks back in the pub... I was out of order and I shouldn't have acted the way I did... Ar've always reacted with my fists and then asked questions later... That's the way I am, but I should never have acted like that with yow... Ar'm sorry..." Gallier's words were awkward but genuine.

"Yow ay been yourself for a while mate..." Tony Giles still did not look up.

"What do you mean?"

"Ar dow know exactly what happened over in Dudley mate, but ar know that since you came here you've been drinking more and more... And I know exactly why..." This time Tony Giles looked his friend directly in the eyes.

"Why?" Gallier was intrigued.

"Cedric Tanner..." Giles's mention of the name cut deeply into Reggie Gallier, but it did not surprise him. "I know how you feel about Tanner because of what happened with your dad..." Gallier had told Tony Giles many details though he had certainly not filled him in on the full picture. "Yow cor hide from it forever Reg... The Reggie Gallier ar

159

know dow run from nothing... He hits trouble full on in the face and he mecks the bad guys pay... Maybe its time you started fighting again?" Giles pushed himself close to his friend and placed a reassuring hand upon his shoulder. "Dow apologise to me... It ay necessary... We've known each other long enough... Apologise to yourself... And to your wife..." Giles's words were sincere and Gallier almost felt choked. Before Gallier could reply, DC Giles spoke again. "There's a fella banged up in cell one... I think you should speak to him... He might be of interest to you..."

"Who is it?" Gallier really was intrigued.

"Cedric Tanner's son..."

Chapter 20

Gallier had the detainee in cell number one brought through into the interview room and as he entered the Detective surveyed him silently. Gallier sat down opposite the man and continued to study his face. At present, the man's eyes were focused intently down upon the table in front of them and Gallier could not make out any details. A dark shadow appeared to cover his eyes and for a very rare moment, Gallier even felt a little apprehensive. He guessed that the detainee was in his early twenties, but his face and demeanour carried a maturity and Gallier almost sensed some kind of kindred spirit to his own. It was as if the weight of the world hung upon the ruggedly handsome, dark-haired man. After a long and calculated absence of sound, DS Gallier eventually spoke.

"Do yow want a cupp'a tay mate?"

"Nope..." The man continued to focus intensely on the table as he shook his head. Gallier lit a cigarette.

"Do yow wanna fake?" The Detective placed his cigarettes on the table and shoved them towards the suspect who began to show signs of amusement.

"You're wasting your time... I will tell you exactly the same as what I told the others... My usual... Fuck all... Nothing..." The man finally raised his eyes from the table and Gallier instantly recognised a haunted intensity that was crazed, frightening, intimidating... The Detective laughed...

"You know... In days gone by I would have bounced you around the room and then sat on you until you told me exactly what I wanted to hear..." Gallier continued to grunt laughter as he exhaled tobacco smoke into the air. "But the truth is ar dow give a shit about what you have done..." The detective placed a charge sheet on the table and then quickly read the details. "It says here that yow'm some kind of street thug? Working for that beat up has-been Dickie Hickman..." Gallier pushed the paper aside with his right hand. "Small-time shit mate... Ar dow give a fuck..." This time the incarcerated man began to laugh.

"So why are you wasting both of our time?"

"I think that you and I could help each other..."

"Fuck off copper... I ay no fuckin' grass... I've heard it all before mate..."

"Just hear me out... This ay what you think..." Gallier picked up the pack of cigarettes and once again offered one to the man before him, Eventually, the so-called criminal pulled one out and accepted a light from the policeman.

"Fine..." The dark-haired man smiled with an arrogance that was beyond his years as he savoured the cigarette smoke.

"So this sheet tells me that yow drive Hickman around in his Jag and provide him with muscle... Basically you knock the shit out of people who owe Dickie Hickman money?"

"A man has gotta eat... Ar'm just a driver and a bodyguard..."

"My question is this Mr Cole..." For the first time Gallier referred to the villain by his surname. "Why are you working for a washed-up has-been like Dickie Hickman when your father is the biggest and most successful drug-dealing gangster this side of fucking London?"

"Do you think you fucking know me?" Cole responded with a fierce and angry intensity and Gallier instantly detected a deep, vicious and festering hatred that was far deeper than even his own.

"No... I do not know you Mr Cole... Or can I call you Michael or Mick? Which would you prefer?"

"You can call me fucking Cinderella for all I give a fuck..." Cole sat back in his chair. His words were aggressive but his actions and manner were ice-cool. Gallier chuckled in amusement.

"You have not answered my question Mr Cole... Why are you making moves in the gutter when your old man is mega rich?" Gallier waited for an answer but there was a long pause.

"Do you know my father?" Cole suddenly leant forwards and his eyes had the same look of violence that Gallier had seen in those of Eddie Fennel, but they were somewhat different to those of Cedric Tanner.

"Cedric Tanner?" Gallier responded deliberately and the mention of the name caused a visible stir in Cole's gaze.

"That bastard is not my father... That piece of shit married my mother when I was a baby... He is not my father..."

"I know..." Gallier had heard the rumours and had even had it confirmed by Tanner himself in Victoria Park... *Maybe Cole was his way of nailing Tanner?* "I know what Tanner did to you as a child Michael..."

"You know? You fucking know?" Cole's eyes grew wide and wild and Gallier was quite confident that he was looking at some kind of monster. "Were you fucked in the arse when you were four fucking years old? Were you so scared to go to sleep each night that you would piss and shit yourself in the unsuccessful hope that it would repulse your abuser enough not to hurt you?"

"No... I can't say I have..." Gallier took a deep breath and then refocused his gaze upon Michael Cole. "You have my sympathy..." The villain laughed.

"Thank you!" Cole proceeded to laugh hysterically. "Your sympathy makes all the difference... It makes up for a childhood lost..." The sarcasm was stinging and Gallier felt genuinely lost for words. Another pause followed as both men smoked their cigarettes in silence.

"So we are agreed..." Reggie Gallier finally spoke. "Your step father had my Dad killed... He also threatened to rape my young nephew..." Gallier shrugged. "I hate him too... We may both come from different sides of the law, but we have a common ground... We can both agree that Cedric Tanner is a total fuckhead, bastard..." Gallier's use of such extreme language caused a grunt of surprised laughter from Michael Cole.

"That he is..."

"So help me Michael... Help me take him down, help me put him away so that he cannot harm anyone else as he has harmed you..."

Gallier was almost pleading. "If you give me a statement, I can arrest him for the historic sex offences..."

"I am not a grass... Not now... Not ever..." Cole sat back in his chair and smugly continued to enjoy his cigarette. Gallier was very confused. *What was it with these villains and their ridiculous codes of honour? Why was Michael Cole protecting his stepfather who had abused him so badly?*

"So you are happy for Tanner to get away with it?" Gallier's frustration was very evident upon his face as Cole continued to display a wild amusement.

"Let me tell you a few things about my stepfather... But just for our ears... There will be no statements... No courts... No witness boxes..."

December 1954

A small boy sat on the stairs and stared obsessively at a tall, well-lit Christmas tree that adorned the large hallway of his Wolverhampton home. It was Christmas Eve and the grand 1920s detached house in which he lived with his mother and stepfather was filled with guests. Occasionally, a well-meaning relative or family friend would attempt to engage him in conversation or comment upon his activity. But he remained focused, mesmerised and oblivious to the outside world. To those around him, he appeared unusual, odd, weird, strange rather than rude. "The things this family have done for that boy! With him being illegitimate an all!" One guest had commented. "He doesn't know he's born, living in a posh house like this!" Another guest had not so subtly observed. But still the boy remained fascinated with the elaborate tree that stood before him. Every so often, he would freeze with utter terror and frantically check the space around him, his face turning back and forth with a twisted look of shear horror and then he would return to the comforting presence of the tree that he had helped his mother to decorate. *That had been a happy day, he had enjoyed his mother all to himself all day and he had actually spoken to her, smiled and been happy...* BUT THEN, he shuddered, *he could not think about it, if he thought about it then he would 'get accidents' and Mommy would be cross at him for the mess in his pants.* He looked over and saw his mother, she wore a sparkly dress and her golden hair hung long across her snow-white face. *She must be a Princess!* He thought to himself.

She caught her four-year-old son's gaze and smiled warmly at him. She did worry about him. He would rarely speak and if he ever did it would only ever be to her or her father. He would regularly soil himself and every time she watched him closely, she could sense that he always appeared to be in fear of something. It tore at her maternal instincts and the fact that she was unable to do anything to help her offspring ripped her heart into a million pieces. He was constantly checking the space around him, shivering, icy cold, as if he was haunted, possessed by some evil spirit that tormented him endlessly. She had tried to speak to her husband about it, but it was always brushed off. Not that her son was really any of her husband's concern. He was not the boy's father and she was thoroughly grateful to the man for taking her in and marrying her with an *illegitimate, bastard child.* She did not love her husband. There was something about him she did not like or trust, but his family were wealthy and she kept telling herself that she should be grateful. She forced a smile as she looked around at the *vile, loathsome* guests who constantly judged her and her child. Her own family were not permitted to be there and she would have to wait until Boxing Day to see them. But her husband's family where there, even though he had not arrived home yet. He had been called to business and she knew that this probably meant that he had gone with a gang of thugs to inflict a vicious beating on somebody. *Why did she always attract men like that? Men who were so insecure and obsessed with themselves that they had to hurt others, Men who were obsessed with dominance and violence.* She allowed her mind to wonder into past memories for a brief moment, but she stopped herself. *Men could wallow in their self-pity, their attention seeking drama and constant search for reassurance, but never women, they had to keep house and look after the children!*

The boy remained on the stairs when suddenly he heard a muffled bang outside of the house. He instantly froze with terror. *He knew that noise anywhere, he listened out for that noise daily, a sign that the nightmare had begun, the slamming of a car door, the ghost!* He bit into his lower lip with such intensity that he drew blood and he felt a sinking feeling as his entire little world was descending into darkness. He could not see the Christmas tree anymore, he could not see his mother anymore, all he could see was fear.

The front door opened and in walked his stepfather. He was short and overweight and was of around thirty years of age. He had an extremely round face with small black eyes that were both piercing and somewhat disturbing in appearance. The child clambered frantically upstairs at the sight of the man and straight into his bedroom. He shut the door and pulled a large teddy bear in front of it before darting under his bed where he would remain, hands covering his 4-year-old ears and his eyes tight shut. *He must hide, he must be quiet, he must not move, or the ghost would find him...*

The little boy eventually fell asleep, drenched in his own urine and filth. He awoke a few hours later and upon realisation of his own wetness and soiled clothing he immediately worried that his mother would be upset. *If only he could get to the bathroom and clean himself.* Slowly, shivering and still terrified he crawled out from under the bed and approached the door. In the cold icy darkness he watched his breath as it arose from his mouth and ascended into the shadowy blackness of the lonely room. He put his hand upon the door handle and summoned up the courage to slowly turn the handle and allow the light from the dimly lit landing to cascade into his bedroom as he opened the door. It was still and quiet and not a soul moved, he looked left and right several times until he was quite satisfied that he was alone and then he ran as fast as his tiny legs could take him over to the bathroom. Once inside he locked the door and he was safe! His mother had told him that he was never to lock the door in case he was to get locked inside, but deep down he wished that he could get locked inside, away from the horrors and truly disgusting physical pain that he endured outside. *It was rude, it was naughty, it hurt.*

The bathroom was cold and damp and smelt of soap, but at least he was safe. He sat himself upon the toilet and looked down at his soiled trousers with shame, but then he heard a sound. The door handle began to move and the small boy felt a pang of terror and then with absolute horror he watched as the latch began to open as whatever was on the outside manoeuvred the door back and forth to loosen it. By now, the little boy could not breathe with panic and dread, the door opened slowly and there in the eerie, silent darkness of the doorway, stood the ghost…

******

The small boy played on a little trike he had been gifted by his grandfather. It was boxing day 1954 and the child had endured a particularly awful Christmas day. His stepfather had gotten particularly drunk, though this did not stop him entering the young boy's bedroom once his mother had fallen asleep and doing what he always did… The next day would begin as a happier occasion. The boy knew that he would be visiting his maternal grandparents who he was rarely allowed to see. He loved his grandad Norman and as his mother drove to their house in Sedgley near Dudley, the young child had actually smiled…

"Wow Michael, that's a fast bike isn't it?" Norman Cole smiled with joy at the rare sight of his grandson playing happily.

"Yes grandad, its super-duper fast!" The boy zoomed past and then suddenly stopped dead in the middle of the yard. "Grandad?"

"Yes Michael?" Norman Cole strolled over to his grandson and dropped to his knee to address the child on the same level.

"Is this bike fast enough to get away from the ghost?"

"There are no ghosts Michael!" Norman Cole laughed at his grandson's comment. "Who told you about ghosts?"

"There is a ghost at my house." Michael's face suddenly changed and his happy smile was replaced with a look of pure terror.

"What's wrong Michael?" The child's sudden change in mood alarmed Norman Cole greatly and he placed a comforting hand on the boy's back.

"The ghost hurts me Grandad." Tears appeared in Michael's eyes and he began to shiver with fear. "He makes me do rude things." As the little boy continued to recount more of his ordeals in greater detail, Norman Cole quivered with anger and tried hard to hold back vomit as tears of distraught sadness began to flow down his cheeks. He eventually composed himself enough to speak for the sake of the boy.

"Michael, you must show me who the ghost is, and then we can make him stop." The little boy nodded with confusion, he had never seen his grandfather cry before and he began to worry that he had done something wrong, but then a small glimmer of hope arose within his young mind. *Would grandad Norman save him from the ghost? Would it all stop?*

******

Norman Cole instantly turned to face his overweight son in law and noticed as he turned that his grandson Michael was now nodding frantically and with fear at the arrival of the ghost. "You sick twisted scum!" Norman Cole narrowed his eyes and set his sights upon the boy's stepfather. "You've been interfering with my grandson and when I tell my daughter you will be finished!"

"Oh dear..." The stepfather spoke in a patronising tone and looked over at Michael with a look of lascivious annoyance. "You naughty boy. I thought it was our little secret. I will have to deal with you later."

The exchange between the stepfather and the young boy enraged Norman Cole yet further and he could not contain his rage any longer as he rushed towards his grandson's abuser. Unfortunately for Michael, Norman Cole was not a man of violence and his stepfather quickly stepped aside and caught the older man off balance with a hard right-hand punch. Norman Cole instantly fell to the floor and cracked a rib and as he tried to get back up, the younger man continued to rain down kick after agonizing kick as young Michael watched on, his hopes of salvation fading fast. Eventually, when the stepfather was quite satisfied that Norman Cole would not be able to get back up, he removed his black silk tie and secured it tightly around Cole's grandfather's neck. "Michael." He demanded the name with a sick and perverted pleasure. "Watch what happens to your grandfather!" The stepfather then proceeded to garrotte the life out of Norman Cole as the young boy watched on, barely understanding the events, but somehow he now knew that his hopes of salvation were being crushed before him. He did not quite understand the finality of his grandfather's predicament, but the images and sounds would remain with him forever as he slowly watched his beloved grandad Norman die.

As he passed, Norman Cole kept his eyes upon his grandson until the last. In that moment, he thought not of his life, not of his only daughter and not of his wife, but of his utter horror at not saving his grandson Michael who's soul was now lost to the evil that had taken his own life from him.

Once he was quite sure that Cole was dead, the stepfather turned to face Michael, his black eyes bulging with a mixture of depraved sexual lust and sheer anger. He slowly and ceremoniously undid his leather belt and his expensive silk trousers loosened around his rounded waist. He removed the belt and whipped it hard off the floor to scare the child and signal his intent. Michael looked helplessly at the floor as the man moved closer to the terrified boy. "You should not have opened your mouth young man!" He grabbed the child by the hair and used his belt to whip him hard across the buttocks with the buckle. Michael yelped at the pain, but he knew that it was nothing compared to what was about to come.

******

December 1973

After listening to a stone-faced Michael Cole recount some of the horrors that he had endured as an infant, Gallier was lost for words. Cole had suffered a truly horrendous and harrowing ordeal as a child and still the detective could not understand for the life of him why the young man would not make an official statement or testify... Eventually, the detective spoke.

"Surely, to get justice for yourself and your grandfather Norman Cole, you could give us a statement? You witnessed Tanner kill a man, you experienced unspeakable horrors yourself! For fucks sake Mick, let me take this bastard down!" As Gallier ranted, his almost 24 hours of being alcohol deprived caused withdrawal symptoms to proceed as he began to sweat frantically and his cool composure was all but gone. He was desperate for a drink, he was sweating and he was frantic... Cole appeared cooler and more composed than ever.

"I trust no-one... Especially not the police..." Micky Cole grinned menacingly... "Vengeance is a dish best served cold..."

Gallier tried to compose himself. He watched the orange glow of his cigarette as it slowly burnt away. It cast a plume of nicotine against the ceiling of the interview room that was already yellow from years of such exposure. *Frustratingly, he was getting nowhere... Cole was not going to talk. Not even those who hated Cedric Tanner even more than he did would 'rat' on the man.*

"Please tell me Mick... If you are refusing to make an official statement, why are you telling me these things?" Gallier was confused and Cole shrugged.

"I dow know really... Maybe I just want other people to know just how sick and twisted that bastard is..." The truth was Cole had an almost resentment for any man professing to hate Cedric Tanner as much as he did... *Nobody had the right to hate Cedric Tanner as much as he did!* The villain closed his eyes and thought a little deeper. "For years I kept a lot bottled up... Kept my mouth shut as I had been taught... All that did was allow people to believe that Tanner was some kind of fucking Robin

Hood… The gangster boss with the flash suit who buys everyone a drink at the bar…" Cole grunted and his eyes narrowed. "All that ever did was turn me into some kind of fucking victim…" Cole's eyes became even deadlier. "I am not a victim…"

"But right now yow'm banged up in this place…" Gallier's tone was patronising and he almost felt harsh, *but he was a police officer…* He cast his eyes back over the charge sheet and shrugged. "Demanding money with menaces… Assault… Possession of illegal substances…"

"That was for personal use…" Cole protested and Gallier could tell that he was a total addict, but a high functioning one that was psychologically damaged and scarred by his harrowing past. *Who was he to judge? (Gallier) He was as much an addict as anyone… The only difference was that his own particular vice was alcohol and it was legal…*

"Maybe so… But like I said, yow ay gewin' nowhere anytime soon… You could be looking at a custodial sentence here Mick… Highly likely with your record…" Gallier guessed correctly in assuming that Micky Cole had a checkered past that was filled with countless violent offences. The villain stroked back his mid-length black hair and sensed some kind of 'deal' offer. "I get that yow ay gunna rat on Tanner… I dow understand it, but I know that your mind is set… But surely you can give me something? A name or something?"

"If you have been keeping tabs on Tanner for a while, you very likely already know everything that I can tell you…" Cole was not lying. He was certainly not privy to the inner dealings of his much-despised stepfather.

"The truth is no… I do not… For the last six years I have left Tanner well alone…"

"So why the sudden change?" Cole was intrigued.

"Lets just say that I woke up… The monster inside of me woke up…" Gallier smiled and Cole nodded.

"The monster inside of me has always been awake…"

"I do not doubt it…" Gallier spoke the truth. "So what can you give me Mick?"

"You can drop all the charges against me? I'm free to go?" Cole was sceptical.

"I'll do what I can Mick…"

"Bull shit…" Cole laughed and Gallier looked on, deep in thought.

"Who was the arresting officer? Who nicked you?" Gallier noticed that there was no name at the bottom of the charge sheet.

"Some DC…" Cole tried to remember the name… "Giles… Detective Constable Giles…" As Cole mouthed the name Gallier smiled inwardly. *Tony Giles was his best mate, surely they could come to some arrangement… But then maybe his best friend had his back all along and had planted Cole there for him so that he could resume his quest against Cedric Tanner? What else could save him from himself?*

"Ok… What can you give me Mick… If it's worth my while I'm sure that I can have a word with DC Giles…"

"So ar've gorra teck your word on that?"

"Unless you wanna do porridge, ar dow see that you have much choice aer kid…" Gallier folded his arms seriously and Cole looked down at the floor for over five minutes…

"Price…" Cole finally spoke. "Davey Price…"

"Who is that?"

"A name… You wanted a name and now you have one…Now do the digging yourself…"

"Yow gorra give me more than that mate!" Gallier extinguished his cigarette into a small ash tray in the centre of the table.

"Davey Price… He's a young villain… Works for Tanner… He likes to think that he's Tanner's second in command… Tanner trusts him but he's a stupid bastard…" Cole had given away as much as he was prepared to give… "Now let me fucking out!"

Chapter 21

The Summerhouse pub stood in Gospel End, Sedgley and sat back from the road that led from Sedgley towards Baggeridge Woods and further on to the nearby village of Wombourne. One of the pub's most notorious and unsavoury regulars was a young villain by the name of Davey Price. Price was in his mid to late twenties and was proud to consider himself as 'number two' to the highly powerful Cedric Tanner. In criminal circles, Price's connection to Tanner made him highly feared, respected and powerful and he loved to flaunt his status through his appearance. He was a thickset man with blonde hair, blue eyes and a head that was almost pig-like. He dressed in the sharpest black suits and modelled himself on the celebrity villains of the 1960s such as the Kray twins from London. He surrounded himself with hardmen who liked to dress in much the same way and the gangsters could often be found playing cards in a far corner of the Summerhouse bar in an area that was reserved almost exclusively for them.

After his brief tip-off from Tanner's stepson Michael Cole earlier that day, DS Gallier had done some further digging himself and he had managed to find out through his would-be ally, Eddie Fennel, that Price was, as Cole had explained, an associate of Cedric Tanner. He had also found out that Price and his cronies regularly used the Summerhouse pub in Sedgley. Of course, it was a few miles outside of Gallier's 'patch' in Cradley Heath, but he had told the newly appointed Inspector 'Clubber' Clark that he was going to chase up information on some suspected armed robbers before setting off towards the Summerhouse.

In the 1970s, alcohol licensing hours in England meant that pubs could only open from 11:00 until 15:00 during the day and then between 18:00 and 23:00 on the evening. On Sunday's, the drinking hours were even further restricted. When Gallier pulled up outside the Summerhouse, he checked his watch and saw that it was 12:20pm. *There was a good chance that Price would be in the pub.* He locked the much-despised CID Morris Marina and then strolled across the car park towards the pub. It was bitterly cold and he rubbed his hands together for warmth as he got closer to the entrance.

"What can I get you Sir?" As Gallier pulled open the double doors and approached the bar, a middle-aged barman greeted him cheerfully. 'Paint it Black' by the Rolling Stones had been a hit record for the British band seven years earlier in 1966 and the song played on the pub's jukebox as Gallier looked across the beer pulls and resisted the urge to buy a drink.

"Ar'm lookin' for a chap called Davey Price…" Gallier surveyed the room and instantly identified a group of three smartly dressed men who were loud and raucous as they played cards in a corner of the room. "Is he in?"

"Er…" The barman stuttered nervously. "Who is asking?"

"Detective Sergeant Gallier… CID…" The policeman held up his warrant card for the anxious bartender to see.

"Is he expecting you? I'm not sure if I have seen him today Sergeant…" The barman squinted to read the name on the warrant card and then lied badly.

"So who are those fellas over there?" Gallier nodded towards the men who were playing cards and then began to approach them, turning his back on the bartender as he tried to protest. " Which one of you lovely lads is Davey Price then?" Gallier spoke sarcastically as he neared the men's table. He could tell straight away that the man to the left was Price. He fitted the description he had been given by Fennel and he appeared to carry an aura of authority.

"Who wants ter know?" Price did not look up from his hand of cards and his voice was low and aggressive.

"Detective Sergeant Gallier…" The Policeman took out his warrant card again but still not one of the three men at the table looked up.

"Do you smell bacon boys?" Price began to laugh and then sniff the air mockingly... "Piggy, pig, pig, oink, oink!" His two accomplices began to laugh hysterically and Gallier smiled.

"So all three of you 'nice boys' work for Cedric Tanner... How does it feel to be down on your fucking knees all day for the big man? Rent boys? Or do you lads work for free? The love of the job?" Gallier placed his warrant card back into his pocket and waited for a reaction.

"Fuck off copper!" One of Price's associates suddenly stood up in a threatening defiance and Gallier noted that he was a huge bear like man. At least six foot five inches tall and at least twenty stone in weight.

"Leave it Jack..." Price suddenly lowered his cards and glared at his colleague. "Sit daahn mate... He's just a very stupid cozzer lookin' for a reaction... Fishin' for handouts..." The villain turned back to face Gallier. "Is that it copper? Yow'm lookin' for a brown envelope?"

"No mate..." Gallier lowered his face so that it was level with Price's "Yow can teck yower envelope and wipe yer fuckin' arse with it!"

"Yeah?" Price smiled. He was far from intimidated. "So what do you want?"

"Do you know that your gaffer interferes with little boys?" The subject matter sickened Gallier and he kept his voice low, but his words did not appear to have any effect on the villain. "Now I'm sure that you and your mates here am all hard bastards and all that bull shit; but do you really wanna work for a bloke that messes with kids?" Gallier's tone suddenly became serious. *Maybe Price did not know the full extent of his employer's sickening antics? Divide and conquer...*

"Ar dow know what yow'm talkin' about..." Price turned away and in that instant Gallier could tell that the villain was very aware of his boss's unsavoury vices, yet he chose to remain oblivious.

"I see... Maybe Tanner ay the only one... Do you like little boys too do yer?" Gallier suddenly became intimidating again and he spoke directly into Price's ear. The gangster froze with anger but managed to hold onto his notoriously short fuse... *The copper was deliberately trying to intimidate him into saying or doing something incriminating and he would not fall for it!*

"I think it's time you left Pig..." Price snarled as he struggled to hold onto his cool.

"Just think about what I said Davey... Do you wanna go down as a sick kiddie-fiddler? A Nonce? Because when Tanner gets busted, and believe you me he will, yow will be tarred with the same dirty, disgusting brush... I will be in touch..." Gallier patted the criminal on the shoulder patronisingly and then stood up. "Right... Enjoy the game boys... Ar'll be around..." As the Detective Sergeant walked away, Price almost broke a tooth as he gritted and ground his teeth in anger.

"Jack?" He slammed his cards onto the table and addressed his huge associate.

"Yes Mr Price?" The bear like man responded obediently.

"Follow that piece of shit outside, teck him round the back so there are no witnesses and then kick the fuckin' shit out of him!" Price's violent command gave him a sense of fulfilment and the big man opposite rose from the table again.

"With pleasure boss..."

The burly criminal, Jack Hudson, emerged out onto the pub car park and looked around for Gallier. *Where did that fuckin' pig go?* He spotted a dark brown Morris Marina near to the side of the road, *and that was usually the kind of car that was used by CID, but where was the driver?*

"Lookin' for summet big man?" As Hudson was looking over at the Marina, a voice sounded from the side of him and he turned to see the smug policeman again.

"Mr Price has asked me to have a word with you..." Hudson grinned as he approached the detective.

"Is that right..." Gallier was unsure of what to expect... "Maybe is you that wants to have a private chat? Get something off your chest?" Gallier took a step closer to Hudson. "I'm sure that not all of Tanner's organisation like little boys? Maybe you could make amends? Do the right thing?" It was a long shot, but Gallier had to be optimistic.

"It needs to be private... Where we woe be seen talking..." Hudson gestured towards the rear of the pub and Gallier began to feel a little hopeful. *Maybe he would finally get one of these bastards to talk!* The detective followed the huge villain around to the rear of the large building, but he prepared himself for any eventuality. Finally, the massive man stopped and turned to face the policeman and grinned again.

"Davey Price says that I am to knock the shit out of yow!" Hudson pulled out a set of brass knuckles and took a clumsy swing at DS Gallier, but the Detective saw it coming and stepped back and countered with a right hook that connected cleanly on Hudson's jaw. The big man winced at the blow and was almost caught off-balance as he quickly tried to correct himself so that he could lunge at his opponent again.

"Yow gorra do better than that aer kid..." Gallier side stepped to the left and then followed up his initial counter with two swift left jabs to the face and then a hard straight right. They were all good punches but despite being dazed and a little shocked, the bear-like Jack Hudson still did not go down. Whilst the villain tried to compose himself again and launch another strike, Gallier noticed a metal dustbin to the side of them. *He could stand there and throw more punches at the cumbersome fat man, but why should he break his knuckles open trying to knock him down when there was an alternative?* Gallier grabbed the dustbin lid and then cracked it hard against Hudson's fleshy, flat nosed face. Blood exploded from the man instantly and Gallier thought that he noticed one of the gangster's teeth fall onto the floor. Finally, the brute went to ground and Gallier finished off by kicking him hard in the groin. Semi-conscious and lying on the ground, Hudson began to whimper as the Detective proceeded to kick down the open dustbin and empty the filthy, rotting contents onto the overweight, supposed tough guy's head. "Now I really do want you to have a think about this..." Gallier got down onto his knees and grabbed Hudson by the hair so that he could raise his head slightly. "Yow dow have to end up like Tanner… That sick bastard is gunna get what is coming to him… Maybe it is time you did the right thing?" Gallier raised Hudson's head further as blood continued to flow from the wounds to his face. "What would your mother think of you working for Tanner?"

"Mar mother's dead… Fuck yow copper…" Hudson finally spoke as he spat blood into the ground and Gallier looked away in disappointment as he tossed the villain's face back into the filth covered ground.

"Fine… Have it yower way… Meck sure you tell that prick Price that ar'm like a dog with a fuckin' bone… Ar will not let gew until yow'm all banged up in nick!" Gallier shook his head and went for his cigarettes. *Was there not a single living soul who had the balls to speak out against Cedric Tanner?*

Gallier gazed into his lukewarm and half empty mug of tea as he tried his best to 'blot out' the festivities of the season that existed around him. His father had died at Christmas and he now found the whole celebratory atmosphere sickening and repulsive. There were still a considerable number of days to go until the 25th and yet again he found himself considering and feeling critical of how Christmas appeared to arrive earlier every year. 'Merry Christmas Everyone' by Slade had been a huge hit for the Black Country band that very year and Reggie Gallier was quite sure that he never wanted to hear it ever again. To say that radio stations had overplayed it was quite an understatement.

"Sergeant Gallier…" The unwanted presence of DI 'Clubber' Clark suddenly appeared at Gallier's canteen table in Old Hill Police station and the Sergeant noted the formal tone of his new senior officer's voice. *It hadn't taken long for the newly appointed DI to change from referring to him (Gallier) as Sergeant instead of the more endearing and friendly term of Reggie.* Gallier looked up from his tea.

"Clubber… What can I do for yer mate?" Gallier knew that by referring to the new DI by the nickname of 'Clubber' instead of the obligatory 'Sir' would cause annoyance. Clark ignored it, sat down and lit himself a cigarette.

"It's about what happened yesterday..." Clark searched Gallier's eyes for signs of guilt but the DS gave nothing away.

"Yesterday?" Gallier played dumb, but he knew what this was about...

"You told me that you were going over to Sedgley to chase up a lead you had on an armed robbery gang..." Clark left a pause and then continued to study Gallier's face. "But I have it on good authority that this was not the case..."

"Is that right..." Gallier narrowed his eyes and stared directly into 'Clubber' Clark's gaze. *Unsurprisingly, he had found another, dirty, bent, crooked bastard who belonged to Tanner and any other drug dealing gangster wannabe that was willing to make a bid...*

"You were warned Reg... You were warned by DI Fowler over in Dudley to leave Tanner's operations alone!" Clark tried to sound assertive but Gallier moved his chair closer to the table and intensified his gaze.

"Do you smell that Clubber?" The DS suddenly interrupted the new Inspector and made a mocking, sniffing sound with his nose.

"What?" Clark was confused.

"Corruption... Dirty, filthy, bent corruption... It dow half fuckin' stink..." Gallier continued to hold the DI in his gaze and Clark shifted awkwardly in the canteen chair.

"I'm transferring you Reg... You leave me with no choice..." Clark was eager to get the conversation finished.

"Where to?" Gallier shook his head... *The depth of Tanner's corruption and influence was even more profound than he had suspected.* "Kidderminster? Plymouth? Inverness? Timbuk-fucking-tu?"

"West Bromwich... I've arranged a meeting there for you tomorrow with DCI Ted Cooper..." Clubber Clark got up suddenly. He had nothing more to say, he was ashamed and embarrassed and the tension between the two officers was untenable...

Chapter 22

Detective Chief Inspector Cooper was a serious man. He was only just above the Police minimum height requirement of five foot eight inches and he had greying dark brown hair and horn rim spectacles that gave him an educated and authoritative aura. He was the total opposite of Reggie Gallier. More of a thinker than a fighter. He could be assertive when he needed to be, but shouting and balling was not DCI Cooper's style at all. His voice was soft and gentle, not particularly friendly and it was definitely straight to the point, but Cooper was a softly spoken man and Gallier could tell straight away that he was transparent and honest. *A refreshing change from the likes of 'Clubber' Clark and DI Fowler!*

"It doesn't make impressive reading does it?" Cooper threw down a lengthy paper document onto his desk as he sat facing DS Gallier in his (Cooper's) large office.

"Sir?" Gallier was unaware of the document's purpose and its contents.

"This is your file Gallier... It was given to me by Detective Inspector Clark at Old Hill... Disobeying orders? Alcoholism? Poor time keeping? Womanising? Violent conduct?" Cooper shook his head in disgust. "Beating up a Police colleague!"

"Sir..." Gallier tried to protest but Cooper cut him dead.

"And worst of all, allegations of corruption!" A severe look of distaste appeared upon Cooper's face and Gallier felt relieved. *The DCI was clearly as sickened by police corruption as he was!* "So what do you have to say for yourself Gallier?"

"Well..." Gallier sighed and adjusted his tie. "I'm sorry to say that some of those things are in fact true... Yes I drink too much, but then most of the fellas in this job are exactly the same! Sometimes I am a bit heavy handed with the villains because, as I am sure you are aware Sir, sometimes that is the only language they understand!"

"And what about the rest of it?" Cooper wanted to like Gallier. He was an intellectual himself, but he also needed tough guys like Gallier around him just as much as he needed the planners and the thinkers.

"The incident with a colleague, he was, still is, my closest friend… We had a falling out whilst off duty and it led to a fight… The issue has been resolved Sir…" Gallier took a sip from a glass of water that stood on the desk in front of him.

"So why have you been sent to me?" Cooper frowned with suspicion.

"Because 'Clubber' Clark is bent Sir…" Gallier placed his glass back onto the table. "If you look back through my file you will see that I was also transferred from Dudley back in the '60s…" As Gallier spoke, Cooper thumbed back through the file to find the relevant information. "I was transferred then for exactly the same reason that I have been transferred now… My senior officers were corrupt and I refused to go along with them… I was a thorn in their sides so to speak…" Gallier spoke with such blatant honesty and sincerity that Cooper found it very hard not to believe him.

"Why should I believe you?" Cooper's tone was patronising, but Gallier knew that he had finally found an ally.

"Have you heard of a villain by the name of Cedric Tanner sir?" Gallier studied the DCI's face as he spoke.

"Yes… Of course Gallier… Exactly the sort of individual we should be striving to bring down!"

"I couldn't agree more so myself Sir… Did you know that Tanner has sold more drugs on the streets of Birmingham, the Black Country and neighbouring towns like Coventry and Wolverhampton than all of the other major dealers combined?"

"I did not know that no…" Cooper was starting to feel impressed.

"Tanner controls all of the major drug distribution from here to London in the south and Manchester in the north… So why do you not know more about him? Why or how has he been able to build such a powerful crime empire?"

"I hope that you are not suggesting that I am corrupt Sergeant!" Cooper's eyes suddenly widened as he misinterpreted Gallier's comment.

"No Sir... What I am saying is that Tanner has become so successful and powerful because he is protected by coppers like 'Clubber' Clark and DI Fowler..."

"And you know this for a fact do you Gallier?"

"Yes Sir..." There was absolutely no doubt or hesitancy in Gallier's voice.

"So where is your evidence?"

"I don't have any..." Gallier shrugged and then sat back in his chair. "But I know that given time I could bring Tanner down, and then in turn he would give up all of the dirty coppers in exchange for a reduced sentence..." As Gallier finished talking, DCI Cooper omitted a short grunt of laughter.

"You have it all worked out don't you Sergeant Gallier..."

"Yes Sir... Give me the time and the resources and I will bring them all down..."

"My principle concern is crime here in West Bromwich... Cedric Tanner is from Wolverhampton I believe?"

"Yes Sir... But I am sure that Tanner's dealers sell gear all over the place, certainly here in West Brom too..." Gallier noticed a blue and white football scarf hanging on Cooper's hat stand. "Are you a Baggies man Sir?"

"Yes... But what on earth does that have to do with any of this Gallier?"

"I'm a supporter myself Sir... I never missed a home game for years Sir... Well apart from when I was working Sir..." Gallier hated 'sucking up' to his senior officers, but he saw a glimmer of hope. "I'm asking you to give me a chance Sir, from one Baggie to another..." Gallier smiled warmly.

"Ok…" Cooper glanced at a calendar on the large, oak desk. "We are halfway through December now… You can have until the end of the year to work on nailing Tanner… But if you are no closer to an arrest by the new year, you will have to refocus your priorities on more local matters…" Cooper could see the relief and joy in Gallier's eyes and he remained confident that he was not being lied to.

"I'm gunna need a team Sir…" Gallier leant forwards eagerly and Cooper could see that the DS was anxious to begin work. "I was thinking, maybe a couple of DC's at least?" Gallier looked around the office at the various photographs and the sparse furniture. "I'm gunna need them for surveillance if I'm gunna build evidence against Tanner…" Cooper nodded and then looked deep in thought for over thirty seconds before smiling and standing up.

"Come with me Sergeant Gallier… I know just the person who will be able to help you…"

DCI Cooper led Gallier down a narrow corridor and into a dark, boxy room that was filled with various dusty files that were all stacked tightly on an array of shelves and racking. In a corner of the room was a small kitchen unit and on top of it stood a metal kettle and a selection of tea making utensils.

"Aidan?" Cooper peered into the deepest corner of the long, cavernous room and a figure slowly emerged into the light. He was a slim, suspicious looking man of average height with fiery blue eyes and a mop of curly, light brown hair which defied Bryl-cream.

"Yes Sir?" The man came closer and narrowed his intense gaze as he studied Gallier closely.

"This is Detective Sergeant Gallier… He is very new around here and he has some important work to attend to. I am assigning you to him for the foreseeable future…" Cooper finished the sentence and then turned to face the Sergeant. "Gallier, this is PC Stringer… But we call him Aid-the aide… He has been with us for a while now. He is a very enthusiastic young constable and I have purposefully been hanging onto him. I am sure that uniform would be eager to have him back... But I have found him to be most useful... He makes an excellent cup of tea!"

"Would you like a cup of tea Sir?" Aid-the aide turned and gazed wide eyed at Gallier and the DS got the impression that the young constable was quite ready to ram a tea bag down the throat of the next officer who asked for a cup of tea before battering them unconscious with the metal kettle! *Gallier instantly liked Aid-the aide...*

"No thanks mate... Ar'm ok right now ta..." Gallier smiled before turning back to face DCI Cooper. "So... About those two DCs I asked for?"

"Erm..." Cooper paused and looked briefly at the floor. "I'm afraid that this is all I can spare at the moment Sergeant. PC Stringer here is keen to learn the ropes and I think that working with an experienced officer such as yourself will be a damn good learning curve for him." The DCI had little more to say and he turned as if to leave the room before quickly looking back. "Oh, and Gallier, please do try not to teach him any of your notorious bad habits that I have read so much about!" Cooper turned back towards the door again and then marched out leaving the two officers in the damp, dark surroundings. Gallier looked around. *The room would be perfect. It was highly likely that Tanner had crooked officers there in West Brom too and Gallier certainly had no desire to socialise with his new colleagues. It would be of benefit for him to remain as inconspicuous as possible as both himself and Aid-the aide carried out their vital investigations into Cedric Tanner...*

"I gather yow dow like meckin' tay mate?" Gallier broke an awkward silence and Aid-the aide shook his head and sighed.

"Fuckin' hell! I've been here fuckin' ages Sarge and all they ever say to me is make the fuckin' tea! Most of those bastards in CID couldn't find their own fuckin' arse holes in a mirror! They couldn't detect a smell in a toilet! All they ever do is 'shilly-shally' around drinking fuckin' tea!" Aid continued to shake his head with a look of profound irritation. "They make me look like a right fuckin' dick head! And that is my pet hate Sir, I cannot stand any fucker making me look like a fuckin' dick head!"

184

"Nobody likes being made to look a dickhead..." Gallier agreed with the constable. "What's your name then chap? Or does everyone just call yer Aid-the aide?"

"Stringer Sir... Constable Aidan Stringer..." Aid-the aide stroked his chin inquisitively. "So what is this special mission Sir?"

"Its very hush hush Stringer... Are you sure you have what it takes for such specialised Police work?" Gallier lowered his voice and adopted a serious tone.

"I was born ready Sir!" The young Constable became further alert and a look of purposeful excitement shot into his eager eyes.

"Ok..." Gallier lowered his voice even further. "First, gew over there, put the tea bag in the cup and then wait for the kettle to boil... Then ar'll have a splash of milk and two sugars!" Gallier kept a straight face throughout as he tapped his new friend on the shoulder jokingly. The young policeman said nothing. He took a deep breath and then set off towards the kettle whilst muttering various obscenities under his breath as he moved...

Chapter 23

A id-the aide breathed into a public Bakelite telephone as he sighed his boredom.

"Nothing to report Sarge... Tanner hasn't moved all day... Maybe he has broken up for Christmas?" Aid-the aide's final comment was laced in sarcasm and the young Constable was sick and tired of watching Tanner's house. The villain lived near to the village of Kinver in a large country house that was situated in a remote rural spot. The only way that the policeman could report back his findings was by driving over to a public telephone box in the nearby village. Due to the nature of the investigation, any kind of radio transmission would have been too risky! Of course, every time Aid-the aide left the surveillance point to report to Gallier, he ran the risk of Tanner leaving the house, but thus far , whenever he returned, Tanner's car was still there.

"What about visitors to the house?" It was getting closer to the end of the year and Gallier needed results and fast. He was sat in the main office of the West Bromwich CID and even though he had now been there for a few days, he had spoken to relatively few people and his presence there was something of a mystery to the other officers.

"Fuck all Sarge... Not even the bloody postman!" Aid-the aide had a dramatic voice that was enhanced by his frequent and over exaggerated use of swear words.

"Right... Keep me updated..." Gallier's voice was filled with disappointment as Aid-the aide replaced the receiver onto the handle. *Another few hours sat watching fuck all! I love my fucking job, beats my former career as a professional watcher of fucking paint drying on a bastard wall!* The young officer was disappointed that there was nobody else around to appreciate his seething sarcasm as he made his way back to the surveillance position. Back in West Bromwich, Gallier chewed on the end of a pencil as he sat on a chair and stared out of the window. He didn't know whose chair or desk he was sat at and in all honesty he didn't really care either. The mood he was in he was spoiling for a fight and he quite relished the prospect of the desk's owner coming over to him to complain.

"Excuse me, but are you DS Gallier?" A wiry young Detective Constable suddenly approached Gallier and the DS wondered how and why the man knew his name.

"Why?" Gallier snapped, but the apparent friendly nature of the DC made him instantly regret his aggression.

"There's a telephone call for you Sarge? From a DC Giles over at Old Hill... I figured that it may have been you he is asking for as I know all of the detectives in here and I have noticed you around over the last few days Sir..."

"Ok... What does he want? DC Giles..."

"He is on the phone Sarge. He is insisting on speaking to you..." The young policeman gestured over to another desk where the telephone receiver lay off the hook on the black, leatherette desktop.

"Thank you..." Gallier smiled a brief thanks and then made his way over to the desk.

"Hello... Tony is that you?"

"Yes... Hello Reg..." The two friends recognised each other's voice straight away. "I cor speak on the phone Reg, but I need to speak with you urgently. Can you get out?" Tony Giles's voice was anxious.

"Yeah, sure... Where?" Gallier was intrigued.

"Over by you somewhere Reg, its too risky over here..." Giles remained anxious and a quiet excitement came over Reggie Gallier. *Was this gunna be the lead that he had been looking for?*

"Do you know the White Swan pub on Bromford Lane?"

"Yes..." DC Giles knew the pub. It was in West Bromwich, but not too far by car from where he was located in Old Hill.

"Ok good... I'll meet you there in twenty minutes..."

The White Swan public house stood on Bromford Lane, West Bromwich and was not far from the newly built Lyng council estate which had been constructed in the 1960s. The estate was typical of many British council developments of the same era and featured a mix of high-rise flats and maisonettes. As with similar developments, the housing was substandard and had only ever been meant as a temporary arrangement to house a booming population after the Second World War. Eventually, the buildings would rot and decay and social deprivation, poverty, crime and anti-social behaviour would become rife.

As Tony Giles entered a small lounge area to the right of the main bar, he spotted his good friend Reggie Gallier straight away. The DS was sat smoking a cigarette and had already drunk three quarters of his Banks's Bitter.

"Do you want another?" Giles nodded to Gallier's pint glass and he already knew the answer to the question.

"Tar…" Gallier drained the dregs of his beer and pushed the dimpled glass towards his friend.

"So… What's all this about then?" DS Gallier asked the question as DC Giles returned to the table with two pints of bitter. "It sounded urgent on the phone…"

"Yes Reg… They found a dead body…" Giles glanced down at his beer and Gallier could tell from the look on his face that it was a particularly nasty one. "On our patch… Clubber Clark and the lads are investigating…"

"I see…" Gallier took a gulp of his fresh beer and waited to find out how the discovery of a corpse in Old Hill had any relevance to him.

"A young lad… Be about 22 years old… They reckon he was brutally raped before he was killed."

"How did he die?" Gallier's thoughts and suspicions immediately shot towards Cedric Tanner.

"He was strangled… Garrotted with a piece of material… Maybe a tie or something? Highly likely that the murder was committed whilst carrying out the buggery…" DC Giles took a drink of his beer and Gallier shuddered inwardly.

"So why are you here Tony? What has all of this got to do with me?"

"Clubber Clark reckons that it's an open and shut case… He's got us all working on it but he has already arrested Eddie Fennel!"

"Eddie Fennel!" Gallier almost spat beer from out of his mouth. "No… No fuckin' way… This ay Fennel's style… Not one bit…"

"I know Reg… That's why I came to you. Clubber Clark is pushing to get Fennel sent down… We all know why…" DC Giles was aware of Gallier's most recent investigations in his new division and he was also growing increasingly aware of some of the crooked, corruption that existed around him.

"It ay Fennel…" Gallier shook his head defiantly. "Why does Clubber Clark think its Fennel? What evidence has he got?"

"The body was discovered on Fennel's business premises and Fennel has a record of extreme violence… I'm sure Clark will be able to manufacture some witness statements so that he can get it all tied up by the end of the week… Dow get me wrong, I dow like Fennel's kind, they are villains, but this just ay right Reg…" As the DC spoke, Gallier began to panic. *Fennel was the only living person who knew of his own vengeful killings of Tummy Collins and Bernard Quinn and surely, if he (Fennel) was being charged with a murder he had not committed, he would give up everything he had on Gallier to try and save his own skin!*

"Where is Fennel now?"

"He's back at Old Hill nick…"

"Can I speak to him?"

"Reg, yow cor do that! What grounds do you have? Besides Clubber will go mad if he finds out."

"As you know Tony, I am currently investigating Cedric Tanner and I have reason to believe that Tanner organised if not committed this murder himself in order to frame Fennel! Tanner has been trying to get rid of Fennel for years…" Gallier did not doubt for one minute that this was indeed the case.

"Well yes Reg, you are probably right, but what about DI Clubber Clark?"

"Fuck him… I won't tell if you dow and it's doubtful Fennel will say anything…" Gallier downed the rest of his beer in one swift action and then prepared to stand up. Is there anything else you can tell me about the victim? Who was he? Where was he from?"

"His name is Alan Norton… A known homosexual from Tipton whom we suspect had been working as a rent boy…"

"Fuckin' hell Tony, Tanner operates over Tipton way a lot… He drinks in pubs over there and he knows all of the rent boys… Fuckin' hell, most of em work for him!"

"Yes… My thoughts entirely Reg, that's why I came to you…"

"Right… Teck me down Old Hill nick right away aer kid… I need to speak to Fennel…"

Eddie Fennel shifted awkwardly in his seat as he waited alone in the interview room. He was not afraid of prison, it was an occupational risk that he had to accept, however, the stigma of being labelled the lowest of the low, a 'Nonce' was a fate he simply could not accept. Especially as he was one hundred percent innocent! Outside of the room, DC Giles and DS Gallier approached.

"We really shouldn't be doing this Reg. What if Clubber finds out?" Tony Giles looked around nervously as the pair reached the door to the interview room. Gallier ignored the remark.

"You stay here and keep a look out… If anyone comes, dow let them come inside… I will talk to Fennel alone…" It had been something of a task for Gallier to sneak into the Police Station without being noticed by his former colleagues, but he had kept his head down and persevered.

"Ok Reg… But be bloody quick! Ar dow like this… Ar dow like this one bit…" DC Giles opened the door and Gallier disappeared inside as the Detective Constable kept his eyes peeled for signs of DI Clubber Clark.

"Hello Eddie..." Gallier sat down opposite the gangster after checking to make sure that they were completely alone in the cold interview room. "Do you want a fake Eddie?" Gallier offered Fennel his cigarettes and the villain took one. As ever, Fennel appeared composed and confident under the scrutiny of the police, but Gallier could tell that it was false bravado.

"Thanks..." Fennel lowered his head as Gallier lit his cigarette and then, after taking back the smoke into his lungs and exhaling, he focused his intimidating glare upon the policeman. "I thought that yow had been transferred to West Brom?"

"I have... But I heard about what happened to that kid and thought I would see if I could help..." Gallier shrugged and Fennel appeared to find his comment somewhat amusing.

"You mean you're scared that I might squeal about those two Gypos we bumped off in Tipton?" Fennel continued to enjoy his cigarette and Gallier said nothing. *The gangster was right!*

"I gather that I'm right in assuming that you didn't kill that kid Eddie?"

"Of course ar day kill that fuckin' kid!" Fennel raised his voice and was offended by the notion that Gallier even had to ask.

"So who did?" Gallier lit himself a cigarette and waited for a reply.

"Isn't it bloody obvious? Cedric Tanner of course... Shagging dead rent boys is exactly his thing and planting them on my property for his gang of bent coppers to find is his way of getting back at me over what happened to those two 'Snetters..." Fennel gave Gallier a knowing look. Everyone in the criminal fraternity, including DI Fowler, DI Clark and the other crooked cops had assumed that it was Fennel who had killed Collins and

Quinn… *The idea that a policeman would murder for vengeance was much too far-fetched!* Only Fennel and Gallier knew the whole truth… "Even if I was into raping and killing young lads, and believe me, I fuckin' am not, do yow really think that ar would be saft enough to leave the body in my own flippin' warehouse?"

"Can you tell me anything? About the victim? Anything at all…"

"Nothing… If fellas wanna get off on other fellas, then that's their fuckin' business, but it certainly ay nuthin' to do with fuckin' me!" Fennel exhaled more smoke into the air before pushing his head back and closing his eyes. *He was beginning to crack, he was letting his guard down… He would have to trust Gallier to help him and this connection with a 'copper' grated upon him…* "You've got to help me Reg… Ar never thought that I would ever ask a copper for help, but after what I did for you with them two gypsies, yow fuckin' owe me mate!"

"You helped me with those gypsies because it was advantageous for you to get Tanner out of the way!" Gallier lowered his voice to an absolute whisper.

"Well it didn't work did it! Yow told me that if we planted those dead Pikeys on Tanner's property, then that bastard would be out of the way for good! I fuckin' trusted you Reg and now look what has happened… They have planted a corpse on my property as payback and now I'm the one gewin' down!" Fennel grunted and shook his head at the irony of the situation and Gallier felt genuine pity… *It appeared as though Tanner was just as untouchable as ever and god help anyone that tried to get in his way!*

Chapter 24

It had been a long hard day and things were looking pretty dismal. The usual barroom hum of the Doughty Arms in Tipton was as it always was and Gallier looked around enviously at the normal, everyday people who were going about their normal, everyday lives. *None of these people were looking at spending the rest of their lives in prison... If Fennel was to talk and give his side of the story, then surely Clubber Clark and the other rotten bastards would come after him next... Why shouldn't Fennel talk? He (Gallier) had involved the known villain in vengeance for his father and the promise that they would get rid of Tanner and his band of bent bastards, but in reality this had backfired and now Fennel was looking at the exact same fate they had intended for Tanner!* Gallier concluded that he would not blame Eddie Fennel, even if he did talk... *Maybe it was just?* No matter how much he thought about it, Gallier could not feel regret or guilt over what he did to Collins and Quinn and this cold lack of remorse bothered him somewhat... *Was he just as bad as the others?*

"I've never been in this pub before I must say..." Aid-the aide interrupted Gallier's thought process. The pair had finished work but Gallier had brought his new colleague and friend over to the Tipton boozer in the hope that they might find some kind of clue or lead. They were certainly clutching at straws, but Tony Giles had informed him (Gallier) that the victim, Alan Norton was from Tipton, so the Doughty Arms seemed as good a place as any to start looking. "So we're looking for Hommos?" Aid-the aide devoured a bag of pork scratchuns and took intermittent sips of beer.

"Homosexuals..." Gallier corrected his colleague with a more respectful term and then continued to look around the room aimlessly.

"So why do you think they might be in here Sarge? Is this one of 'them' pubs? And what are we looking for if we do find some?" Aid-the aide was a stickler for detail, good planning and preparation and Gallier didn't quite know what to say.

"Ar really dow fuckin' know aer kid... As far as I've always known it's just a normal pub. I've been coming in here for the last 20 years!" Gallier shrugged and Aid-the aide was becoming quite dismayed by the vast quantities of alcohol that the DS was casually putting away.

"But Sarge, if we don't have a plan, we will end up looking like fucking dick heads! And you know that I cannot stand being made to look a dick head!" Aid-the aide remained calm, but the intensity of his words were genuine. Gallier smiled to himself. *He had a lot more to lose than being 'made to look a dick head!'* For a few seconds, Gallier wondered what Aid the aide would think if he knew the truth... *That they were trying to find evidence so that they could get a crazed gangster by the name of Eddie Fennel off the hook so that he (Gallier) could continue to get away with the cold and calculated murder of the two gypsies that murdered his father!* In Gallier's mind, Aid-the aide appeared to be a very 'black and white' person. There was right and there was wrong. The law was the law and anything that fell foul of this was unacceptable. Gallier admired this way of thinking and it reminded him of himself before the unfortunate killing of his father... Still, the same question echoed through his mind, vengeance or justice? *Were they the same thing?*

Her skirt was as short as ever and the way that her skinny calves filled out above the knee attracted Gallier instantly and as they always had. It had been quite a while since Gallier had seen his designated 'bit on the side' Gemma and as Christmas was growing ever closer, he had been intending to take her out for a meal and then enjoy her 'company' for a while, but work had been demanding and both himself and Aid-the aide had been working hard and fruitlessly to try and build a case against Cedric Tanner. What angered Gallier, was that as he sat with Aid-the aide at a small table near to the bar, the attractive brunette had walked into the pub and was arm in arm with another man! For a brief minute, Gallier's problems with Cedric Tanner, Eddie Fennel and everything else seemed to fly out of his mind as a jealous rage came over him. *Gemma was his bird!*

"Who the fuck is this?" Much to the surprise of Aid-the aide, Gallier suddenly rose to his feet and approached Gemma and her male companion.

"Oh fuck off Reggie… You're not my fucking owner! Run off back to your wife and leave me alone…" Gemma had clearly been drinking and both her and her male companion appeared to be somewhat upset.

"Fine…" Gallier looked at the floor and tried to remind himself that he was a middle-aged man and not a lovesick teenager. Though he was genuinely hurt. He had been in love with Gemma for quite a while and the fact that she was now 'swanning around' with another man added further insult to his dismal and depressing day. He turned as if to back away, but the man alongside Gemma could not help but make a snide comment…

"Maybe its time she found herself a real man!" In that moment, Gallier did not recognise the effeminate tone of the man's voice and the policeman lost his temper. Without further comment, Gallier smashed the man in the jaw with a hard right hook and instantly Gemma's companion fell to the ground. With a pent-up aggression that was further fuelled by copious amounts of alcohol, Gallier proceeded to put the boot in as he kicked his victim who was already doubled over on the floor and clutching his ribs. Upon sight of the disturbance, Aid the aide instantly got to his feet and made his way forwards so that he could try and restrain his Sarge, but his presence was not required.

"Leave it Reg! He's fucking gay! There is nothing going on between me and him…" Gemma had somehow positioned herself between Gallier and her companion and the tiny but feisty brunette barked her command.

195

"What? But you two are holding hands?" Gallier instantly felt a fool as he realised that the barroom had descended into silence and all eyes were now upon the spectacle that was continuing to unfold.

"Oi!" The Landlord swiftly appeared on the scene and Aid-the aide in particular felt embarrassment. "You lot out! We woe have no trouble in here!"

"Excuse me Sir..." Aid-the aide addressed the pub landlord. "We will be out of here in one minute..." The aide to CID nudged Gallier on the shoulder and whispered to his colleague. "Maybe this hommo, er, I mean homosexual could help us?" Before Gallier could answer, Gemma continued to speak.

"We are out tonight consoling each other... Peter here has had a very distressing day... His boyfriend has just been murdered!" Gallier and Aid-the aide's attention was suddenly well and truly aroused and the aide to CID instantly approached the pub landlord as the sound of the barroom went back to its usual hum.

"Sir, I am deeply sorry for the disturbance...." The policeman took out his warrant card and discretely showed the landlord. "We are in the middle of a very complex investigation. I would appreciate it if we could remain in your premises for a few minutes so that we can continue to conduct our investigation... I can assure you that there will be no more violence..."

"Fine... You've got ten minutes... But any more trouble and yow'm out! Copper or no copper!" The landlord was a strong-minded man who would not allow trouble in his bar!

"Look... I am so sorry..." Gallier helped the beaten man back to his feet. Apologies did not come easy for the burly detective. "It was a misunderstanding... Can I get you both a drink?"

"Fuck off Reg… You've done enough damage… We've both had enough of angry, bully-boys kicking the shit out of people to last a lifetime!" Gemma grabbed the man's hand as if to lead him away when Aid-the aide returned from the bar.

"I am so sorry, but I could not help but hear what happened to your dear friend… You have my upmost sympathy…" Aid-the aide adopted a sympathetic tone. "I know that this must be a very difficult time for you both, but both myself and my colleague, Detective Sergeant Gallier, are Police officers and we may well be able to help you?" The aide to CID had judged the situation perfectly and had taken exactly the right tone and approach that provided Gemma and her companion with compassion and reassurance. Gallier was impressed. *His own 'old school' approach of knocking down doors and beating on villains until they confessed was coming to an end and before him stood the future… Preparation, careful planning and adaptability…* Gemma's male companion turned and looked at her with a slight look of hopefulness that was tinged with sadness.

"Yes Peter…" Gemma spoke reluctantly. "They are coppers… I think you should tell them…" She did not look Gallier in the eyes. *He had pissed her off with his jealous display of possessiveness, but deep down she was flattered… He still loved her…*

"Well, I ain't bloody talking in here!" Peter steadied himself as he pulled away from Gallier. He was a thin and fragile looking man but with podgy cheeks and effeminate looking brown eyes. "The walls have eyes!"

"That is perfectly understandable Sir…" Aid-the aide remained calm and compassionate.

"My house isn't too far from here…" Gemma suggested somewhat apprehensively. "My mom will be there but she will leave us to it…"

"Ok... Let's go to your house... We can talk there..." Peter wiped blood from his face and nodded sadly.

Gemma's mother brought fresh cups of tea into the living room of her house on Robert Road, Tipton and then disappeared back into the kitchen as the four adults more or less filled the small council house's lounge. Reg Gallier could not help but gaze at his cup of tea with disappointment. He had anticipated a night on the beer and weak tea in an elaborate, bone China tea set with far too much milk just was not going to cut it!

"Here... Drink this..." Gemma pulled out a half empty bottle of Bells blended Scotch whisky from an old 1930s cabinet and poured a generous measure into Peter's tea. Gallier looked at her expectantly but she pretended that she hadn't seen him.

"So... Please, tell us what you know... In your own time Sir..." Aid-the aide exuded professionalism and Gallier looked on hopefully.

"I loved him..." Peter spoke through tears. "He loved me too, but we could never be free with it..." He shook his head with grief as the tears continued to flow. "Even my own mother keeps asking me when am I gunna find a nice wench and settle down! She just doesn't understand... Nobody understands... Only Alan understood and now he is dead..."

"Alan Norton?" Gallier interrupted unsympathetically.

"Yes..." Peter nodded and looked at the floor sadly as the salt in his tears cut into the wounds that had recently been inflicted by the Detective Sergeant.

"What happened to Mr Norton?" Gallier continued his line of questioning as Aid-the aide made meticulous notes.

"He was murdered..."

"Sir, could you please take us through the events leading up to Mr Norton's death?" Aid-the aide looked up from his notebook. "When did you last see him?"

"We were working…" Peter looked at the floor with embarrassment and shame.

"You worked together?" Aid-the aide continued with his sympathetic tone.

"Yes…"

"You're gunna have to give us more than this aer kid, I could have been in the pub getting pissed right now!" Gallier's outburst of annoyance was planned as Peter looked back towards Aid-the aide trustingly… *He was the much friendlier policeman, maybe he genuinely could help?* Gallier and Aid-the aide had ascended into their first good cop/bad cop routine seamlessly.

"You tell us in your own time Sir…" Aid-the aide knew exactly what Gallier was trying to do.

"We both worked for him…" Peter looked up and a look of hatred and fear entered his eyes.

"Who is him? Prince Charles? Edward Heath? Alf Ramsay? The man from bloody U.N.C.L.E?" Gallier retained the 'bad cop' act.

"Tanner! Cedric Tanner!" Peter eventually spat the name venomously and Gallier smiled.

"And what did you do for Mr Tanner?" Aid-the aide's eyes widened as they grew closer to extracting the information they required.

"We worked for him on a personal basis…" Peter gulped sadly… "We let him fuck us and do whatever the fuck he and his perverted clients wanted…" Peter looked shamefully at the floor again and a brief and awkward silence filled the room.

"When did you last see Alan, Peter?" Gallier resumed the questions.

"A few days a go…"

"At what time?" A stickler for detail and accuracy, Aid-the aide asked the question.

"About mid-day?"

"Twelve o'clock pm?" Aid lowered his left eyebrow and raised his chin inquisitively.

"Yes, about then… We were entertaining some of Tanner's clients together, then Tanner came in and told Alan he was needed elsewhere… I never saw him again…"

"So what happened to Alan?" Gallier demanded.

"He was killed by Cedric Tanner, I'm sure of it… Tanner's a sick bastard, he enjoys hurting people…"

"But how do you know for a fact that Tanner killed Alan? Where is your evidence?" Aid-the aide placed his biro down. His actions were calm and restrained but he was beginning to feel a little frustrated. Reg Gallier on the other hand was beginning to feel pleased. *If they could get a statement from Peter and an alibi from Fennel's wife then at least Eddie Fennel would be off the hook and there would be no chance of Fennel talking about his (Gallier's) involvement with the gypsy killings…*

"I know it was Tanner, I just know it!" Peter was beginning to feel frustrated and bitterly angry over what had happened to his beloved.

"Yes…" Aid-the aide left a deliberate and patronisingly sarcastic pause… "But did you see Tanner do anything to the man?"

"No…"

"Don't worry Peter… What you have told us is most useful…" Gallier suddenly switched to 'good cop'. "Would you be willing to make an official statement outlining exactly what you have just told us?"

"Reg, Tanner will kill him if he finds out!" Gemma had been silent throughout, but she suddenly protested.

"Its ok Peter… We can keep you safe, if what you are saying is true then Tanner will be locked away in prison for a very long time…" Gallier smiled reassuringly.

"Sarge, can I have a private word please?" Aid-the aide spoke.

"Of course Constable Stringer… Excuse us for one moment please…" Gallier and Aid-the aide disappeared into the hallway and out of earshot of the other two.

"Sarge, we cannot guarantee this man's safety, there is nowhere near enough evidence here to get Tanner off the streets… I think it is unwise of you to advise otherwise… Sir…" Aid-the aide was concerned.

"Yes Aid, but it is all we have and if we do not do something then that sick bastard Tanner is gunna keep ruining people's lives…"

"But it would be very dangerous for Peter Sir… I don't think that we should be taking risks with the safety of the public…"

"Aidan…" Gallier smiled and laughed. "One day you are going to make a very good Chief Constable… The press love all that do-gooder bull shit… But right now I wanna nail that prick Tanner… Do you wanna be Aid-the aide forever or Detective Constable Stringer?"

"I'm not happy Sarge…" Aid-the aide looked concerned…

"Dow worry aer kid… Go back in there and take the statement and then we need to go and speak to a wench about an alibi…"

Chapter 25

"Who is this PC Stringer fella?" Detective Constable Tony Giles cast his eyes over the two statements Gallier and Aid-the aide had taken from Peter and Fennel's wife. Both Gallier and Aid-the aide had enjoyed speaking to Fennel's spouse. She was a particularly attractive Irish beauty and both men had commented afterwards on how Eddie Fennel was a 'lucky man!'

"He's the young chap who is working with me on the Tanner investigation… He's a good lad… A bit 'by the book' for my liking but he will learn!" Gallier took a gulp of his beer as the pair (Giles and Gallier) sat in the same spot at the White Swan on Bromford Lane, West Bromwich.

"How come its Stringer's name on the paperwork and not yours?" Tony Giles was slightly confused.

"Because if Clubber Clark see's my name on it he's gunna know that we are onto them… Besides, if there's any come back and it goes 'tits up', I don't wanna bloody deal with it!"

"He who dabbles deals!" Giles smirked. Now he understood perfectly.

"Exactly… You can give these statements to DI Clark and he will have no choice but to release Fennel… And I got my man Stringer to type up multiple copies so dow let Clubber Clark even think about ripping them up and shoving em' in the bin!"

"Ok…" DC Giles sighed. *Clubber Clark was gunna be pissed off and he was going to have to deal with it…* "Clubber's gunna go mad…"

"Let him… If he's got a problem tell him to speak to Detective Chief Inspector Cooper… He'll shit his pants…" Gallier smiled smugly.

"You do know that there is nowhere near enough evidence here to charge Tanner? So what if he was with the victim several hours before his death?" Tony Giles was right but Gallier already knew it.

"Yes I know… But at least a man is not going down for a crime he did not commit…"

"I guess…" DC Giles narrowed his eyes as he thought. "But there are those who would argue that Edward Fennel is a serious criminal anyway so what difference would it have made?" There was a time when Gallier would have agreed whole heartedly, but then only Gallier and Eddie Fennel knew the real reason as to why the Detective Sergeant was so eager to get the villain released!

"Maybe…" Gallier just shrugged and went back to his beer.

"You will have to warn this bloke though Reg…" DC Giles looked back at the statement for the name of Alan Norton's boyfriend. "This Peter Hartshorne… Tanner won't be happy and you can guarantee that Clubber Clark will let him know exactly who made the statement…"

"Yes I know… Leave it with me…"

Back at the Police station in West Bromwich, Aid-the aide lined up all of his handwritten notes from his observations of Cedric Tanner and studied them very carefully. It was getting closer to Christmas and the New Year and both Aid-the aide and DS Gallier were very aware that once January came, unless they had significant leads, their investigations into Tanner, a villain from outside of their 'patch', would have to stop.

"Oi, Stringer!" One of the DCs in the office had taken a phone call on the 'informant's phone'. The informants phone was a special line that was set up in every CID office so that witnesses and informants could speak to their point of contact at any point without having to go through the station's switchboard system. "There's a bird on the phone who wants to speak to yer!" The officer and the half dozen others in the office found it highly amusing that the 'lowly' aide to CID would have an informant.

"What does she want? A cuppa tay?" Another colleague made the wise crack and the other officers found it highly amusing. Aid-the aide said nothing. He stood up and made his way over to the phone. He was intrigued by the call and was oblivious to the mockery and banter as he picked up the receiver.

"Hello…"

"Hi, PC Stringer?"

"That's me…" Aid- the aide recognised the voice.

"It's Gemma, from the other night? You took a statement from my friend Peter Hartshorne…" Gemma sounded anxious as she spoke quickly.

"Yes Gemma, how can I help you?"

"It's Pete, he's really worried… He has heard that Cedric Tanner is looking for him and that Tanner is on the war path!"

"Right… Where are you now?" Aid-the aide's heartbeat was racing but he remained calm and professional. *He had warned Gallier about this!*

"We are both at my mom's place in Tipton, but we are very scared PC Stringer… Is Reg there?" She was still annoyed with Gallier for the way he had reacted to Peter in the Doughty Arms the other night, but she always felt safer when he was around.

"DS Gallier is out of the office at the moment I am afraid… But as soon as he gets back I will notify him of your predicament…" Aid-the aide was very aware that he was not being particularly helpful, but what else could he do? *He could send a uniform patrol around there, but who could he trust? Would he be giving Hartshorne's position away to one of Tanner's pocket men?* "Just hang tight where you are for now and DS Gallier will sort everything out when he gets back…" Aid-the aide tried his best to sound reassuring and he could tell that the voice on the other end of the phone was disappointed and scared…

"Where is Reg? Is he in the bloody pub?"

"No…" Aid-the aide lied.

"Ok… Please tell Reg to come straight away… He said that he would protect my friend…"

Aid-the aide was sweating as he reverse parked the CID Morris Marina saloon on Robert Road, Tipton near to Gemma's mother's house. Gallier had returned to the office shortly after the young PC had come off the phone and upon him hearing the news, the pair had climbed into the car and made the relatively short journey over to Tipton.

"I don't like this one bit Sarge... I was worried this would happen... This is exactly what I was talking about the other night." Aid-the aide brought the car to a standstill, but Gallier did not share his anxiety... *This was exactly what he had expected and planned to happen!*

"Dow worry aer kid... We knew this would happen... Now we've gotta use it in our favour..."

"What do you mean?" Aid-the aide shot Gallier a look that was more suspicious than confused.

"That kid Peter knows more about Tanner's operations than he is letting on...The other night he just wanted to talk about what happened to Alan Norton... But now he's scared... Now he knows that he is in the shit and he NEEDS to get Tanner banged up..." Gallier emphasised the word NEEDS. "So now he is gunna tell us all that he knows and give evidence in court to save himself from Tanner..."

"But Sarge?" Aid-the aide understood very well and he did not approve. "We can't run around like this jeopardising people's safety! What if you are wrong and the kid can't tell us anything else?"

"Yow've got a lot to learn aer kid.. Sometimes you have to take risks... What else are we gunna do? Every second that Tanner is out of jail, people are in serious danger... It's up to us to do whatever it takes to send him down..." Gallier's point was not up for negotiation and he got out of the car before Aid-the aide had chance to reply.

"Come in..." Gemma greeted the two policemen at the front door. She had been looking out for their arrival from behind the net curtains in the living room and she was anxious for the two officers to come inside before they were spotted.

"Hello you..." Gallier resisted the urge to smack her shapely back side which was exaggerated by the tightness of her denim jeans. "Can you answer a question for me bab?" Gallier's words were random and unexpected and the pretty brunette answered hesitantly.

"Yes... What?"

"You know when folks play golf, what is that thingy called that they use to hit the ball off?" His question was so irrelevant and bizarre but she answered straight away, curious as to just where the Sergeant was going with this line of questioning.

"A tee?"

"Yes please Gemma... Milk, no sugar..." Gallier chuckled and Aid-the aide couldn't help but smile to himself. *He had heard them all!*

"Oh piss off Reg! This is serious!" Gemma wasn't impressed with the comment but she still trudged off into the kitchen to make them a drink. Gallier wanted her out of the way for a while. *Maybe Peter Hartshorne would speak more if she wasn't around?* Slowly, the living room door opened and cautiously, Peter Hartshorne peered out to check that the coast was clear.

"It's ok Mr Hartshorne... It's me, PC Stringer and my colleague DS Gallier... You remember us from the other night?"

"Aye up!" Gallier found his comment amusing but it went over the heads of the other two men.

"Of course I bloody remember you!" Hartshorne was visibly anxious. "You promised that you would arrest Cedric Tanner and keep me safe!"

"Mr Hartshorne, I must point out that we did not promise to make any arrests... As for your safety and welfare we are here now to discuss this..." Ever the professional diplomat, Aid-the aide tried his best to ease the situation but Reggie Gallier was nowhere near as tactful.

"The truth is Peter, you are not safe... You are far from bloody safe... Cedric Tanner and his goons are searching for you and when they get hold of yer, I can guarantee that it will not end well for you... What they did to yower mate Alan is nothing compared to what they will do to you aer kid..."

"But you told me that you would keep me safe!"

206

"Yes... But guess what? That statement you gave us the other night was nowhere near enough to arrest Tanner...All you did was tell us that you and Alan were with Tanner a few hours before Alan was killed... What does that prove?"

"But you did not tell me that at the time!" The horror and fear was beginning to build in Peter Hartshorne's eyes... Gallier had him exactly where he wanted him...

"The long and short of it is that you are gunna have to give me more mate..."

"What do you mean?"

"If you wanna stay safe from Tanner, then you need to give me everything you know about the man and put it in a statement... That's the only way we can get Tanner off the streets..."

"I don't know what you mean..." Hartshorne looked at the floor sadly.

"Ok... Well we might as well get going then... Good luck..." Gallier began to walk back towards the front door when just as he anticipated, Hartshorne protested.

"Wait..."

"I'm listening..." Gallier turned on his heel. "Let's go and sit down..." The Detective Sergeant pointed back into the living room and the three men walked through and sat down.

"I know where he stashes his drugs..." Hartshorne began to speak but Gallier pretended not to be interested.

"Let's wait for the tea to come... I'm parched..." after a few moments of awkward silence as Gallier watched Peter Hartshorne squirm in his seat, Gemma came into the room with a tray of tea. She passed the drinks around and then sat down herself next to Peter. "You were saying Mr Hartshorne?"

"I know where Tanner keeps his drugs..." As he spoke, Gemma looked at him with alarm and tried to protest. "No, its ok Gemma... Sergeant Gallier here needs more information to get Tanner banged up... I've got nothing to lose have I?" His eyes were sad and worried. " Tanner wants to kill me anyway so I might as well tell them everything I know…"

"Please do continue…" Gallier looked over at his colleague Aid-the aide and was pleased to see that the junior officer had taken out his pocketbook and pen to make notes.

"I went there a few times with him… Tanner gets driven everywhere in his Rolls Royce these days… He sits on the back seat smoking big cigars and drinking cognac and he always has a 'companion' with him… Sometimes male… Sometimes female…"

"What is the companion for?" Aid-the aide asked the question and Gallier groaned inwardly…

"What do you think Constable?" Hartshorne's reply was extremely camp in its tone.

"Do you have a registration number for the Roller?" Aid-the aide was ever the stickler for detail.

"It's parked right outside his house… He lives in a big place near Kinver… Not that he's from there originally… He was born and bred in Wolverhampton… I believe that he inherited much of his crime empire from his father many years ago…" Hartshorne said nothing that Gallier didn't already know.

"Yes… You were saying that Tanner took you to the drug distribution depot?" Gallier was annoyed that Aid-the aide had disrupted the flow of information with his rudimentary questions.

"Tanner likes to keep his boys and girls dependant on him… Not just financially, he also likes to get them addicted to opiates… That way he can control us with drugs and get us to do ANYTHING for ANYONE…" Hartshorne suddenly became emotional. He took a deep breath and then continued. "Me and Alan did many things… Sick things for a lot of very sick people…"

"The drug storage unit?" Gallier did not want to hear gruesome details… He wanted to finally nail Cedric Tanner…

"Yes… It's very near to where we are right now… Laburnum Road… Do you know it?" The Road was literally less than half a mile away from their current location and had been right under Gallier's nose the entire time…

"I know it very well… I was born and brought up around here…" Gallier was surprised. The street was in a residential Council estate. *Not exactly where he expected drugs to be stashed!* "It's on the Tibby…" The 'Tibby' was an abbreviation used for the Tibbington Estate which was near to Gallier's family home on the Lost City. "Are you sure? I can't see Tanner tecking his Roller down there… It would be on bricks with all the wheels nicked within minutes!"

"I am quite sure Sergeant… Not many folks are brave enough to steal from Cederic Tanner… I believe he had to switch buildings after a policeman discovered his old storage unit on an industrial estate…" Hartshorne was quite right and Gallier knew this as he had been the policeman that had found the old drug storage unit back in the 60s!

In due course, Hartshorne gave Gallier and Aid-the aide all of the information they needed and it was all safely recorded in Aid-the aide's pocket notebook… All they needed to do next was go back to DCI Cooper so that he could obtain a warrant from a magistrate… Things were beginning to look up!

Chapter 26

The PYE Pocketfone model PF2 first came out in 1971 and was utilized by the emergency services as well as the British Army during the 'troubles' in Northern Ireland. It was a cumbersome and rudimentary piece of communication kit that had many flaws including the ability of amateur radio enthusiasts, as well as those that were linked with organised crime, to be able to listen on air to dialogue between Police officers and the other emergency services such as the fire service or Ambulance crews. They were rarely carried by CID as it's often pompous members saw the PYE pocketfone radio as an item that was akin to uniform or the 'Woodentops' as they were generally known. Despite currently operating as a plain clothes officer, Aid-the aide still carried a pocketfone on a regular basis, especially on occasions when he felt there may become a need for backup. As Aid-the aide sat in the passenger seat of the CID Marina, Gallier drove as the pocketfone was blaring away and proving to be quite a source of irritation for the Detective Sergeant.

"Does that bloody thing ever shut up?" Gallier drove quickly as he hurried the Marina Northwards along the A41 towards Wolverhampton. Aid-the aide was quite surprised as they appeared to be going in a different direction, away from the target address in Laburnum Road, Tipton. He said nothing. *Maybe Gallier knew an alternative route?* "I don't know why you carry it anyway... When I was a woodentop in the '50s, we day need no bloody radio! I never had to call for backup, I just gave em' a damn good hidin'!" Aid-the aide did not doubt for one minute that such uncouth and unsophisticated methods were employed by the Sergeant. *But it wasn't 1959 anymore, things had moved on!* "Can you get any Elvis Presley records to play on that thing? Or a bit of Johnny Cash?"

"I bloody hope not Sarge!" Aid-the aide laughed. He was a young man and by 1973 Elvis 'The King' Presley was not quite as 'cool' as he had once been. The raid on the address at Laburnum Road had been authorised by Cooper and a warrant had been issued but Aid-the aide was adamant that he should bring the pocketfone in case any backup or reinforcements were required.

"What have you brought it for? Its doing my bloody head in!" Gallier continued to drive briskly.

"Because if this drugs raid all goes tits up, I'd like us to be able to call for back-up Sarge... I like to be prepared for every eventuality..." Aid-the aide had his doubts. He firmly believed that there should have been more officers involved. "I really think that we should have a bigger team to do this Sir..."

"I told you didn't I, we cor trust anyone... If we let any other officers know what we are doing, how do we know that they ain't gunna gew straight back to Tanner and tell him or his associates that we are on our way... Besides, if we were sat back at the nick trying to round up woodentops who can find their arseholes with both hands, we'd be waiting around all bloody day!" Gallier had a point on both accounts and Aid-the aide could not deny it.

"Just as well that I have the pocketfone then Sarge..."

"Dow worry aer kid... Remember Hartshorne said that there was only ever a couple of blokes guarding the merchandise at one time... It will be fine... Remember, hard and fast and meck sure you put the bloody boot in!" As Gallier drove on further towards Wolverhampton, Aid-the aide became quite sure that they definitely were heading in the wrong direction.

"Sarge, are we going the right way?" The aide to CID peered backwards over his shoulder. "I thought that Tipton was that way?"

"It is..." Gallier smiled... "I gotta pop somewhere first and see a man about a dog... Or dog heads should I say!" Gallier found his comment amusing but Aid-the aide had literally no idea what the DS was talking about. "Yow can wait in the car!"

When Gallier and Aid-the aide finally reached the target location on Laburnum Road, Tipton, both officers were raring to go. They pulled up the Morris Marina at the side of the road near to the house and both men got out.

"Yow ready aer kid?" Gallier was eager and the look of excitement and enthusiasm in Aid-the aide's eyes filled the Sergeant with reassurance.

"Yes Sarge, lets go!" The young constable placed the PYE pocket radio into the inner pocket of his suit jacket and then both men got out and moved around to the back of the car. Gallier opened up the boot and before them lay a large and powerful looking sledgehammer. The handle had been painted white and Aid-the aide could not help but wonder why it had been painted? "Why is the handle painted white Sarge?"

"It makes it official..." Gallier's response was somewhat vague but before the aide to CID could question further, Gallier nodded towards the house and barked the hallowed words. "Go, go, go!" Within seconds, the two policemen were at the front door and Gallier slung the mighty implement with all his might and instantly the structure was caved inwards and open. *He had definitely done that before!*

"This is a raid!" Aid-the aide shouted enthusiastically and he was straight away greeted by a longhaired man in his early twenties who came straight at him with a cricket bat. The junior detective ducked instinctively as the bat made contact with the door frame and as the villain was off balance, the aide to CID was able to launch himself onto the man, grabbing his head into a head lock and forcing his weight down on top of him.

"Fuck off copper!" The hippie tried to protest but Aid the aide forced his arm into an awkward goose lock and the villain screamed out.

"Shut up yer bastard!" Aid-the aide slipped the handcuffs from his pocket and then locked the man's hands down to a large cast iron radiator as Reg Gallier looked on. In fact, the DS was pretty impressed.

"Good work Stringer..." Gallier pulled out a carbon copy of the warrant that DCI Cooper had arranged with the magistrate and held it high in the air so that the handcuffed hippie could see. "This is a warrant for us to search this place under this misuse of drugs act 1972... Are you here on your own?" Gallier remembered that Peter Hartshorne had informed them that there were usually two henchmen guarding the location at any one time.

"No comment..." The man on the floor did not look up as he spoke.

"Fine... I can smell Moroccan woodbines already, so we must be in the right place... Stringer, search the place... Leave no stone unturned..."

"Yes Sarge..." Aid-the aide moved away from the man on the floor and moved off into the living room. A few seconds later, after searching a number of boxes he shouted back excitedly. "Fucking hell Sarge, there's enough drugs in here to keep Amsterdam and Keith Richards going for months!"

"Oh dear..." Gallier walked over to the hippie on the floor and stood over him imposingly.... "Who do you work for kid? Who does all this shit belong to?"

"No comment..." The man remained unresponsive so Gallier pulled him up by his long hair and slapped him hard across the face.

"Oh my goodness... Sometimes these things happen during the struggle of the raid..." Gallier's tone was sarcastic and patronising. "Now if you do not tell me who these drugs belong to I will have to assume that they belong to you and believe me you will be going to jail for a very, very long time!" Before the hippie could answer, Gallier heard a commotion on the next floor so he immediately hurried up the stairs to the source of the noise.

"Move and I'll blow this pig bastard's head off!" Another longhaired man had Aid-the aide by the scruff of the neck and held some kind of gun to the policeman's head. This man looked different to the first, he had a much more assertive manner and in his eyes was a look of wild and unhinged madness.

"Don't move sarge! He's got a gun!" Aid-the aide kept as still as he could as he looked at Gallier. He did not show his fear but the reality was that he was absolutely terrified.

"Gun?" Gallier laughed and much to Aid-the aide's horror the Detective Sargeant began to move closer. "It's a bloody air pistol!" Gallier continued to chuckle as Aid-the aide slowly moved his eyes around to see.

"I said fuck off copper, stay back you bastard!" The longhaired man continued to panic and rage.

"Does your sister like it when you use dirty words like fuck? Does she get all excited and go weak at the knees, or is it your mother you like to get down and dirty with?" Gallier was no longer laughing as he moved closer and closer, never once diverting his gaze from the crazy eyes of the armed man. "You filthy, in-bred, longhaired piece of piss..." Gallier continued with the insults in the hope that he would coerce the villain into making a move so that he could strike back. "Tell me... Was your old man your father or your uncle or both?" The DS got closer still.

"I said stay back! Fuck you!" The longhaired gunman finally lost his cool and brought his weapon around to shoot at Gallier, but in that instant, Aid-the aide took his chance and grabbed hold of the man's right arm, forcing it wide. The single shot 177 pellet ripped through the air, just passed Gallier's left ear and at that point the Detective Sergeant grabbed him.

"Fucking hell mate, what do you use for after shave? Dog shit?" Without further comment, Gallier punched the man hard in the stomach and forced him to the ground. "Here..." The DS pulled his own handcuffs from his pocket and handed them to Aid-the aide. "Cuff him and have him sit on the floor with his hands behind his back..." Gallier picked up the 177 air pistol and inspected it closely. "You would have thought that a man like Cedric Tanner would invest in better security than this!"

214

"But Sarge, would you trust Laurel and Hardy here with a bloody sawn off shotgun on this estate?" Aid-the aide spoke as he handcuffed the villain as instructed. Gallier laughed and then looked at the vast quantities of illegal drugs that appeared to fill every room.

"So…" Gallier walked over to the suspect who was handcuffed and on the floor with his hands behind his back. "As it stands, you and your mate downstairs have been caught in possession of a fuck load of illegal drugs, you have both attacked a police officer with weapons and you have done all of this whilst in possession of a firearm…"

"I thought you said that it was just an air pistol?" The villain mumbled his response.

"Yes… But in the wrong hands it is still a deadly weapon…" Gallier shook his head patronisingly. "It isn't looking very good is it aer kid… I think you are gunna have to try and help yourself mate… Who do you work for? Who does this belong to?" Gallier knew full well who it belonged to, but all he had so far was a statement from Peter Hartshorne… He needed more evidence if he was to keep the investigation going into the New Year.

"No comment…" The villain looked upwards defiantly.

"Ok… Fine… Have it your way…" Suddenly, Reg Gallier grabbed the man by his feet and yanked him across the room towards the landing and the top of the stairs. The villain tried to curse and protest but Gallier yanked him even harder and pulled him down the staircase by his feet as the man winced at the pain in his back. Once at the foot of the stairs, the DS continued to yank the hippie until he was lay out alongside his comrade in the hallway who Aid-the aide had cuffed earlier. "So which one of you pair of bastards is gunna tell me who owns this place?"

"I thought I told you to fuck off!" The wild, 'longhair' who had just been dragged down the stairs feet first spat in the direction of Gallier and possessed the look of a rabid dog.

"Or maybe I could telephone Mr Tanner and ask him to come down here himself?" Gallier's tone was smug as he pulled out a cigarette. The two villains said nothing. *They were surprised that Gallier already knew*

215

who their employer was so why was the copper asking? "What do you think he will do to you when I tell him that you are both informants and that you tipped me off about this place in exchange for this?" Gallier pulled out two crisp twenty pound notes. He placed them both in each of the pockets of the two men and then went back to his cigarette. This time, Gallier's words had a reaction and the younger villain, the first man that Aid-the aide had cuffed began to cry.

"You can't fucking do that!" The second man protested and Gallier finally lit his cigarette.

"I fucking can mate..." Gallier breathed smoke into the atmosphere and Aid-the aide looked on with mixed thoughts and emotions. *The behaviour of his senior officer was not exactly 'by the book' and he had many questions over Gallier's conduct, however, ultimately, Gallier was only doing whatever it took to try and bring down a dangerous criminal... Was it ethical? Was it just?* "Its up to you..." Gallier continued to speak. "You can cooperate with us and tell us all you know about Tanner, or I can get him down here right away... I am sure that he will be very surprised that we know about this place and he will be eager to find out who tipped us off... You have been a big help lads, leading me and my colleague here to the drugs and being so helpful... I am sure that Mr Tanner will be very impressed with your contribution to the police effort and the Drugs Act of 1972..." Gallier looked over to Aid-the aide. "Stringer, gew outside and contact Tanner on that wireless, phone thing..."

"No wait!" Just as Gallier had anticipated, the first and younger hippie protested. "What do you want to know?"

"I want you to give me a full statement back at the station on Cedric Tanner and what he does here... If you do the right thing then Tanner will go away for a long time and we can have a word with the judge about showing some leniency towards yourself... This of course will depend on what you have to say..."

"Ok..." The villain pushed his tear-filled face into the floor and sighed deeply.

"Good... And you Sir?" Gallier looked at the other villain.

"Whatever..." The hippie had lost his defiance and Gallier chuckled to himself as he continued to enjoy his cigarette.

"Constable Stringer, can I have a word please?" Gallier gestured for Aid-the aide to come closer and the two men moved well out of earshot of the two hippies that remained handcuffed on the floor. "Use your pocket thing to get some uniform vans down here and ask for DCI Cooper... We will get everything bagged up and back to the station where we can question these two idiots even further..."

"But Sir..." Aid-the aide had concerns. "As soon as we get back, these two will change their tunes. They will say that they were made to talk under duress and we will have no evidence other than Peter Hartshorne's statement linking Tanner to this place..."

"Good point..." The aide to CID had not told Gallier anything more than he already knew. The DS narrowed his eyebrows and stroked his chin in a mock concern as he peered past Aid-the aide as if he had noticed something lying on the floor. "Look, back there... What is that on the floor?" The DS pointed past Aid-the aide and the young constable turned around and looked himself.

"I don't know Sarge..." The aide to CID walked closer and saw what seemed to be some kind of ticket book lying on the floor. On top of it was the club logo and emblem of Wolverhampton Wanderers Football Club.

"What is it?" Gallier asked as he took a drag of his cigarette.

"It appears to be some kind of football ticket." Aid-the aide picked it up and then handed it to Gallier. The constable was not a football supporter and he had very little idea about these things, but Reggie Gallier certainly was a football fan.

"Wow! I don't believe it! It's a football season ticket for the Wolves, and look inside..." Gallier opened up the book to reveal the owner of the ticket. "Read the name aer kid..."

"Cedric Tanner..." Aid-the aide was certainly not impressed as it all made sense to him now as to why they had had to go to Molineaux in Wolverhampton first... He felt quite sick...

"Excellent work detective... Now we have the statement from Hartshorne and potentially the other two over there and now the football tickets linking Tanner to the drugs... It will at least be enough to bring him in and extend the investigation into the New Year!"

"Sarge, this isn't right..." Aid-the aide shook his head in disgust... "We both know where that ticket came from..."

"No Stringer..." A look of anger, frustration and sadness came over Gallier's face... "What isn't right is that Cedric Tanner sells this shit to kids all over the Midlands... What isn't right is that Tanner interferes with kids... What isn't right is that Tanner murdered Alan Norton..." Gallier took a long, deep and emotional breath before concluding. "And my father..."

"What?" Aid-the aide had not been privy to this information.

"Yes..." Gallier gritted his teeth but darned not raise his voice to loud in case the two hippies could hear him. "He had my old man killed, so now you can see why we must take this opportunity to take Tanner down once and for all because believe me, he will not allow us to get this close again..."

"But the law is the law Sarge... I joined up to make a difference... Not to plant-" Aid-the aide stopped himself and lowered his voice. "Not to plant evidence and be just as bad as the villains!"

"So we are just as bad as Tanner now are we? For wanting to achieve justice?"

"Look Sarge, I am really sorry to hear about what happened to your father, I really am, but you need to ask yourself something... Is this justice or vengeance?" Aid-the aide was beginning to annoy the Detective Sergeant.

"What's the difference?" Gallier replied, his eyes were cold and his expression was blank. "Get your pocket phone, put the call in and let's get this lot back to the nick... Then we will talk to DCI Cooper and interview the suspects..." Gallier looked at his watch. "In the morning you can decide what you are gunna do... If you wanna bring Tanner to justice then we will go and nick him ... If you wanna make a complaint about my conduct then go ahead in the morning… But at least sleep on it first… I have come too far to get this close to nailing Tanner and I will not give it up just to protect my career…" Gallier turned away from the aide to CID before turning back again. "I know right from bloody wrong… So what if I have my own methods of doing things… That does not make me the same as DI Fowler and Clubber Clark!" The young officer said nothing… *He was undecided…*

Chapter 27

As he drove into work the next morning, Gallier's mind was filled with many concerns, emotions and thoughts. What would Aid-the aide decide to do? In the short time that he had known the young officer, he had been impressed with his policing and detection skills and he had grown fond of the youngster's gruff sarcasm and almost awkward sense of humour. *It was certainly frustrating that the aide to CID was threatening to put an end to the Tanner investigation by complaining about the football ticket and Gallier knew that ten years ago he would have been thinking exactly the same thing as PC Stringer, but his experience and frustrations had hardened him… He knew full well that Cedric Tanner was evil and he knew exactly the threats and horrors that Tanner inflicted upon society, so why couldn't Stringer just turn a blind eye and keep quiet about the Wolves season ticket? Surely it was the right thing to do? Or was it? Maybe he (Gallier) should not have gone after those Gypsies with Fennel? Maybe he should have gone for the big man himself, Cedric Tanner?* But that was not what Gallier wanted… *He wanted to bring Tanner to justice and watch him squirm as his entire empire fell apart around him… Death was too good for the man!*

DS Gallier also felt a strong sense of excitement and anticipation. He had not left the Station until very late the previous night and he was sleep deprived, but the adrenaline of what was to come that day was more than enough to keep him going. Both himself and Aid-the aide had questioned the two hippies until late into the night and just as the aide to CID had anticipated, they had both gone back on what they had said at the drug storage base on Laburnum Road and they were both now refusing to talk. *They were going to have to rely on the football ticket to help link Tanner to the address…* In his mind, Gallier anticipated the worst-case scenario. Aid-the aide would complain to DCI Cooper about the football ticket, but at least Gallier would gain the pleasure of arresting Tanner first! Even if later he did get off on lack of evidence, Gallier would today smash into Tanner's fancy house in Kinver and would bring the drug lord in for questioning. *At least it would wipe the smug grin off Tanner's face for a short time if nothing else!*

It was a Sunday morning and the day before Christmas Eve and Gallier was well aware that most people were at home enjoying the start of their festive celebrations with family, but Gallier could not even think about that. He thought of his wife and daughter and how he had snuck into the house late the night just gone whilst they slept and had snuck out again early that morning whilst they were still asleep. *He really should buy some kind of card and present for his wife at some point, but he really did not know when he would get the chance... He would be busy interrogating Tanner in the interview room and he would not miss that for the world!* As he drove on and got closer to the police station in West Bromwich, his thoughts turned to DCI Cooper. *What would Cooper say when Aid-the aide went to him with his concerns over the football ticket? Would he tell Stringer to get on with his job and not ask such questions about senior officers? Would he order Tanner's instant release and then suspend Gallier?* DCI Cooper was a straight laced and fair man and Gallier figured that he probably would release Tanner and he (Gallier) would be in the shit... *How ironic it was that all he was trying to do was bring down Cedric Tanner and his band of crooked police officers and in return it would be him that would get kicked out of the force... It wasn't fair... It wasn't fair that his dad was dead and it wasn't fair that Tanner and his crew were living the life of Riley when they deserved to rot in jail... It had consumed him... It had taken over his life to the point that his relationship with his wife and child was in tatters, his health was deteriorating on account of his obscene alcohol consumption and all he could think about was nailing Cedric Tanner... When he woke in the morning he thought of it, when he went to bed at night he thought of it and when he awoke gasping for breath and in a cold sweat constantly throughout the night, he thought of it... He needed closure, he needed to escape... He needed Cedric Tanner!*

Gallier pulled his Ford Cortina onto the Police Station car park and was surprised to see DCI Cooper's Rover P6 parked in its usual place. It was Sunday and there was no reason for Cooper to be in work? *Shit! If Cooper was in then that meant that Stringer would be able to go and tell him about the season ticket and their visit to the Wolverhampton Wanderers football ground before they even had chance to arrest Tanner!* Reg Gallier punched the steering wheel in frustration. *Now, it all depended on Aid-the aide and what he intended to do… His future and that of Cedric Tanner and his own wife and child lay in the hands of the lowly aide to CID… What was gunna' happen next?*

The CID office was typically quiet as it usually was on a Sunday morning, but Gallier spotted his colleague Aid-the aide sitting on his own at the end of the room with a cup of tea and surrounded by copious notes. The young officer looked tired and Gallier would not have been surprised if the man had of been there all night, such was his dedication… DS Gallier shook his head with frustration… He admired the shared dedication to bringing down Cedric Tanner, *so why couldn't the youngster just keep his bloody mouth shut about that fucking football ticket!* As Gallier made his way over to his colleague, DCI Cooper suddenly appeared in the doorway of his own office which was at the side of the main CID room.

"Morning Reg… Can I have a word please…" Cooper's tone was grim and Gallier figured that Aid-the aide had already spoken to him.

"Yes Sir…" Gallier forced a smile and then followed the DCI into the office.

"Sit down please Reg…" Cooper sat down at his desk and gestured to the empty chair that was opposite.

"Is this about the Tanner case Sir?" The Tanner case was the only thing Gallier had worked on since he had come to West Bromwich so it could not have been anything else. "I updated you last night Sir, me and Stringer are going over to Kinver this morning to arrest him…" Gallier was literally desperate to have that one last pleasure… After that it didn't matter... *He didn't matter...* "We have statements linking Tanner to the drugs we seized yesterday and items were found at the scene linking Tanner to the property... We've got him Sir, just give me a few hours in the interview room with him!"

"Cedric Tanner is dead Sargeant Gallier..." Cooper's words made no sense to the DS...

"What?"

"Cedric Tanner is dead... Looks like he was murdered last night and his body, well what's left of it was discovered in the early hours of this morning..."

"How? Why?" Gallier was suddenly filled with an immense emptiness... All he had worked and strived for for so long was suddenly irrelevant... It was as if he was irrelevant... He had been robbed... Robbed of the chance to achieve the final justice for his father and robbed of the opportunity and pride of being the man who finally brought down the mighty Cedric Tanner.

"I don't know Reg... All I know is that he was killed and it sounds like quite a nasty one by all accounts..."

"How do you know?" Gallier finally spoke, he had been lost for words.

"Yesterday, when you asked me about arresting Tanner this morning, I had to clear it with Staffordshire Police first as Tanner lives within their boundaries and not ours. So when the murder came in to them this morning I received a telephone call explaining that we would be unable to make the arrest..." Cooper could see the sheer disappointment in Gallier's eyes and he got up, walked around to the other side of the desk and patted the Sargeant on the back. "You and Stringer did good work.... You should be proud of yourselves..." The senior policeman looked at his watch. "Go home Reg, it's the day before Christmas Eve... Spend time with your family... Then come back refreshed and ready to start work on Divisional investigations..."

"No..." Gallier shook his head and stood up. "I'm gunna go over there and find out what has gone on for myself... I really wouldn't put it past Tanner to have made all this bull shit up... He probably has bent coppers over in Staffs just like he has them here!"

"Don't be stupid Reg... Its not our patch... Leave it to the carrot crunching, country bumpkins to sort out... They don't get much of this kind of action out there... They'll be pissing their pants with excitement!" DCI Cooper was usually more 'prim and proper' in his dialogue with junior officers, but he understood that Reggie Gallier was a man who appreciated the cold hard truth without the bull shit.

"Sir, please let me go and take a look..." Gallier was desperate... "Also, if Tanner really is dead, it is more than likely that whoever killed him is from our patch... Just let me suss it out... Remember what I told you about the crooked coppers he had working for him? Maybe they are involved in this?" Gallier was not going to take no for an answer and Cooper simply could not be bothered with the argument as it was more than likely that the Sargeant would drive over to the crime scene regardless of what he said.

"Ok... Fine... You do what you need to do Reg, but I really do think that you are wasting your time..." Cooper sighed as he pulled his Crombie coat down from off the hat stand. "I'm going home to have Sunday lunch with my wife and maybe I will have a small sherry later on..."

"Thank you Sir..." As Gallier turned and hurried towards the door, Cooper suddenly spoke again.

"And Reg, if the Staffs boys disapprove of your presence and won't let you in, you will have to abide by whatever they say... Is that understood?" DCI Cooper spoke with the tone of a disciplinarian School master and Gallier felt patronised.

"Perfectly understood Sir..." Gallier burst out of the office and hurried over towards Aid-the aide who stood up to greet him.

"Sarge!" The aide to CID spoke in hushed tones so that he would not be heard by DCI Cooper. "I've come to a decision about the football ticket..."

"That will not be necessary..." Gallier was mortified that he would not be getting his 'big moment' of taking Tanner down and Aid-the aide could see the disappointment in his eyes.

"Why? What's happened?"

"Apparently, Tanner is dead... Come on, get your coat... We are gewin' over there now..."

The car journey over to Kinver consisted mostly of one long awkward silence. Aid-the aide was at the wheel and Gallier simply gazed out of the window in disbelief as he tried to comprehend the news that he had just received. Briefly, he wondered about what Aid-the aide would or would not have said to Cooper, but it really did not matter now and he figured that he would probably never know which way the young policeman would have gone. *Maybe that was for the best?*

Aid-the aide parked the CID Marina outside of Tanner's large house near to Kinver and straight away a hive of police activity was evident. There were several police vehicles at the scene and it was quite clear to both Gallier and Aid-the aide that the small sleepy village was throwing all of its police resources at an occurrence which was significantly out of the ordinary. The two men (Gallier and Aid-the aide) climbed out of the car and were immediately accosted by a middle aged, uniformed officer who was guarding the property at the main gate.

"Sorry gentlemen, this is a crime scene and you are not permitted to enter..." The 'woodentop' spoke and Gallier pulled out his warrant card.

"Detective Sargeant Gallier, West Midlands Constabulary... We believe that this crime scene has every bit to do with us... Who is the officer in charge here?" As Gallier spoke, the podgy Staffordshire PC felt quite unsure of what to do. *He was outranked, but the Sergeant was from a neighbouring force. He would have to let the CID lot sort it out.*

"Eh, Detective Inspector Lawson Sir... He is just through there..." The PC gestured back towards a crime scene tent that had been erected on the driveway of Cedric Tanner's house.

"Thank you…" Gallier had already marched past the constable as he mouthed the words and Aid-the aide followed on curiously.

"Who the devil are you?" DI Lawson was a middle-aged man with a pencil moustache. He tried to speak with a well-spoken, upper-class accent but it poorly masked a dialect that Gallier figured came from the working-class areas of the Potteries at Stoke on Trent.

"DS Gallier, West Midlands Constabulary… This is DC Stringer…" Gallier deliberately exaggerated Aid-the aide's rank and the aide to CID smiled inwardly. "And you are?"

"Detective Inspector Lawson!" Gallier's audacity and the tone of his voice infuriated Lawson. "West Midlands Constabulary? What on earth are you doing here Sergeant?"

"Sorry Sir, but we were in the middle of an investigation upon the deceased and as most of his business operations took place upon our patch we feel that we have every right to be here… If you have any issue with this, please feel free to take it up with my DCI?"

"That will not be necessary Sargeant… You can please yourself, but do not touch or remove a thing… This is my crime scene!" Lawson looked down at a large, coarse blanket that covered the remains of Cedric Tanner and the awful, unmistakable stench of burnt flesh filled the vicinity. The smell inside of the tent was disgusting and even the most hardened of Detectives were finding it hard not to retch and vomit. "I'm afraid it is a particularly nasty one Sergeant Gallagher…" Lawson mispronounced Gallier's name but the DS could not be bothered to correct him. "In 25 years of policing, I must say that this is by far the worst!"

"I see…" Gallier could not help but harbour a sick satisfaction… *He hoped that Tanner's demise had been suitably horrific…*

"From what we can tell so far, the victim had his penis removed before being shot in both kneecaps and then set on fire… I suspect that our killer wanted the victim to burn to death slowly whilst not being able to move on account of the knee capping…" Lawson looked at the floor before becoming seriously concerned by Gallier's actions as the DS uttered a grunt of satisfied laughter. "You find this amusing Detective?"

"All I can say is that it could not have happened to a more deserving bastard..." All of the other officers present were shocked and appalled by Gallier's words and unprofessionalism. "Lets see him..."

"As you wish... Though I must warn you Sargeant, it is grim... Remove the blanket..." Lawson looked away as he barked the order and a uniformed officer pulled up the material as he himself also looked away and gagged.

Tanner's remains were charred and burned, a gaping hole stood in the place where his penis used to be and a fatty, foul smelling, semi-liquid oozed around the corpse.

"We found his bloody penis in the shed over there..." Lawson pointed to a nearby wooden shed and still he did not return his gaze to look at the remains. Gallier said nothing... He had seen all that he needed to see and Aid-the aide struggled to stop himself from vomiting. Gallier took one last look at the corpse and then smiled grotesquely. *He desperately wanted to have arrested Tanner... But at least the bastard did not get off easily!*

As Gallier and Aid-the aide walked back towards the car, the young officer suddenly pulled off to one side and vomited violently into a bush. It had been a truly distressing crime scene and Gallier could understand why his colleague was reacting in such a way.

"Excuse me, but are you a policeman?" As Gallier drew level with the car, an elderly gentleman approached him.

"Yes... Can I help you Sir?" At first, Gallier thought nothing of the man, but he remained professional and polite.

"Something bad happened here last night didn't it?" The old man looked back up the driveway towards the tent which was clearly visible to the public. Also, the horrific smell of burnt flesh continued to fill the vicinity.

"I'm afraid that I am unable to disclose any details Sir..." Gallier smiled but hoped that the man would soon be on his way.

"I saw something… A car was parked nearby last night… A Vauxhall, an old one… A Vauxhall Cresta, you know the ones with the American looking fins?" The old man described the vehicle and Gallier nodded. "I have the registration number… Maybe it will be of use to you in your investigations officer?" As the old man spoke, Gallier noticed that Aid-the aide was still vomiting and was not within earshot.

"Is that right Sir? Could you write the registration number down on this piece of paper for me please?" Gallier pulled out a small, scruffy piece of paper from out of his jacket pocket and handed the old man a slightly chewed pencil.

"Certainly…" the old man scribbled down the registration number and then handed the paper back to Gallier. "I hope you catch him!"

"Oh, I am sure that we will Sir…" Gallier smiled. "And one more thing Sir…" Gallier lowered his voice and moved closer to the elderly man. "This is a very complex and difficult case and it is very important that you do not breathe a word of what you saw to anyone else… Your life may depend on it!" The detective whispered the last part dramatically and the witness looked concerned. "Not even to another Police officer, you just cannot know who you can trust!"

"I see…" The old man tapped his own nose twice… "Mum's the word!"

"Thank you…" As the old man trudged off back towards his own house which was a fair few yards away, Gallier turned back towards Aid-the aide who had now ceased vomiting and had come back over to join the DS.

"Sorry Sarge! I will have to get used to that sort of thing!"

"Yes…" Gallier placed the paper into his jacket pocket. "You will see just as bad if you work on the roads though, some of the messes they pull out of car crashes…" Gallier shook his head. "You would never drive a car again if you thought about it too much…." The two men walked back towards the CID Marina and climbed in for the drive back to West Bromwich.

I'm guessing that's us done for Christmas now Sarge?" Aid-the aide parked the car at West Bromwich police station and both men got out. "I'm off to go and spend Christmas with me bird!"

"You've got a lady friend have you Stringer?" Gallier thought of how Aid-the aide reminded him of himself as a younger man and how he never had time for a serious relationship.

"Yes sir…"

"Fair play aer kid…" Gallier smiled. "Just dow meck the same mistakes that I have done… Meck time for your family, meck time for yer wench… Dow let this job teck over… Because it will…"

"Ok Sarge…" Aid-the aide was not paying his senior officer much attention. He was looking forward to spending Christmas with his woman and several pints of ale! "I'll get off then shall I?"

"No…" Gallier was deep in thought and his reply surprised the aide to CID. "We still have a little work to do…" The Detective Sergeant pulled out the crumpled piece of paper from out of his jacket pocket. "Go to Margaret in the office. She's still in, I just saw her. Ask her to send one of them telex things to Hendon… I need you to find out who this vehicle belongs to…"

Epilogue

Gallier gazed at a glass tumbler filled with whisky as he sat at a random desk and waited for Aid-the aide to work his magic. Sometimes the information on the telex would come back within minutes, sometimes it was significantly longer... It had been an eventful day... That morning, Gallier had expected to come to work, achieve his ambition of arresting Tanner only to see him walk away and then be suspended himself, he had almost accepted this fate, *but none of this had happened...* He drained the whisky into his mouth and straight away poured himself another. He felt numb... As if the carpet had been quickly pulled out from underneath him... Everything he had strived for was no longer relevant. Everything he had worked for was gone... For nothing... A waste of time which had probably been at the cost of his health, his marriage and his relationship with his only child... He took a sip of the whisky and was surprised see Aid-the aide emerge into the room.

"That was quick!"

"Yes Sarge..." Aid-the aide clutched the piece of telex information in his right hand. The telex system had originally been developed in America in the 1930s and it was a way of sending written messages via a machine that generated a small print out of the required information at the other end. "It appears that they are not very busy today Sarge as no fucker wants to work on Sunday the 23rd of December!" Aid-the aide placed the paper down on Gallier's desk and made his point with a sarcastically humorous tone.

"Would you like a drink?" Gallier held up the half empty scotch bottle as an invitation.

"Er, no Sarge... Like I said, I wanna get off now to be with me bird..."

"Fuck off then aer kid..." Gallier managed a brief and friendly laugh. "Have a good Christmas an dow get too pissed..."

"Thank you Sir... You have a good Christmas too..." Aid-the aide was eager to find out the outcome of the telex check he had just been asked to make, but he knew that Gallier probably wouldn't tell him anything at this stage... *He was tired... Whatever it was could wait until after Christmas...*

When Gallier was quite sure that he was alone in the CID office, he downed his whisky and then poured himself yet another before opening up the telex... The name inside did not surprise him one bit... The Vauxhall Cresta spotted at the scene of Tanner's murder belonged to Michael Cole of Riddings Mount Estate, Old Hill... Cedric Tanner's stepson... Gallier took another drink of his whisky and cast his mind back as he remembered how Cole had recounted to him in the interview room of Old Hill Police station how he had been so sickeningly abused by his Stepfather, Cedric Tanner as a child... Suddenly the reluctance of men like Eddie Fennel and Michael Cole to speak to the police made absolute sense to him. Men like Fennel and Cole did not need the police to hold their hands to attain justice, they simply took it for themselves, an eye for an eye, a tooth for a tooth... *Exactly the same as he had done with those that had killed his father...* He took a deep breath and for the first time in years things felt a little easier... *Was it finally over? If anyone deserved vengeance against Cedric Tanner more than himself then it was certainly Micheal Cole...* Gallier thought of the words that Cole had said to him back in the interview room.

'Thank you! Your sympathy makes all the difference...'

Gallier said the words out loud and then smiled... Cole had said these words in sarcasm. At that time, the villain really could not have cared less about Gallier's sympathy, but ultimately, it would be this sympathy that would help him quite literally get away with murder... *It would make*

ALL of the difference... Gallier could quite easily have handed the telex over to DI Lawson of Staffordshire police to assist in the Cedric Tanner murder investigation, but instead, he held it up in front of his eyes and watched it burn as he introduced it to his cigarette lighter... *What was done was done... An eye for an eye, a tooth for a tooth...* But was it Vengeance... Or Justice?

Also available by Thomas J.R. Dearn.

Author and musician Thomas J.R. Dearn was born in the Black Country area of the West Midlands and has a strong interest in early to mid-twentieth century history. He studied Music at Wolverhampton university before embarking upon a long and successful career as a schoolteacher. Thomas now lives in Worcestershire with his wife, three children, Rottweiler/German Shepherd cross and miniature Dachshund. He enjoys football and is a supporter of Aston Villa and Halesowen town football clubs. Thomas is also a classic car enthusiast and collector of vintage guitars.

Check the website, Facebook or Twitter for news of future releases:
www.onceuponatimeintheblackcountry.com